Additional Praise for

LONELY PLACES

"Grief and trauma manifest in the eeriest of ways in the compulsively readable *Lonely Places.* Kate Anderson turns a longing for home, community, and healing on its head, sucking readers into a macabre mystery that twists memory into lies amid an atmospheric and bone-riddled rural setting. Not to be missed!"

—Nicole M. Wolverton, author of *A Misfortune of Lake Monsters*

"Among the aspens of Kate Anderson's *Lonely Places*, readers will find themselves overcome with claustrophobic uneasiness as Chase and her family try to set down roots after years of traveling. With each chapter, no matter how innocuous things first appear, dread grows beneath the surface until it breaks through with a supernatural crescendo that'll twist the heart. This poignant tale about trauma, forgiveness, and the meaning of home is one I'll never forget."

—Crystal J. Bell, author of *The Lamplighter*

"Creepy and atmospheric, the haunted woods are a character themselves in this slow-burn horror. With its themes of sisterhood, healing, and family trauma, *Lonely Places* is a poignant and important story that stays with you."

—Tatiana Schlote-Bonne, author of *Such Lovely Skin*

"*Lonely Places* lingers long after reading. This haunting exploration of trauma and family is sure to rivet readers with its visceral, atmospheric storytelling."

—Elizabeth Tammi, author of *Outrun the Wind* and *The Weight of a Soul*

"Haunting, traumatic events propel *Lonely Places* from a quiet sibling story to a layered, gripping coming-of-age plot that pits a malevolent aspen grove against a disillusioned and dysfunctional family."

—Kerrie Faye, author of *Dead Girl*

LONELY PLACES

KATE ANDERSON

LONELY PLACES

KATE ANDERSON

Mendota Heights, Minnesota

First Edition
First Printing, 2024

Book design by Kate Liestman
Cover design by Kate Liestman
Cover illustration by Kelsey Oseid

Flux, an imprint of North Star Editions, Inc.

This is a work of fiction. Names, characters, places, and incidents are either the product of the author's imagination or are used fictitiously, and any resemblance to actual persons living or dead, business establishments, events, or locales is entirely coincidental.

Library of Congress Cataloging-in-Publication Data (pending)
978-1-63583-101-6 (paperback)
978-1-63583-102-3 (ebook)

Flux
North Star Editions, Inc.
2297 Waters Drive
Mendota Heights, MN 55120
www.fluxnow.com

Printed in Canada

This is for all of us.

"All good things are wild and free."

—*Henry David Thoreau*

Chapter One

The forest came upon them suddenly, trees closing in overhead so that sunlight dappled the road in a shifting kaleidoscope of light. An army of trees: tall and straight, papery white bark marred by knotholes like battle scars. Ancient and solemn aspens with leaves that fluttered in the wind, murmuring secrets to one another as the car passed underneath. Wildflowers made vibrant silhouettes against the backdrop of white trees: poppies the color of blood, columbines the color of sky, and Indian paintbrush the color of fire.

Chase pressed her hand to the window. Everything was still and quiet in the soft half-light. Dad stopped whistling for the first time in hours, and even the steady whoosh of the tires on the salt-bleached pavement faded. The silence was like slipping into a hot bath, and for half a heartbeat, Chase understood why Mom and Dad had wanted to come here. It was like they'd left the world behind and the only things that existed were their family and the trees.

Guthrie rolled down her window, flooding the car with air that smelled sweet and clean, like snow melting in the spring. She leaned against the window trim, face turned toward the sky. Chase could see the trees reflected in her eyes—eyes that were oddly world-weary for someone just ten years old. She strained to hear what Guthrie was whispering to herself, wishing she could claw her way into her sister's mind and unspool her thoughts, but the wind snatched Guthrie's words away, and all Chase caught were fragments: *quaking* and *toadstools* and *far-flung.*

"We're almost there," Mom said, twisting around from the front seat to drop her hand on Chase's knee. It was heavy with rings: polished sea glass set in dull copper, and looped wire with rough-cut gems. Chase itched to pull away, annoyed at the way Mom was acting like this was all normal, like there was nothing unusual about having a father who always, always put his own wants above the rest of the family's needs, and a ten-year-old sister who hadn't spoken a word to any of them in six months.

"Almost where, the middle of nowhere?" Chase shifted, shaking off Mom's hand.

Dad sang a snatch of Arcade Fire under his breath, a lyric about chasing the wild places before they disappeared. "Come on, Chase, I thought this was what you wanted. Some stability, a couple of years in the same place—"

"I wanted to go home." The words felt like broken glass in her mouth. "To Boone."

Dad's jaw flexed when she mentioned the town he had grown up in—the town they had left years earlier—but all he said was, "The whole country is your home. How many seventeen-year-olds can say that?"

They had lived in all of the contiguous forty-eight states by the time Chase was twelve—if you could call a month spent in a Missouri campground or two weeks tracing the coastline of Lake Michigan "living" somewhere. She wasn't sure she could. Her parents should have taken a hint from the way all of her childhood drawings of their family showed them standing in front of a house with a picket fence instead of the converted school bus they wandered the country in. To her, living somewhere would always mean a house with their name on the mailbox and flowers in the yard, like the one they had left behind after Dad's parents died when she was eight.

Energy thrummed off Dad from the driver's seat. He was always moving: fidgeting with his sleeve, shaking his foot so hard that his whole chair jiggled. It annoyed Chase to no end. The only time she ever saw her father still was when he was in front of a canvas, paintbrush in hand. Then he'd tilt his head to the side and all the nervous energy that was usually tangled up inside of him settled. Even his breathing slowed down. The only things that existed for him were the brushstrokes and the paint, a world of his own creation.

Now he jerked the steering wheel to the side, rolling to a stop on the gravel shoulder a few feet away from a faded sign.

"For old time's sake," he said, grinning at Chase in the rearview mirror as he unbuckled his seat belt and flung his door open. Mom and Guthrie followed, but Chase took her time, making them wait as she rummaged under her seat for a pair of high-top sneakers and laced them to the very top. She felt no sense of urgency. They must have stopped to take pictures at a thousand road signs on a thousand miles of dusty shoulder over the years.

When she finally got out, Mom and Guthrie were gathering wildflowers among the trees, while Dad propped his phone on the hood of the car so that the camera framed the sign:

PANDO ASPEN GROVE

"The trembling giant," Dad said, sweeping his arms out at the aspens ranked on either side of the road. "Each of these trees is a genetic clone, and they're all connected to a massive underground root system. It's the oldest and largest organism on earth." He bent over the camera to set the timer. "Sadie, Gus—picture!"

Guthrie already had a crown of white daisies tangled in her hair, and she held another ring of flowers out to Chase.

Her eyes were as deep and still as a pool of dark water in the forest.

"Put it on for me," Chase said, ducking her head so that Guthrie could reach. "How do I look?"

Guthrie smiled and flashed a double thumbs-up but didn't say anything. A twinge of guilt thrummed through Chase at her sister's silence, and she shoved it away, just as she had for the past six months.

"Ready?" Dad asked. Mom put her arms around Chase and Guthrie, and Dad pushed the button on the camera, then jogged to take his place on Guthrie's other side.

The air was hushed, like they were swimming underwater. Even the motes of dust in the sun hung motionless as the camera flashed, capturing the family as they stood on the edge of something big and new and unknowable.

Guthrie had always been the quiet sister: withdrawn where Chase was outspoken, soft where Chase was hard. She clung to Mom's side wherever they went, and if strangers tried to talk to her, her eyes would glaze over as she stared past them, like she was trying to convince herself they weren't there.

"She's just shy," Mom would protest whenever Chase said Guthrie looked like a deer in headlights. "Lots of kids are at her age."

Chase tried to point out that most kids Guthrie's age didn't celebrate Halloween on one coast and Christmas on the other. No wonder Guthrie was afraid to talk to strangers. She had never been around one long enough to get to know them.

Then, after that night in the woods six months ago, Guthrie's introversion bloated into something all-consuming and bitter. Her nightmares left her sweating and gasping for breath. Her eyes dilated to empty black holes every time someone left the room. Sometimes Chase worried that Guthrie was fading away, her edges becoming less and less distinct, the line blurring between reality and the world she inhabited alone in her head. Maybe somewhere in her mind, she was still in the woods, lost and calling for her parents and sister until her voice faded away like the light in the sky at dusk.

Chase thought her parents would have to pay attention to Guthrie's alarming silence. But Dad watched Guthrie withdraw into the shadows and just said, "Still waters run deep."

"You have to do something," Chase had spat at her parents one night after finding Guthrie cornered by a skunk outside the bus when she had run out to grab a forgotten book. She had been crouching in the dirt long enough that her calves were cramped, waiting for the skunk to wander away instead of calling out to her parents or Chase for help. Chase's voice shook, her chest tight with anger—at her parents for their inaction, at herself for her part in Guthrie's silence. "This isn't healthy. Guthrie needs stability. She needs to know that we'll always be there when she needs us. She needs *roots*."

"Just because we're not rooted down doesn't mean we don't have roots," Dad said. "And stability is just another word for pressure. I don't want to force Guthrie into a box that doesn't fit her."

"Oh, come on! Stop using Guthrie as an excuse. If you're really concerned about her, you would take her to, like, a child psychologist or something. This isn't for Guthrie. This is for *you*."

"Chase—" Mom began, but Dad held up one hand to stop her.

"You're right," he had admitted. "This isn't just for Guthrie. This is for all of us."

And now the car was deep in the woods, the road twisting like the roots that lay underground. Chase thought about those words as they drove: *This is for all of us.* As long as she could remember, Dad had been chasing something that she didn't understand—chasing something that she didn't think he would ever find. The last wild places, maybe, the ones ruled by the trees and the sky and the birds. The places he created with paint and brush.

Pando Aspen Grove seemed like it could be one of those wild places. There was something unsettling about the liminal space, the trees that stood in lines, the shadows that beckoned. Chase unconsciously clenched her jaw as a skeletal staircase, twisted and blackened by fire, flashed past. *Just all that's left of some hunting lodge that burned down*, Chase told herself, watching it until it disappeared into the endless ranks of white trees.

Guthrie clicked her tongue in time with the turn signal as Dad made a right onto a rutted dirt road that was bracketed on either side by bullet-riddled metal signs: NO TRESPASSING and PROPERTY OF THE US FOREST SERVICE. The car jolted and bounced, squeezing between trees that grew so close to the road that Chase could have reached out and run her fingers over their smooth bark, and plucked one of the round silver-green leaves that waved like flags as they passed. Twice, there were slim saplings a few feet tall in their path. Their springy trunks bent under the car as Dad eased his way over them.

"I'll have to get back down here with clippers and a chainsaw to clear out the road," Dad said. "No one has been here in a while, and the mature trees send out shoots that'll take root and grow into saplings if nothing stops them. Next time, we might not be able to make it through."

The sprawling reach of the forest made Chase uneasy, the roots rolling over and consuming everything in their path like a hungry beast.

They followed the road for more than a mile, always climbing, until it was little more than two ruts that wound between the aspens. Finally, when Chase thought her head was about to split open from the bouncing, the road opened into a small clearing, and they rolled to a stop.

"You've got to be kidding me," Chase deadpanned.

They were at the top of one of the larger hills. Aspens stretched as far as she could see in every direction, not quite blocking her view of snowcapped mountains in the distance.

"Welcome to the Fitzgerald Fire Lookout," Dad said. "Our new home."

Chapter Two

"We're really going to live here? Up in that?" Chase challenged her mother as they unloaded the car. Dad was already clattering up the spindly staircase that marched back and forth along one side of the tower, his arms full of boxes.

Mom shook a pillow deeper into its pillowcase, then tossed it at Chase. "You're lucky. This tower was once a private vacation rental, and it was completely remodeled before the Forest Service decided to reopen it. Most of the other lookout towers are just glorified tents on stilts."

"Haven't you ever read *The Shining*?" Chase mumbled, tilting her head back to stare up at the lookout. It stood at least fifty feet over her head. The squat, square building at the top was crowned by a round tower paneled in rusty tin that shone blood red in the setting sun.

Mom laughed. "Haven't *you* ever read *Into the Wild*?"

"That one doesn't exactly work out well in the end, either," Chase pointed out. "The guy starves to death in a school bus."

"Oh, all right then, *Desolation Angels*. Here—" Mom passed Chase her backpack and another pillow. "Take this up to Guthrie. She's probably already staking out her bed."

"Guthrie isn't up there," Dad said, jogging back down the stairs for another box. "I left her down here with you."

Chase dropped the pillow; a little cloud of dust rose around her feet. "Where is she, then?" She could taste the edge of panic in her voice, bitter, like the rind of a lemon. The three of them blinked at each other, and suddenly it was like they were six months in the past, coming back together at the campsite for dinner and realizing that no one had seen Guthrie for hours.

Mom bit her lip and glanced around. "Maybe she's exploring the other side of the clearing."

But Chase knew better than that. Guthrie didn't explore—not anymore. She didn't explore, and she didn't talk, so she wouldn't call out if she needed help.

"I bet I'll be able to see her from the deck," Dad said, turning back to the stairs. "You two look for her down here."

Chase spun away from Mom, her heart pounding in her ears, and jogged to the edge of the clearing. The aspens formed a tight circle around the crown of the hill where the lookout stood. Branches from one tree wove into the branches of the others, and underbrush, thick with raspberry thorns, filled in the spaces between. She prowled along the edge, searching for a footprint or a broken twig to show that Guthrie had passed through.

It was so quiet. So still.

A shiver crept up Chase's spine, caressing each knobby vertebra until the hairs on the back of her neck stood up, like she was being watched. The unseen scrutiny was heavier than the familiar gaze of her parents, and it left her feeling like she was forgetting something.

It was the same sensation as when a word was on the tip of her tongue, or as when a dream faded away. Like the trees wanted her to remember something . . .

"Gus!" she called, but the forest swallowed her voice, and the world was silent.

The soft chatter of the birds overhead, the rippling whisper of the wind through the leaves, the shuffle of her feet over the rocks that marked the edge of the clearing—all of the sounds that made up the background noise of a summer day in the woods were gone.

"Gus!" she shouted again. She felt the word leave her mouth, her breath a little explosion in her throat, but the sound dropped like a stone in the still air. Whirling around, she caught sight of her parents: Dad above her, leaning over the railing of the deck with a hand shading his eyes, Mom calling out for Gus as she prodded the underbrush on the other side of the clearing. Her voice came to Chase muffled and a half-second too late, like it was the sound from a radio broadcasting from far away.

Movement flickered in the corner of Chase's eye, and she turned back to the trees to see a flash of red. Red like poppies, red like blood, red like the stripes on Guthrie's shirt.

Chase's heart stuttered, then raced to make up for the beats it had missed. Not Guthrie's shirt, but a cardinal, its feathers a bright flash against the muted palette of the aspens, the repetitive silver-green and gray. It rose in the air, its beak opening and closing in silent song, and soared over Chase's head, before folding its wings to its body and plummeting toward the ground like a bomb.

The bird hit the base of a huge tree, its neck breaking with a sharp snap. All the sounds came rushing back in, flooding over Chase in a muted roar that reminded her of waves on the beach. The ocean, rolling in and out, carrying things to and fro. Softening corners and reshaping edges until they were like drawings. Unrecognizable.

Chase closed her eyes, concentrating on breathing slowly through her nose. Guthrie wasn't the only one who had become anxious. Driving all day and staring out the window into the sun, the monotonous hum of the car, the way her ears popped as they changed elevation: It was enough to make anyone hear things that weren't really there.

Or not hear things that are *there*, Chase corrected herself.

But the bird was real. It was lying right there at her feet, its head twisted to the side, its wings loose and twitching in the breeze. Chase knelt in the dirt on the edge of the clearing and looked into the shadows of the forest that rolled before her like waves on a storm-tossed sea.

With the sun going down, darkness crept across the open clearing, swallowing the car, the last few boxes waiting to be carried up the stairs that led to the lookout. Chase. Inside the woods, the white aspens were like ghosts.

"Guthrie?" Chase tried again. Her voice came out in a harsh whisper. She didn't want to release her sister's name into the woods, didn't want the trees to hear.

On the other side of the broad tree where the bird had died, leaves rustled. Guthrie came into view little by little, her face pale like moonlight. She was holding something that shone in the dark, cupped in her hands like a bird's egg.

A skull, barely larger than Chase's thumbnail. The bone was feathered at the edges like one of Dad's paintings, and it tapered to a sharp point.

"What were you doing?" Chase hissed, grabbing Guthrie by her thin shoulders. "You shouldn't go into the woods."

Her heart pounded, echoing an unspoken last word: *alone*, *alone*, *alone*, *alone*.

Guthrie tilted her head to the side, like she wasn't sure why Chase was upset. Chase was the one who had left Guthrie alone in the woods that night, and now—

Guthrie pointed at the crumpled red bird on the ground.

"It flew into the tree," Chase said. "Don't touch it. In fact, you shouldn't be touching that, either—"

But when Chase reached to take the bird skull, Guthrie closed her fingers around it and pressed it to her chest. Her eyes, the same deep brown as their father's, flashed as she curled her lip over her teeth in a silent snarl. Chase dropped her hands and took a step back, twigs snapping under her feet. Her heart pounded along with the throbbing at the base of her skull, and it took her a few breaths to feel like she was getting enough oxygen. Shivers raced across her body, and she swallowed hard, staring at the way Guthrie hunched her shoulders around the skull, one finger stroking it greedily. She had never seen her sister like that before. Guthrie was a gentle shadow with eyes soft as a baby deer's; she apologized with every movement, meekly fitting herself in the gaps and crevices left between Chase and their parents. Even before she stopped talking, Guthrie never argued when Chase told her to do something. But this was a declaration: The skull belonged to Guthrie.

Chase's lips were dry, and she wet them before speaking again. "Fine. Just come on; we were all looking for you."

Guthrie turned her eyes on Chase, and there was no hint of fierce insistence left on her face. Her lips twitched into the shadow of a smile, and she slipped her free hand into Chase's.

"I found her," Chase called as she led Guthrie back to the lookout in the center of the clearing. Mom met them at the bottom of the stairs, huffing out a strangled sigh as she pulled Guthrie tight against her chest.

"There you are! You need to let us know before you go into the woods," she scolded.

The stairs creaked and swayed as they clambered up—one, two, three, four, five flights. Chase was panting for breath by the time they reached the narrow deck at the top. The air was thin and insubstantial in her throat. *High altitude*, she thought, as black spots flashed across her vision. She drew in a long, slow breath, steadying herself with one hand on the rail. Like the stairs, the deck, and the walls of the lookout itself, the rail was silvery wood, splintered and rough from wind and rain.

Dad came out onto the porch, letting the screen door

bang closed behind him. "Gus! Already out exploring? See anything cool?"

Guthrie's eyes lit up as she opened her fist to show him the tiny skull.

"Beautiful," Dad murmured. "Look how delicate it is. The bone is so thin, it's almost like an eggshell."

"You're not going to let her keep that, are you?" Chase asked.

Guthrie scowled. Dad frowned. Even Mom looked perplexed by the question. Chase was the only one who looked at the skull and saw death instead of art.

"I don't see why not," Mom said. "It should be just fine if we soak it in some bleach. Come on, Gus, let's see if there's any under the kitchen sink."

Mom ushered Guthrie inside, leaving Chase and Dad standing together at the railing. He wrapped one arm around Chase's shoulders, the fabric at the elbows of his worn flannel shirt strained and threadbare. "Just look at that view," he said in a voice thin with longing. "What do you think? Could we be happy here?"

He offered her the forest like it was a gift, watching her expectantly as she took in the rolling sea of trees. A clear lake nestled at the bottom of the hill, aspens crowding right up to the edge of the water. On the other side of the lake, another hill rose. This one was a patchwork of silvery-green aspen and darker pine trees. The great blue dome of the sky turned to deeper indigo as the first stars appeared above them.

She looked back at the tree in the clearing where she had found Guthrie. The cardinal was still visible at its base, a bright stain that stood out in the dark.

"There's a dead bird at the edge of the woods," she said, shaking off her father's arm and turning to go inside.

Chapter Three

The inside of the lookout was bright with light that shone on warm honey-oak paneling. Soaring windows offered a view of the surrounding forest from every angle. A set of matching twin beds stood under the windows on either side of the room with a ladder descending from a dark opening in the ceiling between them.

Mom stood at the counter in the tiny kitchen opposite the front door, unpacking boxes of food they had bought at the grocery store in the last town they had passed through: canned chili, rice, granola bars. A pot of water simmered on the stove with an open box of spaghetti next to it.

"I know it's late for dinner, but I have to eat something more substantial than road trip snacks," Mom said over her shoulder. She popped the lid off a jar of tomato sauce and emptied it into a saucepan, then turned to face Chase, wiping her hands on the hem of her T-shirt. "Ready for the grand tour?"

Chase cocked one eyebrow and gestured to the room. "I think I can see it all from here."

"Haha," Mom said. "There's a little more to it. Come on. You too, Guthrie."

Guthrie rolled off the bed she had already claimed, pointing to the ladder, her head tilted to one side in a question.

"Great place to start, Gus," Mom said. "The cupola is where Dad and I will sleep. Go on up."

Murky darkness settled over Chase like a shroud as she

climbed into the cupola. The air was still and hot. She groped along the wall for a light switch, finally finding a chain that lit one bare bulb.

Guthrie prodded at her from below, and Chase hauled herself into the tiny space, stepping to the side to make room for her sister. It was just large enough for a full-size bed and a pair of nightstands. There were no windows set in the walls up here, and Chase's skin immediately began to crawl with claustrophobia.

"Look up," Mom called from below. Chase tilted her head back. The ceiling was one large, domed skylight that framed the purple-blue swirl of the sky above the bed. Chase tapped Guthrie on the shoulder and nodded at the view.

"There's the Milky Way. It looks close enough to touch, doesn't it?" she said.

Guthrie's eyes were wide and full of stars. For what felt like the thousandth time, Chase wondered what her sister was thinking about. When she looked up at the night sky, surrounded by trees, did she remember that night in the woods six months ago? Had she counted each cruel pinprick in the black velvet sky while she waited for her family to find her? And when she lost her voice from calling to Chase—was that when she decided to stop talking altogether?

"There's more to see down here." Mom's voice was slightly muffled, but it was enough to make Chase jump. She pulled herself out of the memory, shaking off her regret and guilt, and turned to go back down the ladder. Guthrie followed, blinking, her pupils shrinking as they climbed back into the light.

"The bathroom is small, but at least it has hot water, which is more than some of these lookouts can say," Mom explained, opening a door tucked behind the ladder to reveal a toilet, a sink, and a narrow shower. "The water is pumped and heated using a solar-powered pump—there are panels on the flat part of the roof around the cupola." She closed the door and gestured to the kitchenette and scarred wooden table with mismatched chairs. "Plenty of space for cooking."

The center of the room held a sagging sofa and a pair of armchairs grouped around a wooden chest. Guthrie heaved the chest open, squealing at the stacks of board games inside: Monopoly, Yahtzee, Scrabble. The boxes were tattered, the corners worn away. Games left behind from when the lookout was still a private rental—probably all missing essential pieces.

"It looks like Guthrie already chose her bed," Mom said. "That leaves the other one for you." Her smile was too tight, and her eyes flicked back and forth between Chase's. "I know there's not much privacy, but I thought we could hang some curtains around the bed . . . give you your own space."

Curtains around her bed. Just like they were still on the skoolie.

One year, Chase insisted to herself. *Then I'll finally go home.*

Home—Boone, North Carolina. That was where her roots were; that was where she belonged. Where her grandparents had lived and her dad had been born, where he had learned to ride a bike and bought his first set of paints. Where he had grown up in a house that was always in the same place. There was a kind of power in that, in looking out a window at a view that never changed and picking out a spot on the sidewalk under a drooping sycamore tree: *That's where I tripped and skinned my knee and got blood on my favorite shoes.* All the places she had seen blurred together into a carousel of memory that could have belonged to anyone. When she closed her eyes and tried to conjure up a picture of somewhere that meant something to her, the scenes she saw were as impersonal as the stock photos that come in picture frames.

Everywhere they'd gone, everywhere they'd lingered, the people were fiercely loyal to where they were, almost as though their entire selves were wrapped up in that sense of place. If that was a crucial step in development, Chase had evidently missed it. How was she supposed to know who she was if they never stayed anywhere long enough for her to find herself?

The answer had to be in Boone. She didn't understand why Dad had left the only place their family had ever belonged—or what he had been chasing ever since.

Chapter Four

In Chase's sleep that night, she dreamt about the woods, about walking through the endless trees with Guthrie. At first their silence was easy and companionable, but it didn't take long for Chase to feel anxious, her throat working as she strained to speak. Guthrie reached for her, smiling sweetly before ripping a piece of tape off her mouth.

Chase startled awake, tangled in the sheets, blinking at the stars outside her window. Her mouth was sticky, and she rubbed at it with her sleeve before sleep found her again. In the dim light of morning, she found a smear of dark blood on her sleeve, her lips sore and chapped from the change in altitude and the dry western air.

The sky was turning the color of orange marmalade and apricot jam. Chase rolled onto her side. From this angle, she could just see the tops of the trees, outlined in gold by the rising sun.

The wooden ladder groaned as Dad eased his way down from the cupola. He was halfway across the room before he noticed Chase watching him.

"Sorry," he said. He was smiling, but his eyes darted from Chase's face to the front door, where his easel and a stack of canvases were tucked behind a desk. A junkie looking for his fix. "I know it's early. I just have to get out there to paint that view."

Dad had dabbled in all kinds of art over their years on the road—painting murals on commission, teaching still-life drawing in a retirement community, doing freelance graphic design to pay the bills—but at heart, he was a landscape painter. His paintings were alive with color and movement, almost sound. Chase didn't have to be an artist to see why this place appealed to him. It already looked like a painting.

"I was already awake," she said.

"Then why don't you come sit outside with me? Keep me company."

She rustled under the covers. She knew she wouldn't be able to fall back asleep—not with the shrill cacophony of birdsong outside. And soon the sun would spill across her bed like fire through a forest.

"I'll make some coffee," she offered, swinging her legs to the floor.

She pulled on a sweatshirt and put on a pot of coffee to brew. She could see Dad on the deck that circled the lookout tower, setting up his easel and opening his paint kit: a wooden box that unfolded into different compartments, each one packed with half-empty, curling tubes of paint and loose bristles from old brushes. The wood was stained with a rainbow of oil colors. Like Dad, it was disorganized and messy. Chase wasn't sure how he ever found anything he needed, but somehow, he managed to create beauty out of the chaos.

By the time the coffee was done, Guthrie was awake as well, sitting up in bed and rubbing her eyes. She made a noise in her throat like a twig snapping when Chase opened the door to go outside.

"I'll be right there with Dad," Chase said, nodding toward their father. He was already studying his paints. "And Mom is still in bed."

Guthrie chewed on her lip, her brown eyes dark and glassy, but she let Chase go.

When they had found her in the woods that night, Dad had

carried her out with her thin arms clasped around his neck and moans blooming on her lips. She'd cried out when branches brushed her arms, burrowing deeper into Dad's arms like the trees were trying to snatch her away.

Now they were surrounded by trees.

That had been one of Chase's arguments against coming to the lookout. "You do realize that Guthrie had a traumatic experience in the woods, right?" she had said. "How could it possibly be a good idea to move her to an isolated lookout tower surrounded by nothing *but* woods?"

Dad had just shrugged. "I can't think of a better place to heal than in the woods."

Now, Chase could hear the trees whispering to one another when she stepped out onto the deck. The sound was like the steady wash of waves on the beach, rising and falling as the leaves trembled in the wind. Like birdsong, it was a mild sound, a background sound that she wouldn't have noticed except for the silence all around them. There was no hum of traffic or call of neighbors; no dogs barking or doors slamming. Even the sky was silent above them, leaving only the sound of the trees and their secrets.

"Thanks," Dad grunted when she put his coffee on the railing next to his easel. Chase sat in a splintery Adirondack chair with peeling paint, wrapping both her hands around her mug to warm them against the morning chill. Even in late May, the mountain air was cool before the sun rose overhead. Sipping her coffee, she blinked at the jewel-bright sky and thought about Fitzgerald, the nearby ranching town: a one-stoplight tourist trap known for its mineral hot springs and a famous land art installation called Sun Tunnels. Fitzgerald had a small general store where they could do their grocery shopping, but the closest Target was two hours away.

That was a problem. Chase would choose hiking over shopping any day, but you don't get paid to wander around in the woods. And making money was one of the things that she had to do before she could move back to Boone.

But even small towns had to have places that would hire a teenager. A diner, or the gas station. Later this morning, when they went into town, she would apply for any job she could.

Mom and Guthrie were sitting at the table when Chase took her mug back into the kitchen. Guthrie grinned at her from under sleep-tousled dark curls, slurping a spoonful of instant oatmeal. The bird skull she had found the night before was in her other hand.

"Are we still going to Fitzgerald today?" Chase asked, rinsing her mug at the sink.

"Yes," Mom said. "I want to go once a week, so we can do the grocery shopping and catch up on email. Today, we should buy some curtains and storage containers for you girls, and—oh, I better make a list or I'll forget something."

While Mom went through all the things they should stock up on while they were in town, Chase pulled a pair of jeans and a T-shirt out of her suitcase and got dressed in the tiny bathroom. Looking in the mirror, she brushed her hair out of her face. Instead of Guthrie's chocolate curls, it was stick-straight and chestnut brown that lightened to honey during the summer. She kept it long enough to sweep the middle of her back, but rarely wore it loose. When she was younger, it was almost always in complicated braids. One of the only things she remembered about her grandmother was sitting between her knees on the staircase at her house so that Grandma could put her hair in Dutch braids.

She should remember more than that. She had been eight when they died; that was old enough to have memories of people who had been such a big part of her life. Before Dad started chasing something unattainable, they had lived on the same street as her grandparents. But even when Chase closed her eyes and tried to think of them, all she could conjure up was the faint scent of cigar smoke and pink roses worked into the pale-yellow nap of the stair runner; her grandmother's eyes framed by thin lines when she smiled, her grandfather's sandpaper cheek pressed to hers as he pointed at stars in the sky.

Dad was still at his easel when Chase, Guthrie, and Mom tramped down the five flights of stairs to the car. He raised one hand as they drove away. Guthrie waved back, but Chase knew that he was just holding up his paintbrush to match the shade of paint to the sky.

Chapter Five

Fitzgerald's main street was two blocks long, lined with old-fashioned buildings that had square false fronts like in a cartoon ghost town. It felt like a ghost town, too. Besides their car, the only other ones Chase saw were crowded around a small diner with a neon sign shaped like an arrow pointing at the door. The word *PANCAKES*, outlined in flickering tubes of light on the arrow, was the closest thing Chase saw to a name.

"Maybe we can get some after our errands," Mom said, winking at Guthrie in the back seat. "I hope they have chocolate chip."

Chase stayed close to Guthrie during the errands: the grocery store to stock up on canned goods, pasta, and a week's worth of produce; the post office to rent a PO Box. At the library, they got cards, and each checked out a stack of books, before taking advantage of the free Wi-Fi to catch up on the world outside of the fire lookout.

"Oh, the Warners finally moved onto their homestead!" Mom thrust her phone into Chase's face to show her a tiny house in the middle of a meadow with a handful of chickens wandering through the long grass. "Marissa says by next year they'll be able to provide seventy-five percent of their own food." She sighed, scrolling through pictures. "You know, that's what drew us to bus life in the first place. Minimalism and off-grid living. Being more self-sufficient."

"Cool," Chase muttered without looking up. Most of

Mom's friends were people they had connected with through the skoolie community, other families who also wandered the country in the name of disconnecting from mainstream, consumer-driven culture and giving their kids different opportunities.

Opportunities like a lack of privacy, no sense of stability, an inability to relate to greater society . . .

After checking everything off on Mom's list, they walked along Main Street toward the pancake restaurant. Chase looked in all the dusty storefronts for help wanted signs, but the only notices she saw were for going-out-of-business sales.

That didn't bode well for her plans. They had never stayed in one place long enough for Chase to work, but when Dad had announced that he had taken a job as a fire lookout, she had assumed it would be easy for her to earn the money she needed to move back to Boone.

The hostess at the diner looked up when the bell over the door rang, grabbing menus from the stack on the hostess stand. "Table for three?" She led them to a table tucked in an alcove by a player piano that was plunking out "The Entertainer."

"Yep, chocolate chip," Mom said, studying the menu. "That's what I'm getting. What about you, Gus?"

Guthrie bowed her crown of dark curls over the menu, running her finger down the list of choices and stopping on a picture of a pile of pancakes topped with peaches and whipped cream. She tapped the picture and grinned.

Chase leaned over her shoulder to read the description. "Sliced peaches smothered in cinnamon syrup with fresh whipped cream and a dusting of cinnamon sugar. Yeah, that does sound good, but I'm going for an American classic: the Elvis."

Mom wrinkled her nose. "Peanut butter and banana? Ew."

“Don’t forget the bacon. That’s the most important part.”

After they ordered, Chase leaned back in her chair and let her gaze drift around the room. The walls were decorated with pictures of the town over the decades. She could see the lookout in several—grainy black and white, Polaroids with rounded corners, faded sepia. It didn’t matter. The lookout and the trees were the same in each one. Lonely. Deliberate. Eternal.

The consistency of the scenes should be comforting—wasn’t something that hadn’t changed after decades exactly the kind of stability she craved?—but she felt trapped just looking at it. If they were finally going to settle down somewhere, it should be in Boone. It should be where they belonged.

“Be right back. I’m going to ask about getting a job,” she muttered, her chair squeaking across the faded linoleum as she stood up.

The hostess, an older woman with a sheet of long silvery hair, was still standing at the front counter. She smiled at Chase and pushed her glasses up her nose. “Can I help you?”

“Hi,” Chase said. “I was wondering if you’re hiring right now.”

“’Fraid not,” the woman said, her smile pulling down at the corners in sympathy. “We’ve got a couple of regulars who will be home from college soon and are planning on their old shifts over the summer.”

Chase’s heart sank. “Oh,” she muttered. “Thanks anyway.”

“You’re new in town,” the woman observed before Chase could slink back to her table. “My name is Bridget Nelson.”

“I’m Chase Woolf.” She gestured to Mom and Guthrie. “My family just moved to the Fitzgerald Fire Lookout.”

Bridget’s face tightened slightly. “At the lookout—is that right? I didn’t know that it was being rented out again after . . ." Her voice trailed off. Chase waited for her to continue, but she just shook her head and pressed her lips together.

"We're not renting," Chase explained. "The Forest Service reopened it as a lookout station because of the drought."

For decades, the US Forest Service's approach had been to snuff out any fire that broke out without taking into consideration that fires were a natural part of a forest's life cycle. The result was forests that were tinderboxes. Without small fires to clear out the deadfall and leave healthy trees that didn't have to compete for resources, wildfires had become all-consuming, destructive forces that could create their own weather patterns and leave nothing in their wake.

Now, the Forest Service took a different approach. Rather than extinguish every wildfire that sprang up, they focused on managing fires—sometimes going so far as to ignite prescribed burns that could be easily controlled.

Even knowing the importance of fires in a healthy forest ecosystem, Chase felt a surge of panic every time she thought about letting something burn, about intentionally allowing the destruction that came with fires.

"Hmm. Well, you're in luck. I might know just the thing. My son owns the camp at Fitzgerald Lake, just below the lookout. He might have something for you."

"There's a camp at the lake?"

"Spruces. It's a summer camp for children. They do crafts and games, go hiking, and every night there's a singalong. You might pop down there and ask Michael if he has any need of you. He and my grandson Wilder are already there, getting the camp ready to open the week after Memorial Day."

"Thanks," Chase said.

"And tell Wilder I said hello, when you see him." The woman winked and went back to her work.

Chase wandered back toward the table, mulling over the

hostess's reaction when she had mentioned the lookout. *After*. The word was heavy with meaning. After what? Had something happened at the lookout, something serious enough that it hadn't been rented out since? The woman had seemed reluctant to talk about it, which meant it was probably one of those small-town secrets that everyone but Chase knew. One of those things that would always mark her as an outsider in Fitzgerald.

She paused to look more closely at a yellowed snapshot of the lookout, searching the photograph for a hint of its secrets. Her eyes caught on a slight figure in the lower corner, a girl with a haze of dark curls around her face who looked about ten—the same age as Guthrie. She wore a short white dress with a collar and knee socks. Her narrow, serious face was turned slightly away from the camera, her dark eyes fixed on something out of frame.

The way her unruly curls framed her face reminded Chase of Guthrie. It wasn't just that they looked alike. There was something else there—the wild spark in her eyes that was so like the expression on Guthrie's face when Chase had tried to take the bird skull from her.

It's whatever Dad is looking for, she thought, and then she heard the waitress.

"Sorry, that must be an old menu. Peaches aren't in season yet. What can I get you instead?"

Chase turned back to their table just in time to see Guthrie's eyes go flat and glassy. The waitress leaned down toward her with the menu. Her smile faded when Guthrie didn't respond.

"There's one with fresh berries and whipped cream, if you still want something with fruit."

Guthrie bit her bottom lip, her throat working. Chase lurched away from the wall, forgetting the girl in the picture, and slid into her chair next to Guthrie.

"I'm here," she whispered, grabbing Guthrie's hand. It was clammy and shaking.

"Is she okay?" the waitress asked.

Chase didn't answer, because the answer was no. Guthrie hadn't been okay since Chase had left her alone in the woods.

Chapter Six

In the middle of the night, the sound of tapping against a window roused Chase from an uneasy sleep. Shaking off dreams of twiglike hands beckoning to her and Guthrie from the trees, she blinked slowly, trying to get her bearings in the suffocating darkness. Her eyes gradually adjusted until the outlines of the room stood out in shades of black and gray. She held her breath because even the quiet draw of her lungs was enough to drown out the sound. It came again, just above her head: something bumping against the window.

Chase sat up and leaned against the window, pressing her face to the cool glass. Outside, the stars looked close enough to touch, like she could drag her hand through the velvet black and come away with a handful of diamonds filling her palm. She remembered what it had felt like to sit on the steps of the skoolie in the middle of the desert and watch the stars come out: the air thin and sweet with the scent of creosote, the heat of the day fading as the moon rose like a sun that burned cold. In the desert, the sky was so big that it dwarfed everyone, even Dad. And that was gratifying to Chase, a reminder that under the endless desert sky, down at the very bottom of everything, Dad took up just as little space as Chase did, and his dreams were just as insignificant.

A flutter of movement in the clearing below drew her gaze. There—half-hidden in the tree line. A wisp of white that swirled like smoke, eyes swimming in a pale, featureless face. Bones woven into hair like a crown. The figure tilted her head back to stare up at the lookout. The eyes were all wrong—empty and black and much too big. They filled the moon-white face, darkness bleeding together and leaving no room for other features.

Chase's heart seized, stuttering to a stop, as she looked into the black holes on the girl's face. She felt like she was being swallowed up, like she would never stop falling. Falling into a place in her mind where no one could ever reach her—

Flumpf. A moth hit the window where Chase was leaning, striking the glass hard enough that a stream of blood, thick and silver in the moonlight, seeped out of its feathery body. Chase jerked away from the window like she had been burned. The ghost of her fingerprints gleamed against the glass for a heartbeat and then, like the figure in the trees, disappeared.

I was dreaming, Chase told herself, clawing her way out of those bottomless-pit eyes. *Dreaming about* that night *when we found Guthrie in the woods. Dreaming about—*

But the thought drifted away from her as dreams do, leaving only fragments.

There was no sign of the moth in the morning, but the blood was still there. It trailed down the window, a river of red. Chase wrinkled her nose and traced the trickle of blood with her pinky. How could one small moth have so much blood in its body?

Dad's easel was already on the deck when she took her breakfast outside. She climbed onto the bottom rung of the railing, leaning into the sky and searching the trees for a hint of the girl she had, maybe, seen the night before. She wasn't convinced that she had seen anything; she had been half asleep when she heard the beat of the moth's wings against the window. Whatever she had seen had probably just been the tattered remnants of her dream.

One of the trees reached a branch toward the lookout, motioning toward Chase in the wind. The drowning eyes of the girl in white looked up at her mournfully. Chase's toes slipped on the edge of the railing, and for one brief moment her heart stopped, hanging suspended in her chest. She wrapped her fingers around the splintered wood and blinked, waiting for the shape in the trees to sort itself into something she could make sense of.

The eyes were dark and ragged around the edges, scars in the white bark of the aspen trees, weeping tears that were the same rusty color as the aspens' sap.

Knotholes. That was all she had seen.

The screen door banged shut as Dad came out onto the deck with a canvas under one arm. "Careful," he said. "You look like you're about to take flight."

Chase dropped back to the deck. "I thought I saw something." She let out a short bark of laughter, relieved and a little embarrassed. "See that tree down there? The knotholes make it look like it's a face, watching us. It scared me last night."

Dad's eyebrows drew together. "Amazing how much they look like eyes. They form as the aspens self-prune, dropping small branches that don't get enough sunlight." He took a step back, studying the view from the deck, then pivoted the easel to face the other direction. "So Mom said that you're going down to the camp at the lake today."

His voice was flat and even, but Chase still bristled. Over the years, Dad had made his thoughts about places like summer camps and wilderness glamping resorts perfectly clear. He even complained whenever Mom insisted they visit a national park, calling the crowded parks "the Disneyfication of nature," a watered-down version of wildness that catered to the lowest common denominator.

Chase didn't agree. Not everyone could pack their family into a school bus like a tin of sardines and wander through the deserts, the mountains, the high plains. Normal people snatched at nature on long weekends and annual trips. They relied on national parks and places like Spruces to fill themselves with nature, to take small sips of the tonic of wilderness.

She hadn't forgotten how she had felt two years ago in Arches when they reached the end of the dusty trail, as crowded as a theme-park line, and clambered along the narrow ledge of red rock into a natural amphitheater crowded with tourists. Delicate Arch had risen out of the desert, ancient and enduring, and Chase had felt . . . wonderstruck. Kinship. Sanctified. Alone and together, all at the same time. It was like a pilgrimage that she had made with those strangers. The trail had been noisy and bustling, full of crying toddlers and complaining teenagers, but at Delicate Arch, everything was hushed and solemn, and Chase felt like she belonged.

She thrust out her chin. "It's my last shot at finding a job. No one was hiring in Fitzgerald."

"Would it be so bad if you couldn't find one? You've got the rest of your life to work."

"Well, I'll keep that in mind if it turns out you have a secret college fund for me," she said snidely.

Dad clucked his tongue. "No secret college fund, but if you really want to go, I know you'll find a way. We raised you to be tenacious."

After breakfast, Chase shook off the tendrils of fear that crept up her neck at the thought of going back into the woods and started down the path to Spruces. It had grown wild in the years since the lookout had last been used, just a hint of a track through weeds that swayed to Chase's knees. If she looked at it straight on, it disappeared into the undergrowth. So she kept her eyes lazy and unfocused, following the curves out of the corner of her eye.

The sounds of the lookout followed her into the trees: the tinkling of a windchime hung on the deck, the *thwack-thwack* of Dad's brush against the canvas, the slam of the screen door. Chase relaxed the tense set of her shoulders and filled her lungs with fresh air that billowed and swirled like the clouds of birds above. Twigs cracked underfoot, birds sang overhead, and the grass parted with a constant *hush-hush-hush* as she followed the path.

The wind had come down this hill, toppling long, straight trees so that they lay across the path like broken femurs. They made their own network through the grass and the wildflowers, the thickets of wild lilac that tangled in Chase's hair and the roots that seemed to creep across the path when she wasn't looking. She stepped onto one of the fallen trees, one hand held out like she was on a balance beam. Even that slight movement was enough for her to lose her tenuous view of the faint path. It disappeared into the swaying grass, and Chase froze. The lookout was above her and the lake was below, but this network of fallen trees might lead anywhere. If she had learned anything from looking for Guthrie in the woods that night, it was that trees couldn't be trusted.

It had been six months since she and Guthrie had gone for a walk in the woods at a campground in South Dakota. They hadn't gone far, just enough to escape the sound of traffic from the busy two-lane highway that led to Mount Rushmore. The campground was kitschy and full of tourists wearing fanny packs and matching T-shirts. It was not the kind of place they normally stayed, but the town had commissioned Dad to paint a mural on the side of the new parking garage.

When Chase finally got bored, she headed back to the

campground, thinking Guthrie could find her way back on her own. Chase wasn't even supposed to have been with Guthrie—*Dad* had promised to go for a walk with her. But he had been distracted, focused on a rough sketch of the mural, and had talked Chase into taking his place. And after everything—after Guthrie had wandered in circles in the woods, her tears tracing tracks on her cheeks as muddled as the footprints she left, after they had found her cowering against a tree, her wide eyes shining white and panicked in the dark, after she started moaning in her sleep and wetting her pants and even after she stopped talking—Mom and Dad had brushed it all off.

Still. Chase was the one who had left her alone in the woods.

Shivering, she stepped off the tree and back onto the path, her mind filled with thoughts of Guthrie alone in the woods. The birds above her were suddenly silent. She could still hear the soft movement of their wings as they moved from branch to branch, but they had stopped singing.

It lured me in, Chase thought, then bit her lip to stop herself from trembling. *The woods lured me in until I was too deep to make it back to the lookout and now—*

And now what? Nothing had changed. She was still on the path to Spruces. The sun was out and a soft breeze carried the scent of wildflowers. It was a beautiful day, and she was out for a walk in the woods.

But now the trees were watching her.

The trees in Pando were covered in dark whorls, knotholes that wept red sap, but she wasn't used to their strange shape, the graceful swoop of the scars that were so evocative of eyelids and eyebrows. Chase knew they were just knotholes, but she could feel their gaze on her as she pushed deeper into the forest, the trees whispering to each other with the quaking flutter of leaves. The tingle on the back of her neck, the way her breathing hitched in her chest and her legs ached to bolt. The only thing that stopped her from scrambling into a run was the fear that if she ran, whatever was behind her would give chase.

Because there *was* something behind her. It was more than just the blank stares of the knotholes. It was the thrum of the sap in the veins of the trees, the soft mantle of silence that had settled on Chase and Guthrie that first day at the lookout.

A physiological response, she told herself. *The knotholes look so much like eyes that my body can't tell the difference. That's why I feel like I'm being watched. But if I look back, there won't be anything there.*

She stopped breathing long enough for her lungs to revolt and blood to throb in her temples in protest, and then she turned around.

The watcher was made of bone and bark, smooth and white with empty eye sockets that reminded Chase of the expression on Guthrie's face when Dad had carried her out of the woods. Antlers curved out of the tree trunk like twisted branches. The tree had nearly consumed the deer skull, and knobs of bark like pearls on a string showed where the vertebrae had already been devoured.

Chase clapped a hand over her mouth to muffle her squeak of shock. Fear passed over her like a flash of heat lightning, and then anxious giggles spilled out. She gasped for breath, bending at the waist to settle her hands on her knees, and caught sight of the deer skull again. It glared at her, and now it was no more threatening than a mask in a Halloween store.

"Nice to meet you," she said, dissolving into giggles again. She felt punch-drunk and silly right up until a voice behind her answered.

"Nice to meet you, too."

Chapter Seven

Chase's heart leapt against her ribs like a bird trapped in a cage as a boy stepped out of the trees. She stumbled back, bumping against the deer skull. The sharp points of the antlers pressed into her back. "Where did you come from?" she blurted out.

The boy shoved a pair of round-framed glasses up his nose with fingers slim and pale as aspen twigs. "From Spruces. You must be the girl from the pancake restaurant. Peanut butter and banana, right?"

"And bacon," Chase added, her heart slowing. She stepped away from the antlers. "Did your grandmother tell you about me?"

He grinned. He had a cute smile, with slightly crooked front teeth that only added to its charm. "Gram knows all the new gossip around town. She said you're looking for a job."

"Yeah. I'm Chase—Chase Woolf. I was just on my way down to Spruces to meet you and your father."

"Wilder Nelson. And I see you've already met Skully." Wilder motioned behind Chase.

Chase glanced at the skull in the tree. "You know about this?"

"Dad showed it to me years ago. It was here when he was a kid. You used to be able to see parts of the backbone, but I guess the tree has grown over it."

"But how did it happen?" Chase asked.

Wilder paused. "You ever see bucks fight? It can get pretty brutal. Sometimes their antlers get tangled. If they can't break apart, they end up dying stuck together. This deer must have charged the tree for some reason. Wedged one of his antlers into the wood, couldn't pull loose, and died here. When all that was left was bone, the tree started to grow over it."

"Lovely." Chase wrinkled her nose.

He snorted, then crossed his arms. "I didn't mean to startle you. I was actually coming up to the lookout to meet you. Gram thought we might be about the same age."

"I'm seventeen," Chase said.

"Me, too," he said. "Eighteen in August. I'll be a senior when school starts. What about you?"

"I'm a senior, too, I guess." She fidgeted with a strand of hair that had been pulled loose by the branches, catching the confused expression on his face. "I'm homeschooled. I just need a few more credits, and then I'll graduate." *And then I'll turn eighteen, and then I'll be out of here*, she finished in her head.

"Cool. You want to come back down to Spruces with me?"

He led the way down the trail, walking backward half the time so he could talk to her. "I just got my lifeguard certification, so I'll be out at the lake this summer. But Dad might have something for you." He batted a branch out of the way, then held it up for Chase. Her skin tingled as she ducked under his arm. "Most of the counselors are other teenagers from Fitzgerald, so it's a fun place to work."

Of course. Spruces sounded like it was the kind of job that people went back to year after year. The counselors had probably all grown up together and now worked together and had all kinds of shared experiences that she would never understand. Summer romances, jokes, feuds—things that wouldn't make sense to someone on the outside looking in.

Someone like her.

I just need to make money, not friends, she thought. God. She sounded like a contestant on *The Bachelor*.

The woods opened onto a rocky shore. The lake was deep green and smooth as a sheet of glass. She could see the lookout tower on the hill over the lake, could feel it watching her with Dad's disapproval of the camp seeping out of the windows and flooding down through the aspens.

Wilder pointed out the buildings as they walked through the camp: the bunkhouses in a wide, grassy field; the boathouse next to a dock that ran out into the water; the mess hall.

"Is that a firepit?" Chase asked, pointing at a circle of blackened stone surrounded by rough plank benches. Alarm bells went off in her head. She knew that Utah—like all of the American West—had been in a drought for years, and it was only getting worse. That was the whole reason the Forest Service had reopened the Fitzgerald Fire Lookout, the whole reason her family was here.

"It used to be," Wilder said. "Don't worry, we haven't had a bonfire in years. We still sit around here at night and sing songs and stuff, but instead of a fire, we pass out glow sticks and eat no-bake s'mores bars instead of roasting marshmallows."

The knot in Chase's stomach loosened as they passed the firepit and came to a log building that gleamed yellow with fresh varnish. A sign reading SPRUCES EST. 1990 hung over the open front door. Wilder jogged up the steps and poked his head inside.

"Hey, I met one of our new neighbors." He motioned for Chase to come up the steps. Inside, a balding man with lanky limbs was hunched over a computer desk. "Dad, this is Chase Woolf. Chase, this is my father."

The man unfolded himself from the desk chair and stood up, holding out a hand for Chase to shake. "Hi, Chase, I'm Michael Nelson. It's nice to meet you."

"Nice to meet you, too." She shifted her weight from one foot to the other. Her throat felt like it had cottonwood fluff stuck in it. Now that the time had come to ask for a job, she wasn't sure how to approach it. *Remember Boone*, she told herself, and drew in a deep breath. "Mr. Nelson—"

"Call me Michael."

"Okay. Michael, I know that it's late in the season and you've probably already hired your staff, but I was wondering if you have any jobs available. I'm saving money for college, and living at the lookout makes it hard to get into town for a job."

Michael crossed his arms and tilted his head. "As a matter of fact, one of my counselors just broke her leg, so she's out for the season. How do you feel about arts and crafts?"

Chase was the least creative person on the planet. It had been her first unconscious rebellion against her father. When she was younger, she used to have a miniature set of his art supplies: an easel, a pack of children's watercolors. But when Dad tried to teach her how to mix colors, hers turned a muddy brown. When he showed her how to use a pencil to outline a scene, she pressed hard enough to tear the paper and break the lead. He finally gave up, drifting away into his own world, and Chase felt a twinge of regret that she couldn't join him there.

"I love arts and crafts," Chase lied. "In fact, my father is an artist."

Michael cocked an eyebrow. "Then this is serendipity. Or as Bob Ross would say, a happy little accident." He reached for a drawer in the filing cabinet next to the desk. It squealed as he pulled it open. "You can take this new-employee form with you and fill it out. Camp starts the week after Memorial Day. It's an easy enough job. We host kids ages eight to twelve from all over the western United States. Sessions run for one week—Monday through Friday—but since they leave on Friday, you have that day off. Then the next week, a new group arrives. Each age group has two art sessions for the week they're here, so you just have to come up with a couple of projects and then repeat them every week. You know, boondoggles, pinecone bird feeders, that kind of thing. The art room is stocked with all kinds of supplies, but if you think of something else you need, just give me a list and I'll pick it up. Here's a counselor shirt and a key to the art room—" Michael pulled a brass key off his keyring, handing it to Chase along with the employment form and a deep green polo shirt embroidered with a spruce tree. "Wilder can give you a little orientation and answer any questions you have."

"Thank you," Chase said, her head spinning like she had just run up all five flights of stairs to the lookout. "I really appreciate this. I'm excited to get started."

"We're happy to have you. Welcome to the Spruces family—and to Pando." Michael was still smiling, but it suddenly seemed tighter . . . forced. "By the way, how is everything at the lookout? I haven't been up there in quite some time."

Chase shrugged. "It's only been two days."

"Of course," Michael said. Now there was a noticeable crease in his forehead, and his eyes were flat and serious. "Well, you and the rest of your family are always welcome here—just in case anything happens up at the lookout."

Chapter Eight

Michael's words rang through Chase's head, his strange offer dampening the elation she felt at finding a job.

In case anything happens up at the lookout.

He had said it like he *expected* something to happen.

Like something had happened there before, something that could happen again.

"What did he mean by—" She hesitated, biting back her words. She didn't want to sound paranoid. Michael had probably just meant it in the context of living in an isolated fire lookout with no cell service. Spruces was the closest thing to civilization in Pando, so of course he would offer help if they needed it.

"By what?" Wilder asked.

"Oh, uh—" She laughed to cover the awkward pause. "By boondoggles? I have no idea what those are."

"You never made boondoggles when you were a kid?" Wilder laughed, too. "They're these complicated keychains you make out of plastic cording. I'm sure there are some in the art room."

He led the way to a small shed with dirty windows, and Chase fumbled with the key Michael had given her. The shelves were stocked with the kinds of art supplies that Dad would scoff at: pom-poms like colorful dandelion fluff, powdered tempera paint, fuzzy pipe cleaners.

Chase made mental lists as Wilder pulled open cabinets and drawers. She would have to scour Pinterest for craft projects next time they went into Fitzgerald. Maybe Guthrie would have some ideas.

"So where are you from?" Wilder pulled out a pencil sharpener and set to work sorting through an enormous box of colored pencils.

"North Carolina," she said. "Boone. But we've been all over for the past few years."

"Oh yeah? Are your parents military or something?"

Chase let out a short bark of laughter at the thought of her dad taking orders from anyone. "No way. My parents are definitely more the hippie type. It's complicated, but we've been living in a skoolie for a while—a school bus renovated to be like an RV."

Chase recognized the bright flame in Wilder's eyes with a sinking heart: wanderlust. Fanaticism. A fervent zeal to throw his life away.

"Come on, there's something else I haven't shown you yet." Wilder grabbed her hand and hauled her out the door, pulling her back across the camp to a sagging barn, where something hulked in the weeds, something shrouded with a tarp, something suspiciously bus-shaped. Chase dragged her feet as Wilder yanked the ragged tarp off to reveal a short white bus sitting on bald tires.

"This"—Wilder stroked the bumper like the bus was his pet dog—"is Georgia Pie."

Georgia Pie. A stupid name for a bus. It sounded like something an old lady would name one of her collectible porcelain dolls. Or Chase supposed it could be the name of a food truck that specialized in peach pie. But Georgia Pie wasn't going to be a food truck.

"I'm going to take her out after graduation next year," Wilder said. The words tumbled out of his mouth as he opened the door and ushered her in. Inside the bus, it smelled like hot sunshine and split leather, the must of foam padding poking out from the cracks in the upholstery, the thick, rich, scent of oil in the sun.

"Dad got a new camp bus last year," Wilder explained. "I did some demo last fall, but it was too cold to work on her during the winter."

Chase glanced around at the mostly stripped interior. "Cool," she lied. "But hey, I better get back to the lookout. I've been gone for a while. My sister might be worried."

Wilder pulled the bus door closed behind them and then walked with Chase back toward the wooded path that led to the lookout. A breeze ruffled the water, sending foamy ripples across the lake.

"What about you?" Chase asked as they turned into the woods, eager to steer the conversation away from skoolies. She picked flowers as they walked, delicate bluebells and snowy-white columbines. "How long have you lived in Fitzgerald?"

"My whole life. My parents grew up here, and my grandparents, and my great-grandparents." He gave a grim laugh. "I guess you could say that our roots run as deep as Pando's."

Jealousy bloomed in Chase's mouth, oily and sour. "That must be nice. To grow up in a place where everyone knows your family."

"Are you kidding? It's the worst. Everyone thinks of me as a kid because they knew me when I was little. And no one ever forgets anything. Everyone knows about—" He bit his words off sharply, clamping his teeth.

"What?" Chase asked. "What does everyone know about?"

"Nothing. Family stuff."

She waited for him to elaborate, but his face turned stormy and he didn't say anything else.

"Can I ask you something?" Chase said. She picked another flower, this one a deep blue coneflower. "About the lookout."

The trail was narrow enough that she could feel Wilder stiffen beside her. "What about it?"

"Did something happen there?"

"Like what?"

Chase hesitated. Her suspicions suddenly seemed very flimsy. What exactly was she basing this theory on? She hadn't wanted to come here in the first place. Wasn't it more likely that she was simply letting those feelings affect how she interpreted people's reactions? Searching for some reason that her family shouldn't be here, letting herself get carried away by inflections and things unsaid?

"Nothing," she said. "Never mind. It's just not my favorite place."

The tense set of Wilder's jaw relaxed, and his fists unclenched, fingers brushing against Chase's before he shifted away. He glanced at the clouds rolling across the sky, dark and tinged green like a week-old bruise. "Looks like it's going to storm. Are you okay going the rest of the way by yourself?"

"Yeah. You should head back before you get caught in the rain."

"I'll see you in a few days." He pushed his glasses up his nose, then picked a daisy from the side of the trail and handed it to Chase before heading back toward camp. "For you."

Chapter Nine

When Chase got back to the lookout, Dad was standing at the bottom of the stairs, bouncing a tennis ball off the wall of the lean-to where they parked the car. "Any luck?" he asked.

"You're looking at the new arts and crafts counselor at Spruces," she said. "Camp starts in a week."

"Oh really?" Dad let his ball roll away, pressing his lips into a tight smile that instantly made Chase's nostrils flare.

"I know what you're going to say," she said. She put on a nasally drawl. "'Places like that don't encourage true expressions of creativity. They just want to churn out as much construction paper detritus as possible. Craft projects that will go straight into the trash as soon as the kids leave the art room. Save them the trouble and rip their projects in half as they walk out the door.'"

"Is that what I sound like?" He seemed amused. "Well, damn."

Chase shrugged. It was easier to make his reaction into a joke than to hear what he really thought. She knew better than to expect any support from him. Dad only supported himself: his ambitions, his career, his goals.

They only pursued his dreams.

But Chase was done ignoring her own. She was going to go back to the only place she had ever belonged, and working at Spruces was how she would get there.

"Well, for your information, that's not what I was going to

say at all," Dad said. "I was going to tell you that I'm proud of you for finding a way to meet your goals, and that this is a great opportunity for you to introduce kids to true creativity. Maybe show them how to embrace their individuality."

Chase blinked. Proud of her? She couldn't remember the last time he had told her he was proud of her. He was usually so wrapped up in his own art that nothing else seemed to matter.

"Oh," she said. "Well, thanks. I guess."

The sky cracked open in a flash of light, and Dad scooped his tennis ball off the ground.

"Come on," he said. "Let's hurry before we get struck by lightning."

His easel stood at the top of the stairs, the canvas blocked out in the first step of a landscape painting. Chase squinted at it before going inside, trying to find the shape of the mountain ridge and trees, but all she saw was a muddy swirl of colors. Dad said she spent too much time looking at what was right in front of her instead of seeing what was really there, which made less sense every time she thought about it.

Dad dragged the easel in behind her just as the storm broke, tucking it out of the way in a corner. Chase shivered at the chill on the back of her neck before he closed the door. The afternoon had been warm, but the temperature must have dropped twenty degrees with the rain.

"There you are!" Mom said. She and Guthrie turned to look at her from where they stood together at the stove. The rich, creamy smell of homemade cocoa wafted across the room. "We were worried you would get caught in the storm."

"I almost did," Chase said. She rummaged through one of the cabinets for a mason jar to put the bouquet in. Her heart fluttered a little as she arranged the flowers so that Wilder's daisy was in front. It stood out among the other flowers, cheerful and bright.

Mom gave the cocoa one last stir, then brushed her hands on her apron. "Well? How did it go?"

"Good," Chase said. "I got a job."

"Nice! I know you were really hoping this would work out. What will you be doing?"

Guthrie ladled cocoa into the mugs while Chase told them about the camp and about meeting Wilder and his dad. The four of them settled on the sagging couch and armchairs as the rain streamed down the windows, blurring their view of the world outside. Maybe it was as futile as a small child covering their eyes to hide from some imagined threat—*if I can't see them, they can't see me*—but something inside Chase loosened, tiny muscles that she hadn't even realized she had been tensing. The tight fist of paranoia that she was always being watched unraveled.

"I think I'll like it," she concluded, sipping her cocoa. "What did you guys do while I was gone?"

"Oh, nothing much. Dad painted, and Gus helped me clear out some of the overgrown raspberry bushes down in the clearing. I'm going to plant a garden. Oh—" Mom turned to Guthrie, laying her hand on her knee. "Show Chase what you found!"

Guthrie set her mug on the chest and scrambled across the room, snatching something white and knobbly off the wide windowsill over her bed: a skull the size of a child's fist with deep, wide-set eye sockets and a sharp jaw with a row of yellowing teeth. A fox, or a small coyote maybe. At the base of the skull, several inches of dirt-covered bone protruded like muddy roots. Guthrie held it like it was a bridal bouquet she had wrenched out of the earth.

Chase's mouth twisted as she examined the skull and its appendage. It was smooth, except for the splintered end, like a femur that had been snapped. It wasn't the jointed string of bones like vertebrae, or anything else that Chase had ever seen.

"What is that thing?" she said with distaste. "The part coming out of the bottom?" *The roots.*

"We're not sure," Dad said. "Maybe some kind of tumor that forced the head away from the spine. Whatever it was probably killed the animal."

Chase shuddered as a chill swept over her, then finished her hot chocolate in one swallow so that her chest ached from the spreading heat. "So was it buried in the garden plot where you were working?"

Guthrie shook her head and gestured out the window toward the trees.

"She was playing while I worked," Mom explained. "I think she found it over by the edge of the clearing somewhere."

Chase frowned. "Weren't you watching her? She shouldn't be alone out there. It isn't safe."

If anything happens up at the lookout . . .

"Relax," Dad said. "I could see her from the deck."

Considering how lost Dad could get in his work, Chase didn't exactly find this reassuring, but she let the subject drop.

Chapter Ten

"Shit," Chase muttered as a thorny tendril caught in the tender skin of her wrist. A bead of blood welled from the wound.

They had been at the lookout for a week, and Mom had made them spend an hour every morning working to clear the garden. She had found shears and shovels in the storage shed, but no gloves, and Chase's hands were paying the price.

"Is this really worth it?" Chase asked, holding up her hands so Mom could see the swollen skin and red scratches. "We can just buy vegetables at the store."

"I know, but I've always wanted to have a garden," Mom said. "Tom, remember how I had just planted my first one in Boone when we got the skoolie and left?"

"Zucchini, corn, and tomatoes," Dad said, leaning on his shovel. "I'm sure it would've been a bountiful harvest."

"You just left it?" Chase frowned, remembering the veiled envy in Mom's voice when she had talked about her friend's homestead.

Mom shrugged. "Hopefully whoever bought our house got to enjoy it. But you're right, you girls have done enough for today. Why don't you and Gus go play? Dad and I can finish this up."

Dad grunted, flicking his eyes toward the tangled mess they still had to wrestle out of the ground, but straightened up and stabbed his shovel into the earth without arguing.

Guthrie's favorite place to play was under the watchful

gaze of the tree that had startled Chase so much in the night. The tree still made her uneasy. Even in the bright light of day, she saw a face in its ragged knotholes, saw reaching, grasping hands in its tangled branches. And as much as she hated the crawling feel of the sightless eyes on her skin, she was wary of Guthrie playing alone so close to the woods, so she strung up a hammock between a pair of nearby trees and read while Guthrie collected bits of nature to arrange at the base of the tree. Offerings on the altar of the forest: handfuls of acorns and bright red berries, the hollow, papery dome of an abandoned wasp nest, a bundle of silver-green leaves that rustled in the wind. She used hanks of plaited grass to tie twigs into crude triangles that looked like some sort of rune meant to invoke wild magic. She wove springy, discarded aspen branches into wreaths.

And she plucked bones from the dirt like they were flowers.

The woods seemed littered with them: mandibles and scapulae rising out of the loamy soil like seashells out of sand. Chase speculated that there must have been an owl or hawk that nested near the lookout, and the tiny bones had been discarded from its roost. Even with this logical explanation, she still didn't like Guthrie's sudden fascination with bones, and she had said so when Mom untangled an old necklace and helped Guthrie string the bird skull on it like a pendant.

"How is it any different from collecting feathers or preserving dragonflies?" Mom had asked.

"It feels morbid."

"Hmm. I guess I just see it as nature."

It was this darker, twisted side of the natural world that Chase felt every time she was among the aspen trees. No matter how brightly the sun shone, under the trees, the light was flat and diffused. Brassy. The woods were filled with birdsong, but it was shrill, the kind of cacophony that put her teeth on edge and made her bones itch.

And the trees were always watching, watching . . .

She draped an arm over her eyes to block out their gaze, the hammock swaying in the breeze that quaked through the leaves above. Tomorrow was the first day of camp. Chase had spent the past week coming up with ideas of projects to do and making lists of supplies she would need, but every time she thought about it, her stomach tilted to the side like she was on a carnival ride. Maybe this was a huge mistake. She didn't know anything about teaching arts and crafts, and this would be the first time in years that she and Guthrie would be apart for more than a few hours.

Well. Not counting that night, of course.

If we were like everyone else, we'd both be in school all day. And next year, I'll be two thousand miles away, she reminded herself.

Sometimes, she already felt like she was that far away from her sister.

She could hear the faint *swish* of long, swaying grass as Guthrie darted along the tree line, humming and occasionally whispering to herself: *bones* and *wither* and *twist.* It was these secret murmurs that Chase tried so hard to catch. Maybe something Guthrie said to the trees would be the key to understanding who she was now, would help Chase find a way to apologize for leaving her alone. But the more she listened for Guthrie's secrets, the faster they seemed to drift away, as fleeting and silvery as her voice.

Other sounds were drifting away, too—the steady *chunk* of Mom and Dad's shovels in the rocky soil, the omnipresent chatter of the birds above. The only things left were Guthrie's soft, indistinct voice and the answering whisper of the wind in the leaves.

But the air had gone completely still. The hammock had stopped swaying, and Chase no longer felt the shiver of wind across her brow. She held out one hand to be sure, then opened her eyes to watch for the fickle twist of the leaves overhead, but they hung limp and bedraggled.

Guthrie laughed, somewhere off to the side, and Chase's eyes darted to the tree where she crouched. The tree whispered back, a hushed give-and-take between the still leaves and Guthrie, like she wasn't just talking to herself this time, like she was actually having a conversation with someone else . . .

Chase rolled out of the hammock, stumbling a little and grabbing onto the trunk of one of the trees that supported her hammock.

"Gus?" she called. Her voice hung in the air like a mote of dust, not quite an echo but lingering far longer than it should. Her chest felt tight in a sudden pressure shift, like the atmosphere had condensed, squeezing all of her molecules into a smaller space. She raked her gaze over the trees, searching for the telltale flutter of leaves where an errant breeze might be responsible for the whispering sound, but they were completely still, held motionless by the same pressure that kept her from taking a step toward her sister.

Guthrie glanced over her shoulder at Chase, then looked back at the tree with the face, and Chase thought she saw the knotholes widen and deepen, yawning into the bottomless pits that had nearly swallowed her up the other night. Her head spun, and her mouth opened, and this time her voice was whip-sharp in the suffocating air.

"Guthrie!"

Her legs steadied enough for her to let go of the tree that she was clutching and stride through the thin grove to Guthrie. She hadn't realized how dizzy she was from getting out of the hammock, but that explained the sense of disorientation, the way the knotholes had seemed to swell.

Guthrie smiled up at her, holding out a wilting chain of dandelions and daisies that she was draping over the tree.

It stared balefully at Chase, the eyes nothing more than knotholes, a trickle of rusty sap leaking from one corner like a bloody tear.

"Were you talking to someone?" But Chase knew, even as she asked, that the answer was no. It had to be, because Guthrie didn't talk to anyone.

And besides, there was no one else around.

Chase reminded herself of these facts over and over throughout the rest of the afternoon, but that night, when the lookout was dark and the moon shone silver on the eyes of the trees, it was harder to make herself believe that there hadn't been someone else at the edge of the woods.

But it was the truth.

It had to be the truth.

If it *wasn't* true—if Guthrie had been talking to someone in the trees—that meant that Chase really had seen a girl dressed in bones at the edge of the woods.

Every time that thought crept in, Chase squirmed at the ridiculousness of it. Pando may be a superorganism, but it wasn't sentient.

She gave up on sleep sometime around midnight. Huffing out a sigh, she sat up and leaned against the frosted glass of her window, staring into the forest below. She squinted, looking for any hint of movement in the trees, and nearly gasped when the shadows shifted—

A small animal, maybe a fox, creeping through the underbrush at the tree line. The bushes rustled as it disappeared deeper into the forest.

This was ridiculous. Chase couldn't spend the next year jumping at shadows, convinced the trees were watching her. Parting the curtains around her bed, she slipped out and padded across the floor to the front door. She jammed her feet into her sneakers without lacing them and turned the doorknob slowly, willing the door not to creak as it opened.

Outside, the air was thin and sharp with cold. Chase shivered and crept down the stairs. The moonlight lay across the clearing like a band of silver. Crossing her arms, she waded through the swaying grass, right up to the tree where Guthrie liked to play.

Forcing out any bit of fear with decisive breaths, she set her jaw and waited for the sound to fade, the air to thicken, the eyes to swallow her whole.

But the leaves only rustled in the benign breeze playing across her skin. She counted sixty breaths before turning back to the lookout.

This time, when she felt the familiar creep of eyes on her back, she didn't think twice about the knotholes that marred the trees all around.

Chapter Eleven

"I'll be back this afternoon," Chase promised over toast the next morning. "Then we can play a game, or go for a walk, or do whatever you want."

Guthrie gave her a sticky thumbs-up, fingers covered in jam. She kept looking out the window, like she was expecting to see someone, but the only one outside was Dad.

"And while I'm gone, you stay close to Mom," Chase added. "Don't go into the woods. It's easy to get lost here. All the trees look the same."

Pressing her mouth into a smile that was so tight it was almost a scoff, Guthrie gave a little half-laugh and shook her head. It was clear she didn't agree about the trees, but she nodded when Chase pressed the point about her staying close to the lookout.

Dad was standing at his easel, staring out over the sea of trees, when she left for camp a few minutes later. The silver-green leaves on the quaking aspens shifted like the sun flashing off waves. He looked up when the screen door banged shut behind her.

"Off to work?" he asked. He was smiling, but his mouth twisted down at the corner like it took a lot of effort.

"Yep." She adjusted her backpack and took a step toward the stairs.

"Hey." Dad grabbed her hand. "Places like Spruces aren't my thing"—his lip curled more—"but you'll be great at it."

Chase jerked out of his grasp. "Wow. Thanks a lot."

"I didn't mean—"

But his explanation was lost under the rattle of her jogging down the lookout stairs. She didn't have time to explain why it was an insult to be told she'd be good at something he reviled.

The camp was bustling when she broke through the trees at the end of the path. Chase recognized the deep forest-green polos of the other counselors. Wilder waved from the pebbly beach where he was lining up the canoes, glossy red like the poisonous nightshade berries that grew in the woods. He dragged the last one into place and then jogged over to meet her.

"Hi," he said. His hair was tousled and messy, like he had just woken up. "Good to see you again."

"Yeah, you too." Her cheeks flushed when he grinned at her.

"Come on, Morning Welcome is just about to start."

Chase followed him toward a clearing where Michael was greeting campers and helping the counselors arrange them into groups.

A girl with olive skin and chin-length black hair sidled along the edge of the mayhem and bumped Wilder with her shoulder. "Hey. Who's your new friend?"

"Willow, this is Chase. She's the new arts and crafts counselor," Wilder said. "Chase, Willow and I go to school together."

"Hi." Willow was like her name: tall and slender with long, springy limbs and bone-straight hair. She gestured at herself. "Archery and ropes course. Wilder used to do the ropes, but I guess he thinks he'll be able to get some color on that pasty chest." She made a face at Wilder, and Chase's stomach tightened at the easy familiarity between them. Besides her family, she had never been close enough with anyone to joke like that. And lately, it seemed like even her relationships with them were shaped more by tension than by laughter.

"Dad needed a lifeguard." Wilder shrugged off Willow's teasing as a bell echoed across the camp.

"To our new friends—welcome to Spruces! And to our old friends, welcome back!" Michael's voice was like the bell he rang to bring them together, deep and resonant. It carried over the small crowd of campers gathered on rough-hewn log benches in the center of the camp. Chase tried to listen as he continued his welcome speech, but her mind was racing ahead to the art project she had planned for the day, mentally going over the steps again and again.

"You okay?" Wilder murmured. Chase blinked, realizing too late that she was staring just as blankly as the knothole-marked trees.

She pulled her mouth into a smile. "Yeah. Just zoned out, I guess."

He flashed her a grin. There was a tiny dimple in the corner of his mouth that only showed when he smiled a certain way—not too wide, not for show. "Gotta pay attention, Woolf. Those kids'll run wild if they sense any weakness. You don't want them to rebel, or you'll end up like the guy in *The Scream*." He pulled a face, his mouth sagging open, eyes wide in exaggerated horror, hands clapped to his cheeks like the Edvard Munch painting.

"Don't worry," Chase said. "They won't know what hit 'em. I'll have them so deep in the creative process that it'll be like an Escher print—no way out." She winced inwardly at the false confidence in her voice. Surely Wilder would see right through it; surely he could tell that she was in over her head. But what could she do? Admit to the boss's son that she had no idea what she was doing?

Michael finished his speech and announcements, and the camp broke up, each age group following their own morning schedule before lunch together in the mess hall.

"Chase!" Wilder's voice again, this time from halfway

across the clearing. His dark green polo stood out in the sea of campers swarming toward their various activities, and Chase realized with a jolt of horror that a pack of eight-year-old Hares was already pouring through the art room doors. Wilder clapped his hands to his cheeks again in another parody of *The Scream* as Chase turned and ran to catch up with them.

All in all, the morning went well. One girl came into the art room with two blonde pigtails and left with them green, but the paint was washable, and Chase was ninety percent sure that it really had been an accident. She was sweeping the floor before lunch when Willow came in.

"Hey." Willow spoke from the doorway. "How's your first day going?"

Chase straightened up. "It's . . ." Her gaze drifted around the room to the chair flipped by the back table, the overflowing trash can, the sticky glue drying on the counter next to the sink. "A lot," she finally settled on.

Willow laughed and came into the room. Her eyes were the same color as the gray, weathered wood of the lookout, but they were warm. More like a fleece blanket than the splintered deck, Chase decided.

"It takes a while to get used to it," Willow said, sweeping an armful of torn paper off one table and into a trash bag. "I think I went to bed at eight every night during my first summer working here."

"When was that?" Chase asked.

"Three years ago. And I was a camper myself for a few years before that. I practically grew up here." She tapped a spot on one of the scarred wooden tables, where *WN* had been carved into the wood in clumsy, crooked letters. "Wilder and I have the same initials—Wilder Nelson and Willow Neal—and now we can't even remember which one of us carved this."

So she and Wilder had known each other since childhood.

Chase wondered what that was like. There must be downsides, of course. She was glad there wasn't anyone who could remember her mouthful of rubber bands and spit when she had braces. Or the way she had tried to speak in verse for six months when she was a tween. No one from her past to tease her with embarrassing nicknames.

But Willow talked about Wilder in that easy, comfortable way that Chase had always envied. It must be nice to share so many experiences with someone that their memories became yours.

"Let's grab lunch," Willow suggested. "The kids get PB and J, but Cookie keeps a stash of frozen pizzas for the counselors."

Chase's stomach growled. Pizza sounded amazing, even the frozen kind with crust like cardboard, and it would be nice to spend an hour talking to someone her own age before she had to face the afternoon sessions.

"Okay," she agreed. "Let me just take this to the dumpster first." She pulled the trash bag out of the can and knotted it.

"So did you move to Fitzgerald, or are you just here for the summer?" Willow asked as they crossed the camp toward the mess hall.

"Neither. My family is living at the fire lookout. For now."

Willow froze. "No shit?"

Chase glanced at her, surprised by her reaction. Living in an isolated lookout tower was unusual, but Willow's face was sour, like she was holding her breath while digging through the trash. "Uh, yeah. We got here about a week ago."

"Like, you actually live in it?" Willow let out a nervous chuckle when Chase nodded. "Oh my *God*, there's not enough money in the world to get me up in that thing."

There it was again. The undertone of distress Chase heard when anyone mentioned the lookout. It was like a hulking shape hidden in the shadows, the kind you don't notice until silence falls and the night grows dark. The twisted expression on Willow's face, the secretive press of Wilder's grandmother's lips when she refused to say what had happened there, Michael's words when they first met: *You and the rest of your family are always welcome here just in case anything happens up at the lookout.*

Chase heaved the lid of the dumpster open and tossed the bag in. "Okay, you have to tell me why everyone is so scared of the lookout. Is it because it's out in the middle of the woods? It's not any more isolated than Spruces."

Willow's eyes widened, her pupils black circles that reminded Chase of the knotholes on the trees. "Nine years ago, Michael found a body there."

Chapter Twelve

Chase's stomach twisted. "He found a body." The words came out flat, like she was reading a sentence out of a book, not talking about someone she knew.

Willow nodded. "Well . . . he found remains. Skeletal remains. Is that still considered a body?"

"Wait, wait—" Chase almost laughed, thinking of the deer skeleton in the tree and the bones scattered through the woods. "Not human remains. Just—"

"No, they were definitely human remains," Willow said swiftly. "Skull and everything. They were under a tree, and the roots were all twisted through the skull cavity like a brain. And there are rumors that something was . . . *wrong* . . . with the body."

Chase shook her head, blinking to try and clear her thoughts. "A body at the lookout. In the tree roots. How did he find it?"

"There was this huge windstorm that brought down lots of trees in the woods—"

"I noticed that," Chase interrupted, thinking of the network of fallen logs that wound through Pando like lines on a map.

"Michael went up to check on the lookout and there were trees down all over the clearing. You know how when trees fall, the roots pull out of the ground, and they're all covered in dirt and rocks and stuff? Well, there were *bones* tangled in the roots of one tree. He tried to pull them out, thinking they were just from a deer or something, but they wouldn't come.

It was like they had become *part* of the tree, like the bones had grown into the roots and the roots had grown into the bones. Then he saw the skull." Willow leaned forward, and Chase got the distinct impression that she was enjoying this. "He started screaming—"

"Hold on. How do you know all these details?" Chase asked. She didn't want to be dismissive, but she didn't see how Willow could possibly know what Michael's reaction had been unless she had been there. And if she had been there, she would have put herself at the center of the narrative instead of Michael.

"Everyone in Fitzgerald knows the details," Willow said as though that settled it. "Michael had a kind of breakdown."

No one ever forgets anything. Everyone knows about—

So this was what Wilder had meant by that. His father's grisly discovery had become the kind of urban legend that was passed around and embellished until even the people involved had forgotten the truth.

"Did they figure out who the body belonged to?" Chase asked. Her shoulders crept up toward her ears.

"Some girl who went missing, like, fifty years ago. Her name was Tessa. I don't remember the details." Willow shrugged; it was clear that for her, the interesting part of the story was the discovery of the body, not the original disappearance. "Come on, I'm starving."

She banged open the back door of a gleaming stainless-steel kitchen. Chase could hear the muted babble of dozens of voices in the mess hall on the other side of a set of swinging doors. Wilder was already leaning against the counter, halfway through a slice of pepperoni pizza.

"Hey," he said around a mouthful of cheese. "How's it going?"

"Okay, I guess," Chase said. "Willow was just telling me—"

"That she's a natural," Willow said in a falsely bright

voice. She shot Chase a sideways look with raised eyebrows. "Right, Chase?"

She clearly didn't want Wilder to know that she had told Chase about the body. It made Chase uneasy, talking about Michael behind Wilder's back like that, like he was just a character in an urban legend instead of Wilder's father—not to mention her boss. But then she remembered the hard look in Wilder's eyes when he had complained about growing up in a small town. He didn't like everyone knowing his family business. It must be refreshing for him to finally have someone in his life who looked at his father without imagining him pulling bones from the twisted tree roots.

She couldn't take that from him.

"I don't know about that," Chase said. "But you said I would get used to it at least."

"Oh. Yeah." Willow's forehead relaxed, her eyebrows lowering back to their normal position.

"Hungry?" Wilder grabbed another slice of pizza for himself and tried to pass Chase a plate, but she waved her hand in refusal. Her appetite had completely vanished when Willow started talking about bodies trapped in tree roots. Instead, she spent the rest of the lunch break trying to distract herself by listening to Wilder's description of a group of nine-year-olds who swore they had seen a giant tentacle reaching out of the lake.

"Too bad you're not staying down here with the other counselors," Willow said as they left the kitchen at the end of the lunch break. "It's a nonstop party after the kids are in bed."

"I'm not a big partier," Chase said. Growing up on a skoolie had made her an introvert, and the thought of being in the middle of a loud group with no escape made her skin crawl.

"Me neither," Wilder said.

"He doesn't even stay in the boys' bunkhouse," Willow said. "Still sleeps in his dad's apartment at the back of the office."

"Two words: private bathroom." Wilder swept out his hands like he was introducing a novel concept. "Plus, the office is the only building in camp that has internet, so while you suckers are watching *Friday the 13th* on VHS for the hundredth time, I'm streaming premium content."

"Porn," Willow told Chase. She choked back a laugh as Wilder flushed and spluttered a denial that didn't convince either of them.

At the end of the afternoon, Chase tried not to think about Willow's stories of bodies tangled in the network of roots below her feet as she followed the winding path up the hill. But it was so easy to imagine that the spindly white trees were bones themselves, bursting out of the rocky soil like a calcified garden. And as she came to the clearing where the skeletal deer reigned like a ruler of rot and ruin, Willow's words rang through her ears:

Like the bones had grown into the roots and the roots had grown into the bones . . .

When she got back to the lookout, Dad's painting setup was abandoned on the deck, the canvas he had been working on that morning still propped against the easel. Chase recognized the rough outline of the mountain range opposite the lookout, but besides that addition, it looked the same as it had when she left.

Guthrie threw herself at Chase the moment she stepped through the door, clutching her so tight around the waist that Chase felt her ribs compress.

"Let me breathe, sis," she gasped. Guthrie ducked her head, loosening her grip.

Dad was sitting on the couch. He looked up from his paperback. "Well? How was it?"

"Good," Chase said, falling into one of the squishy armchairs. "Tiring. I can't believe I have to go back tomorrow."

"You'll get used to it," Mom called from the kitchen, where she was elbow deep in bread dough. "Did you see Wilder again?"

"Yeah. And I made another friend, too. Willow," Chase added.

"That's great," Mom said.

Guthrie tugged at Chase's hand, trying to pull her out of the chair and gesturing at the table. One of the board games from the chest was laid out, ready to play. Chase pressed her lips together to keep from groaning out loud. All she wanted to do was let the chair swallow her, but she had promised Guthrie they could play a game when she got back.

Chase dragged herself out of the chair. "Okay, Gus, what are we playing?"

It was a battered edition of Scattergories, a game Chase had never heard of. A faceted die with twenty letters of the alphabet lay in the middle of the table, along with a timer.

Chase pulled the instructions from the box and skimmed through them. "So we roll the die to see what letter we have to use. Then we have three minutes to come up with something for every category using that specific letter." She looked up from the rule sheet. "Seems easy enough. You understand all the rules?"

Guthrie nodded and handed her a pencil and a sheet of paper, but the paper already had writing on it.

"What's this?" Chase asked. "'Dear Natalie, you wouldn't believe the view—'"

"Oh." Mom laughed. "You'll think it's silly, but I actually started writing a letter to Natalie. You know, my friend from the skoolie meetup group? We used to text all day long, and I miss talking to her, so I figured I could write about all the things going on throughout the week and then mail it when we go to town. Kind of old-fashioned, but—" She shrugged.

"I don't think that's silly," Chase said. "I think it's sweet."

Guthrie rolled the lumpy die to choose a letter for Scattergories. It landed on T. The timer started with a buzz. Chase bent over her list, studying the categories. The first one was *a girl's name*.

A girl's name that started with T. The first one to pop into her head was, of course, Tessa, but she didn't want to write that. She put down Tammy instead.

Next category: *capital city*.

For someone who had spent her life on the road, Chase didn't have a very good grasp of geography. Mom and Dad had never spent much time teaching her about things like capitals. Was Toronto a capital city? Guthrie probably wouldn't know even if it wasn't, so Chase wrote it down.

The incessant ticking of the timer crawled into her skull like a bee. It made it hard to think. Across the table, Guthrie was writing furiously, but more than half of Chase's list was still blank when the buzzer sounded.

"That was way harder than I thought it would be," Chase complained. "I could only think of four things. What about you?"

Guthrie smirked and slid her paper across the table so Chase could read it. Every category had something written by it in Gus's loopy handwriting, and the paper slipped from Chase's hand when she saw what Guthrie had written.

Tessa

Tessa

Tessa
Tessa
Tessa
Tessa
Tessa
Tessa
Tessa
Tessa
Tessa
Tessa

"What is this?" Chase hissed, shoving the paper back across the table with shaking hands.

Guthrie took it, her smile fading. She shook her head, shrugging, and tried to give the paper back, but Chase wouldn't take it.

"Why did you write this?" Chase demanded.

Guthrie shrugged again.

"Don't say you don't know—tell me. Here, write it down." Chase rolled one of the pencils to Guthrie. She picked it up uneasily, like she wasn't sure how to hold it.

She didn't write anything.

When Gus had first stopped talking, Mom had bought her a small whiteboard and marker that she could carry around. Guthrie doodled on it and occasionally used it to play tic-tac-toe with Chase, but as a communication tool, the whiteboard turned out to be useless.

It seemed that whatever was stopping Guthrie from talking—fear, or anxiety, or maybe even anger—wasn't limited to just her voice. She didn't want to communicate with them at all, at least not in any meaningful kind of way. Sure, she found ways to answer direct questions, and she never failed to get her meaning across, but when it came to sharing her thoughts or feelings—sharing who she really was inside—she was as silent as the aspen grove on a day without wind.

"What's wrong?" Mom asked, turning away from the counter. Her hands were still sticky with bread dough.

"She wrote the same thing for every category," Chase said.

"Oh. Well, maybe she just didn't understand the rules."

"No, that's not it. She wrote *Tessa*." The name was light and bubbly, a name that should trip off the tongue and dance in the air. But in her mouth, it felt rough and heavy.

"So?" Dad asked, coming to the table to look over Chase's shoulder at the paper.

Chase bit back rising hysteria. Blurting out Willow's disturbing story about a body trapped in the tree roots would only scare Guthrie and come across as a small-town urban legend to Mom and Dad.

"So I just want to know where she heard that name." She turned back to Guthrie. "Like, was it someone we met in Fitzgerald? Someone who told you something about the lookout? Or maybe you saw it written in one of the books that was here when we moved in?"

Guthrie held up her hands, wide, questioning, helpless. She didn't know. Her eyes were still round, and she flinched back like she was afraid Chase would yell at her again.

"It's okay," Chase said, forcing herself to take a deep breath and let it out slowly. "I'm sorry. I'm not mad. It's just that someone told me a story about a girl named Tessa today at camp, and so it seemed strange that that was what you wrote."

"Oh." Dad frowned. "Just a coincidence. Tessa isn't an uncommon name."

"Yeah," Chase agreed. "I'm sure that's all it is."

But she balled up the paper and threw it away as they cleaned up the game.

Chapter Thirteen

Mom and Guthrie were already outside when Chase left for camp the next morning. She lingered by the garden, watching Guthrie, who stood at the edge of the clearing, eye to eye with the black knotholes on a slim tree, leaning forward like she was sharing a secret with a friend.

"I think she's talking to that tree," Chase said to Mom.

Mom glanced up from the weeds she was pulling. "Maybe she is."

"You don't think that's strange? That she'll talk to a tree, but not to us?"

"Don't you remember Jesse?" Mom said, brushing the hair off her face and leaving a smear of dirt across her forehead.

Chase scowled at the mention of her childhood imaginary friend. "That was different. Jesse wasn't a tree. And I still talked to you guys. *And* I was a little kid."

"You were nine," Mom pointed out. "Gus is only ten. And if you think about it, it makes more sense to talk to a tree. At least that kind of has a face."

Of course she had to say that. The hairs prickled on the back of Chase's neck. "Just don't let her wander off, okay?"

She thought about Jesse all the way down to the camp, telling herself that Mom was right and imaginary friends were perfectly normal. She had read in a secondhand psychology textbook that she had found in a Little Free Library that children often used imaginary friends to fill needs that weren't otherwise being met, or to practice emerging skills in an environment they could control.

That lined up with what she remembered of hers. She had invented Jesse, named after her favorite character from *Tuck Everlasting*, about a year after they left Boone. They had been on the road long enough for the novelty to wear off, long enough for Chase to start feeling lonely. At first, she had just imagined Jesse sitting next to her on the couch as she read about him, but it wasn't long before she was formulating whole conversations with him in her head. Sometimes he even made her laugh. He was a friend she could take with her wherever she went, a friend she never had to catch up with.

Eventually, she had learned to manage life on the road, and she hadn't needed him anymore. Jesse had drifted away, replaced by fantasies about going back to Boone and plans of how to get there.

It was easy to see how talking to the trees filled Guthrie's needs. She had never had friends, and so she invented them. She had spent her life drifting on the wind like a kite without a string, and so she literally personified being rooted down by latching on to a tree.

An idea started to take root as Chase stepped out of the woods, her gaze sweeping over the dozens of children racing around the camp.

She went to find Michael during lunch. He was in the office, standing at the desk with the phone tucked against his shoulder, scribbling something on a sheet of paper. He smiled at her, holding up a finger to indicate he would just be a minute.

Chase glanced around the room as she waited. The walls were covered in large, framed pictures, each one showing a group of kids in bright T-shirts posing with a hand-painted banner: Spruces 1990, Spruces 1991, Spruces 1992. She jumped forward a few decades, looking for Wilder, and found a tiny, round-faced version of the boy she knew perched on Michael's shoulders. A woman who had the same dark curly hair as him stood next to them, her hand on Wilder's back to steady him, her smile as bright as the sun.

Wilder's mother.

He hadn't mentioned her.

She searched the other pictures for the dark-haired woman, finding her with Wilder and Michael summer after summer. Chase's mouth hitched into a crooked smile as she watched Wilder grow taller and lose his baby fat. The first year that he had glasses, he also had a sullen expression that was out of place on his face. Michael had the pinched, baggy look of someone who had lost a lot of weight in a short time.

And Wilder's mother was gone.

Chase glanced at the year painted on the banner: eight years ago. The year after Michael had found the body at the lookout.

She jumped as Michael hung up the phone, backing away from the photograph as though he could tell what she was thinking. He turned toward her, smiling.

"Hey there, Chase. Everything going okay?"

"Yeah," she said. "I just had a question for you. Well, more of a favor, I guess."

"What can I do for you?"

She told him about Guthrie and how boring it was at the lookout. "It got me thinking . . . she would probably love camp." This was a lie, or at least an exaggeration, but Chase felt like she had to sell it. "There's not much for her to do up at the lookout. She even started talking to the trees," she added, forcing a laugh like it was just a quirk, but Michael's face hardened, so maybe he agreed that it was concerning.

"So I was wondering if she could come to camp with me," Chase finished in a rush. "Not overnight. Just during the day. I'd even be willing to work for free so she could attend."

She felt a little sting as she offered it, but it would be worth it. As much as she needed to save money, Guthrie was more important, and if Chase could give her an opportunity to be around kids her age, make friends for the first time ever, she was going to do it. Besides, then she wouldn't have to worry about her parents letting Guthrie wander off into the woods while Chase wasn't there.

"You'd be willing to do that?" Michael asked.

Chase swallowed. "Yes."

"You're a good sister."

"She makes it easy."

Michael crossed his arms, leaning against the edge of the desk. "You said you're saving money for college? May I ask what you want to study?"

She shrugged. Her fantasies about college had been mostly about going back to Boone and sinking herself into the kind of community she had always hovered outside of. She hadn't thought much about the actual school part.

"Chase, I'm impressed with your generosity, but I won't ask you to give up your paycheck. Guthrie is welcome to come to camp this summer. What's one more kid?"

"Really?" Chase was flooded with relief. "Thank you so much. She'll be so excited."

"Happy to have her. How old is she?"

"Ten on the Fourth of July."

"That makes her a Wildcat. I'll let Laura know to expect her tomorrow. You're doing great here, Chase. I'm glad you're with us this year." He winked at her as he went back to work. "So is Wilder."

Chapter Fourteen

"This will be fun," Chase promised as she and Guthrie walked to Spruces the next day. "You'll make some friends. Someone to play with."

Someone other than the white-barked trees with their soulless, staring eyes that wept sap like blood. Guthrie had been talking to them again when Chase got home yesterday afternoon, sitting on the ground with her arms wrapped around her bent knees, a flower crown perched on her head.

"I hear you talking to the trees sometimes," Chase continued. "Are they like imaginary friends?"

Guthrie ducked her head, chewing her lip. She looked embarrassed to have been caught in such a childish game.

"I used to have one, too. It's totally normal. But once you meet some other kids, you won't need an imaginary friend anymore."

Guthrie looked up at her doubtfully. Yesterday, she had met Chase's invitation to attend camp with a blank expression, her eyes staying empty through the ensuing argument as Chase tried to convince their parents to send her to Spruces. As always, Dad had protested the idea of trusting "the establishment" more than themselves. Mom had seemed torn until Chase pointed out that this was why they had come here: to give Guthrie some stability. That had tipped the scales in Chase's favor, and they had all agreed—some of them more reluctantly than others—that Guthrie should at least give Spruces a try.

"We're going to make nature collages today," Chase said to distract Guthrie as the path wound past Skully. She could feel its empty gaze on the back of her neck. "You'll be good at that. You always find such interesting things by the lookout."

Guthrie shrugged. She picked flowers as they walked, twirling them in her hands until the stems were bruised and broken, and discarding them along the path behind them. They reached the edge of the forest, blinking as they stepped out from the diluted light under the trees. Without the flowers or underbrush to pluck at, Guthrie's hands twisted around each other, helpless and empty. Chase laced her fingers with Guthrie's to still them.

"You don't need to be nervous," she said. "Everyone is so nice. Look, that's my friend Wilder." She pointed at the clearing where the campers were gathering on the benches for Morning Welcome. Wilder waved, jogging over to meet them.

"You must be Guthrie," he said.

Guthrie stared past him, her eyes fixed blankly over his shoulder. Wilder glanced back, trying to follow her gaze, but Chase knew there was nothing there. Guthrie wasn't looking at anything in particular, she was just avoiding Wilder.

"Wilder, can you show us where the Wildcats sit?" Chase said. "I want to introduce Guthrie to her counselor."

"Yeah, they're right over here." Wilder led them over to a young woman with short pink hair who was trying to wrangle a group of squirming ten-year-olds. Guthrie clung to Chase's side, but the counselor finally managed to coax her to sit down after Chase promised to have lunch with her.

"She's pretty shy, huh?" Wilder said as his father rang the bell to signal the beginning of Morning Welcome. He and Chase slipped to the back bench where Willow was saving them seats.

Chase hesitated, but Wilder and Willow—and Guthrie's

counselor, and Michael, and all the campers that Chase was so desperate for Guthrie to play with—would find out soon enough.

"Not just shy. She doesn't talk."

"She doesn't talk?" Willow repeated. "What's wrong with her?"

Chase's shoulders stiffened. This was always the reaction people had—that Guthrie was somehow defective.

"Nothing is *wrong* with her," Chase hissed. "She just doesn't talk."

Willow held up her hands in surrender. "Sorry! I just meant, like, does she have autism or is she Deaf or something?"

"There's nothing wrong with being autistic or Deaf, either," Wilder pointed out. "But I think Willow is just trying to ask if there's a reason she doesn't talk."

The tight knot in Chase's lungs relaxed enough for her to draw in a breath. "She had a traumatic experience a while ago. She still talks a little, like when she's playing—" *Or to the trees*, she thought. "—but she doesn't talk *to* anyone anymore."

"That must be rough," Wilder said.

"It is," Chase admitted in a low voice that she prayed wouldn't carry across the benches to Guthrie.

Her morning art sessions went by quickly. She handed out paper bags to the campers and took them to a grove of trees at the edge of the camp where the counselors had hung hammocks. After their nature walk, she let them spend the last fifteen minutes gluing everything they had found to cardstock. Some of the kids used leaves or flower petals to make figures, but most of the collages were messy and dripping with glue. Chase winced as she hung them up to dry, imagining Dad's grimace if he could see what she was calling *art*.

When it was time for lunch, she stood in the doorway of the mess hall, her ears ringing from the cacophony of laughter and shrieks, and searched the roiling mass of children for her sister. She found Gus sitting at the very edge of a table, knees turned to the side and half hanging off the bench like she was trying to take up as little space as possible. She was picking at a sandwich but not eating.

"How's it going?" Chase murmured, crouching down next to her. "Are you having fun?"

Guthrie pulled the crust off the bread and shook her head. Chase's heart sank at the emptiness in her eyes. They looked like a light that had burnt out; they looked like a cracked glass that could never be filled.

I don't want to force Guthrie into a box that doesn't fit her, Dad had insisted when they came to Pando.

That's not what Chase was doing, though. She wasn't trying to make Guthrie be something she wasn't or trying to force her to change who she was. She was just trying to give Guthrie a shred of normalcy and stability in their wind-scattered lives.

But maybe Guthrie doesn't need that, a voice whispered in Chase's head. It sounded suspiciously like Dad. *Maybe what she needs is for what's normal for her to be enough.*

"You have art right after lunch," Chase said. "I bet your collage will turn out amazing. I have to go get ready, but I'll see you soon, okay?"

Guthrie hunched forward, her shoulders rounding as she sank into herself.

After lunch, the Wildcats burst into the art room with Guthrie trailing behind them. She caught Chase's eye and raised her eyebrows, tilting her head back through the door toward the woods.

"In a minute," Chase said, waiting for the kids to sit down at the tables covered in butcher paper. "Do you want to help me pass out the bags?"

"She doesn't talk," a girl named Madison called out. With

her hair in tight French braids and her nose tipped up at the end, she looked like the bossy kind of girl who everyone wanted to impress. "We don't think she can."

Chase gritted her teeth. "She *can* talk. And just because she chooses not to doesn't mean we shouldn't talk *to* her. She's a Wildcat, too."

"How do you know?" Madison asked.

"She's ten, same as you," Chase said.

Madison and her friends tittered. "No, I mean how do you know she can talk? *We* haven't heard her say anything." There was a rustle of agreement from the rest of the group. Guthrie wilted against Chase's side.

"Because she's my sister," Chase said. "And she's smart enough to communicate *without* talking. Can any of you do that?"

The question came out sharper than she meant it. *Cool it*, she told herself, taking a deep breath in through her nose and blowing it out through her mouth. She couldn't let these kids get under her skin, but it was hard not to.

"So she knows sign language?" a boy with furrowed eyebrows asked. "I know some signs because my cousin is Deaf, but Guthrie didn't answer me when I tried to talk to her."

"Well, no, she doesn't communicate with sign language," Chase said. "I just know what she means by her facial expressions and gestures. We can have a whole conversation without her saying anything. Isn't that cool?"

"Like this?" Madison turned and whispered to a friend, crossing her eyes and waggling her eyebrows. The friend let out one shrill giggle, clapping a hand over her mouth when Chase glared at her. She had to regain control of the situation before Guthrie realized they were making fun of her.

"Let's do our Spruces cheer before we start art!" Chase said, trying to sound peppy and upbeat. "On three!"

The kids shuffled into a circle with their hands overlapping in the middle. Guthrie lay her hand on top. "One, two, three, *Spruces*!" they screamed, flinging their hands in the air. Chase's ears rang.

"Okay, let's get started," Chase said. "Today we're going to take a look at art in nature. I'm going to take you on a walk, and I want you each to collect things to use in a nature collage. Leaves, flower petals, twigs, small rocks—anything you want." She passed out the paper bags and organized the kids into a ragged line, before leading them out of the art room.

When they reached the hammock grove at the edge of camp, Chase told the kids to stay where she could see them, then let them scatter among the trees. The woods were sparse here, the trees thinned to make room for half a dozen hammocks—nothing like the tangle of limbs at the lookout. Most of the kids stayed close to her, stripping silver-green leaves from the branches and picking wild sage and petals from wildflowers while they chattered about their time at the lake that morning. Wilder had only let them paddle the kayaks along the shore, but he promised that they could go to the floating dock in the middle of the lake tomorrow. Now they were debating the lake monster rumors.

"Not as big the Loch Ness Monster, of course," the boy who knew sign language assured the others. "But my brother told me something grabbed his foot when he went to the floating dock last summer, and I think I saw a fin sticking out of the water."

The other kids squealed, half dismayed, half impressed. Chase pressed her lips together to keep from laughing.

A sudden shriek silenced the conversation about the lake monster. The kids bunched up around Chase as the panicked cry came again. Chase twisted around, trying to find the source of the sound, but it seemed to echo all around them. She couldn't pinpoint which direction it had come from.

"Shh—" she hissed, holding a finger to her lips to quiet the rest of the group. She quickly scanned the huddle of kids, counting. Her heart sank as she realized that two were missing: Guthrie and Madison.

"You okay?" she called, straining to hear. The air had grown thick and silent. "Madison and Gus, come back to me! It's time to go back to camp."

A burst of wind swept through the crown of the trees, the gentle whisper of the quaking leaves growing into a confused babble that filled Chase's ears. When it died away, she could hear Madison calling, "Stop it!"

"Stay here," Chase muttered, shaking off the sticky hands of the other children and heading deeper into the woods. "I'm coming! Where are you?"

"No, don't," Madison moaned from somewhere over Chase's left shoulder. Chase veered that direction, batting away branches and crashing through the underbrush until she saw three slight figures tangled together: Guthrie, Madison, and a paper-white face with swollen black eyes.

Chase's head spun, but then she blinked and the face was gone. It was just a tree with knotholes for eyes. Guthrie was reaching for Madison's braids, which were tangled in the branches, but Madison was thrashing and pulling like an animal in a trap.

"Stop, stop, stop!" Chase said. "The more you pull, the harder it will be to get you untangled. Just hold still and I'll get you loose, okay? Everything is okay."

"She grabbed me," Madison sobbed. "She won't let go."

Guthrie held up her hands, shaking her head, but Madison moaned and batted them away.

"She's just trying to help you," Chase said. "She didn't grab you."

"She was talking to someone, and then she grabbed me." Madison was shaking so hard that the tree trembled as Chase untangled her braids from its branches. Her hair was full of twigs when Chase was finally done.

"There. See? You must have gotten it caught during that burst of wind a few minutes ago."

Except Madison had cried out *before* the wind.

Chapter Fifteen

The rest of the afternoon was a complete and utter failure.

There wasn't enough time to do the collages once they got back to the art room, so Chase just passed out paper and colored pencils to let the kids draw while she finished cleaning Madison up. The girl's cheeks and neck were covered in shallow scrapes that Chase dabbed with a wet paper towel before sending her to see the nurse. Madison was crying more than Chase thought necessary, and the other girls fought over who would get to walk with her. When Chase wouldn't let any of them go—she could literally stand in the doorway and watch Madison to be sure she made it the hundred yards to the office—they huddled around a table muttering about her and glaring at Guthrie.

Guthrie refused to go with her counselor and the rest of the group when the hour was up. Chase didn't blame her, so she let her sit at the back of the art room with colored pencils during the last two sessions of the day, which Chase held inside. She didn't want to risk another incident like the one with Madison, so instead of taking the kids to the woods, she got out the plastic lacing cord and tried to show them how to make boondoggle keychains.

But considering the fact that she still didn't really know what boondoggles were, it did not go well.

By the time the last group had left, Chase felt deflated. Used up and wrung out. All her hopes for the day had slipped away and been replaced by something hard and raw. She straightened up the art room, peeling gobs of half-dry glue from the table and sweeping pine needles and bits of leaves off the floor. Guthrie was still lost in her drawings at the back of the room, and she didn't look up until Chase turned off the lights.

"Let's go," Chase said. Her voice sounded fake: hollow and forced. She tried to make herself smile as Guthrie stacked her papers neatly and put the colored pencils away.

The path through the woods was strewn with the flowers Guthrie had picked and discarded that morning, the bruised petals bright spots against the dirt. She gathered them as they walked, skipping ahead of Chase, blossoming with each step she took deeper into the woods.

"See?" Chase could imagine Dad saying as he tilted his chin up in triumph. "See? She doesn't need to go to camp. This place is good for her. This place is good for *us*."

Would he still think that if he saw the way Guthrie squealed with morbid delight when they reached Skully?

"Why are you so interested in bones all of a sudden?" Chase asked as Guthrie stared into Skully's empty eye sockets. The words felt brittle in her mouth, like they might crack between her teeth. Why was *she* the only one in her family who seemed to remember that the bones Guthrie lined up on her windowsill had once made up the frameworks of living, breathing creatures?

Guthrie looked away from the bones protruding from the tree just long enough to shrug. She tugged at the antlers as though she wanted to free them to add to her collection, but the tree held tight, just as the shared roots of Pando had held Tessa's bones for all those years.

"Gus, let's go," Chase snapped. Her stomach twisted as Guthrie trailed one hand over the high, smooth dome of the skull in farewell.

"You know, I thought going to camp would be fun for you," she said. Her mouth curled, more grimace than smile. "I was trying to help. But it didn't really work out, did it?"

She bit back what she was really thinking: that Guthrie hadn't even tried, that she could have made an effort to be friendly even without talking to the other kids.

Guthrie left her side as they approached the lookout, skipping over to the tree where she liked to play. She lay the bouquet of wilted flowers that she had gathered from the path at the base of the tree and leaned in to whisper something that Chase couldn't hear.

"How'd it go?" Mom called from where she and Dad were working in the garden. Her face was hidden under the brim of a wide, floppy hat, but Dad's head was bare and Chase could see the smug set of his jaw. He already knew how it had gone.

Chase clenched her teeth. "It was a disaster. You want me to say you were right? Fine. You were right."

"I don't want you to say I was right," Dad said.

"She's over there talking to a fucking tree instead of us. How does that make you feel? Because it makes me feel like shit."

"Chase—" Mom protested, but Chase was already halfway to the lookout. She stormed upstairs, blinking back angry tears. She had been so sure that going to camp was what Guthrie needed, but it was like she didn't *want* to come out of the place she had retreated to after that night. Like she was happy there, in a world that Chase couldn't access.

Dad's easel was set up on the deck, the painting he had been working on since they arrived at the lookout clamped in place. Chase's fingers clenched with a sudden urge to splash black paint across the canvas, blotting out the view that she could never share with him.

Living in a space under three hundred square feet had taught Chase and her parents how to tiptoe around one another and avoid uncomfortable conversations, and so when she left for Spruces the next morning, they all pretended that nothing had happened. Dad tipped an invisible cap to her from his easel on the deck and told her to have a great day, and Mom ran after her to give her the water bottle she had forgotten. Guthrie handed her a bluebell that she tucked behind her ear.

"Nice flower," Wilder murmured when she met him and Willow for Morning Welcome. A little thrill raced across her skin as he reached out to straighten it.

"Thanks. Gus gave it to me."

"She didn't come with you today?" Willow asked.

"No, that's not going to work out," Chase said. "My mom wants her to stay at the lookout to keep her company."

She didn't know why she was lying. Willow and Wilder had both seen Guthrie with the Wildcats yesterday—surely they had noticed how uncomfortable she was.

"My little sister doesn't come to camp, either," Willow said. "She doesn't like it."

"Your sister probably doesn't talk to the trees, though," Chase muttered.

"Not the trees, no," Willow said thoughtfully. "Although she did spend about three years telling us that the vacuum was her girlfriend, until they broke up because the vacuum wanted children and she didn't."

Chase choked on a laugh. "Wait, what?"

Willow shrugged. "Kids are weird."

The rest of the Wildcats didn't seem surprised not to see Guthrie again, either. Chase felt a ripple of irritation as soon as Madison walked into the art room, but she bit her tongue and forced herself to think of her first paycheck and how it would pad her shabby savings account.

When the last group of campers burst out the door a few hours later, leaving paint smeared on tables and torn pieces of paper in their wake, Chase leaned against the wall and breathed. Her throat was raw and her voice was hoarse and all she wanted to do was close her eyes. Who knew that helping kids make construction paper collages would be so tiring?

At least she didn't have to come back tomorrow. Friday was the day that the campers went home, giving Chase a three-day weekend. She had big plans for her time off: a book and a hammock set up under the trees at the edge of the clearing.

Wilder was standing just outside the art room door when Chase opened it. She stumbled back, choking on a nervous squeak and managing to turn it into a laugh.

"Wilder," she said, laying a hand over her eyes and waiting for her heart to slow. It didn't. "You scared me."

He grinned. "Ha. Sorry. Are you heading back?"

She nodded.

"I'll walk you partway," he offered.

"Thanks." She grabbed her water bottle and flicked the lights off, closing the art room door behind her.

"So. How was your first week as a camp counselor?" Wilder asked. The sounds of the camp faded as they strolled along the edge of the lake and into the woods.

Chase let out a strangled laugh. "Oh boy. Maybe don't ask me that until I've had a chance to sleep for about twenty hours straight."

Wilder laughed. "That's fair."

"How about *you*? How was your first week as a lifeguard?"

Another laugh. She liked his laugh—it made her feel warm inside, like she had swallowed the sun.

"Don't ask me that until I've had a chance to sleep for about twenty hours straight." He echoed her words, rubbing the tip of his sunburnt nose. "It's actually way more exhausting than you would think. Sitting on the lifeguard stand all day in the sun. I was practically seeing things by the end of the afternoon yesterday."

"Like what?"

He kicked a pebble along the path. "You know that giant tentacle I told you the kids were talking about?"

Chase laughed. "You're joking."

"You caught me. No giant lake monsters." He looked at her sideways, smiling, and her stomach did a funny little twist.

"That you know of, at least," she quipped.

"Right."

They walked in silence for a moment before Wilder cleared his throat. "I really did think I saw something, though. In the woods, across the lake. By the path that leads up to the lookout. I kept seeing movement out of the corner of my eye. Like someone moving through the trees. But when I looked right at it, there was nothing there."

Chase's skin prickled. "The way the sunlight catches on the leaves when they're fluttering in the wind. That's all."

She shivered, pushing forward through the trees. Skully rose out of the underbrush ahead of them. Wilder paused, shoving his hands into his pockets. "Hey, I actually wanted to ask you something." His voice was casual, but his eyes darted away from her face. "Do you want to do something this weekend?"

Chase felt a rush of tingling heat. She was drawn to Wilder like a moth to a flame, but there was no clause for a boyfriend in her plan to go back to Boone. "Like what?"

"I'm going to finish stripping the bus tomorrow. I was wondering if you would help me draw a floor plan on Saturday, and then we could watch a movie or something."

Ah. The bus. The tight twist in her chest relaxed with a pang that only hurt for a moment.

"For a second, I thought you were asking me out," she joked to cover her disappointment. She hadn't spent a lot of time around other teenagers, but she had read the books and watched the movies, and she didn't have time to play the games. It was best to define the bounds of their relationship right now, before either of them got any ideas.

"Oh?" Wilder looked straight at her. His eyes were hazel with flecks of gold like embers rising from a fire. "And you would have said . . . ?"

"No."

He made a face, wincing. "Just like that, huh?"

"I told you I'm saving up for college, right? It's kind of an all-encompassing goal for me. I can't afford to get sidetracked by anything." She lifted one corner of her mouth in a rueful smile. "But you just want help with the skoolie, right?"

"Uh, yeah. I just want help." He rubbed the back of his neck. "So what do you say? How long did you live on a skoolie? You must know everything there is to know about it."

"Nine years," Chase said. "And I know some stuff, but I didn't design or build it. I mostly know how annoying it is to have to climb over my sister's bed to get to mine, or have to convert the couch to a table every time you want to eat something."

"Still, you've really lived it. You can stop me from messing it up. I could really use your advice," Wilder persuaded.

Chase would be happy to never set foot on another bus, but Wilder's enthusiasm was contagious. So instead of telling him her advice was to tow the old bus to the junkyard and be grateful for the roots he had in Fitzgerald, she said, "I'll think about it. But no promises."

Chapter Sixteen

"Make-your-own-pizza night on homemade dough. Natalie emailed me the recipe, and I've been waiting to try it out," Mom announced when Chase walked into the lookout. "Then I thought we could go for a hike. There's supposed to be a rope swing about half a mile away."

"Yeah, Wilder mentioned that," Chase said dryly. "A girl fell off and broke her leg in three places earlier this spring. She's the one I replaced at Spruces."

"Oh." Mom pursed her lips. "Well, we don't have to swing on it. We could just enjoy the hike. There are so many wildflowers—"

"Mom. I'm so tired. The only thing I want to do is crash."

Mom took in a deep breath and spoke without letting it out. "Okay. Maybe we can hike another day. What do you want on your pizza?" She gestured at the table, which was so loaded with toppings that Chase couldn't see the wood grain.

"Uh—" After rubbery frozen pizza for lunch four days in a row, Chase couldn't stand the thought of more marinara and mozzarella. "I'm not really hungry."

"Fine. Guthrie? What about you? Do *you* want to make pizza with me?" There was an edge to Mom's voice that told Chase she was irritated. Well, so was Chase. She was exhausted after her first week of work, and her conversation with Wilder had left an ache in her chest that was half disappointment, half reluctant relief.

It would have been hard to say no if he had been asking

her out, but she didn't have to worry about that, because he just wanted help with his build. With his stupid bus. With a dream that would never match up with reality.

So why was she actually considering helping him?

Because it was Wilder, she admitted to herself, and she already craved his presence like a cat craves the sun.

Chase went out to the deck while Guthrie started pointing out what she wanted on her pizza. Dad was slumped in one of the Adirondack chairs, chin resting on his hand.

"I told her you wouldn't want to go hiking," Dad muttered. "She should have gone earlier today instead of waiting for you to get home, but she thought it would be safer with three people."

"Why didn't *you* go with her?"

"Busy."

Chase glanced doubtfully at the canvas propped on the easel by the railing: the vague, hulking shape of the mountains with just a hint of trees. It hadn't changed much in the last few days, which suddenly explained Dad's reticence.

When Dad's painting was going well, he was buoyant and alive. He kissed Mom every time he saw her and told jokes that made Guthrie laugh and Chase roll her eyes. He read voraciously and remembered everything he heard and could have insightful conversations about a dozen different topics. When he was like that, Chase understood why Mom would follow him anywhere.

But over the years, there had been a handful of times when his inspiration had dried up, and his personality had gone with it. He sunk into himself, and his eyes went flat and dull. The person he was disappeared, and the one who took his place was sullen and melancholy. When this happened, it was like all the light in the family went out.

And right now, Pando seemed pitch black.

Why are we fucking here? Chase thought.

She sat next to Dad in the wake of his rippling darkness for a few more minutes before going back inside, climbing into her bed, and pulling the curtains closed without saying anything to Mom and Guthrie. She slumped against her pillow and reached for her book on the shelf over her bed. She was reading *Little Women* again, and all she wanted to do was sink into the March household and let the day, the week, the last nine years, roll off her.

The book had gotten pushed toward the edge of the shelf, and her skittering hand knocked it between the bed frame and the window. Groaning, she rolled onto her stomach and plunged her arm into the gap next to her mattress, fingers scrabbling for the book and coming up with nothing but dust bunnies.

"Shit," Chase muttered. Her grandmother had given that book to her, and it was one of the few things that had survived the purge of their possessions when they moved into the skoolie—too important to leave lying on the dusty floor.

Chase slid off the bed and heaved the heavy frame away from the wall. It screeched, moving just half an inch. Gritting her teeth, she pulled again until the gap between the bed and the wall was big enough to reach into. Crawling across her mattress, she thumbed on the flashlight on her phone and aimed it into the dark gap. The book lay on the floor, but as she reached for it, the light from her phone flashed over something on the wall that made her bite her tongue.

Tessa

The word was carved into the wood in sharp, jagged letters, all angles and lines like scars. And like scars aching to herald a coming storm, Chase could feel the name settling into her bones.

Maybe Guthrie had carved it while Chase was at camp—her idea of a practical joke after Chase's overreaction the other day.

But Chase had barely been able to move the bed. There was no way Guthrie, with her arms like twigs and her wrists like hollow bird bones, would have been able to.

There was only one other explanation.

Tessa, the girl whose body Michael had found tangled in the tree roots, hadn't just gone missing in Pando all those years ago.

She had gone missing from the lookout.

Chapter Seventeen

Had Tessa slept in this bed?

Had she gazed out at this view?

Had she walked on this path?

When Chase went outside the next morning, it wasn't just the eyes of the trees that she could feel watching her. Everywhere she looked, she felt the invisible influence of a girl who had lived and died in this place.

She didn't say anything about Tessa's story to her family—not yet. There was no point until she knew all the details, and she was determined to get them today at the library in Fitzgerald.

She went straight for the lone computer at the back of the room while Mom and Guthrie returned their books. Clicking on the guest profile, she drummed her fingers on the desk as it booted up. The cursor stayed a tiny, rotating hourglass for an excruciatingly long time, but she was finally able to click on the internet browser and open a new window.

Her fingers hovered over the keyboard as she thought about what to search. She decided to start with Michael's discovery of the body, since it had happened more recently. Maybe reading about that would lead her to more details about the initial disappearance. She typed in *Fitzgerald Fire Lookout + human remains*, then added the year, realizing all of a sudden that it was around the time her family had left Boone.

The first result that popped up was a short piece mentioning how a downslope windstorm had uncovered human remains at the Fitzgerald Fire Lookout and authorities were working to identify the body. Chase navigated back to the search results and skimmed through them for an updated article, clicking on one dated a month later.

Human Remains Discovered at Fitzgerald Fire Lookout Those of 1970s Fire Lookout's Missing Child

A decades-old mystery has been solved, and a former US Forest Service employee can finally lay his daughter to rest.

It's been forty years since Richard Shaw and his wife and daughter came to Pando. What was meant to be an opportunity for the Shaw family to heal after the death of their older daughter became a new nightmare when nine-year-old Tessa vanished just a month into the summer. An extensive search followed, spanning all of Pando and the surrounding area, but Tessa was never found.

"It was a difficult time," Mr. Shaw said when

A pop-up blocked the rest of the article, demanding that Chase become a subscriber to finish reading. Heart shrinking down, she closed the window without continuing to the payment page. She had read enough to know what she needed to search for. There had been a part of her that had still been hoping the name carved on the lookout wall was just a coincidence, but here it was in blue-lit black and white: Tessa Shaw, the daughter of a fire lookout.

She pressed her palms to her face, squeezing her eyes closed so that lights flickered on the backs of her eyelids. Just knowing that Tessa had lived at the lookout wasn't enough to sate her curiosity—she needed the details. Had Tessa waited like Guthrie had, alone, afraid, falling deeper and deeper into a well of darkness as voices echoed off the trees, every snapped twig or rustle in the underbrush an unfulfilled promise?

Opening her eyes, she typed Tessa's name into the search bar and watched as the screen filled up. Many of the results were from regional news outlets, giving the same bare-bones information the first one had, but as she scrolled down, other types of results appeared. Reddit posts hypothesizing that Tessa Shaw might be a Missing 411 case, and conspiracy theories that she had been abducted by a secret government agency. Her name even popped up on a cryptozoology site.

"What the hell," Chase murmured. She didn't have time to read through all of the articles and sites, so she sent them to the printer.

"Ready to go?" Mom appeared over her shoulder just as the printer grumbled to life, spitting pages lifelessly onto the floor.

"Did you know about this?" Chase leaned to the side so Mom could see the screen. "A girl went missing from the lookout in the '70s. Her body was found there just a few years ago."

A line appeared between Mom's eyes. "I didn't."

"I found her name carved on the wall by my bed." Her eyes darted to Guthrie sitting in an armchair, already engrossed in one of her books.

"We have to tell Gus about this. It makes me nervous that she's gone into the woods alone. She needs to know how dangerous it is."

"You and I both know that she's fully aware of how dangerous it is."

There was a bite to Mom's voice. It was the closest she had ever come to acknowledging Chase's blame in what had happened that night. Chase clamped her mouth closed, trying to swallow down her shame and guilt.

"Guthrie wants pancakes," Mom said. "Let's just enjoy the rest of the afternoon. Dad and I will talk about Tessa Shaw later."

Chase gathered the papers from the printer without looking at them. She folded them in half and stuffed the thick packet into her back pocket, determined to find out what had happened to Tessa Shaw so she could warn Guthrie away from the same fate—no matter what Mom said.

Later that night, Chase closed the curtains around her bed and spread the pages of information across the blankets.

There were only a few articles about Tessa's original disappearance, and these were scanned copies of faded newspaper articles. Chase figured most of the newspapers from 1977, the year Tessa had gone missing, were on microfilm. She would ask about that the next time they went to Fitzgerald, but unless the tiny regional library had a hidden periodicals section, the microfilm machines were probably in one of the larger towns, far-flung in this sparsely populated part of the country.

Chase settled on an article that had been printed in the *Salt Lake Tribune* a month after Tessa vanished.

Search for Missing Nine-Year-Old Comes to an End

One month after Tessa Shaw vanished from the Fitzgerald Fire Lookout, search operations have officially ceased.

In the last four weeks, hundreds of volunteers and search and rescue teams have scoured the wilderness in Pando and the surrounding area, finding only one clue to the child's fate that left more questions than answers.

On the morning of June 20, 1977, Tessa Shaw and her parents, Richard and Donna, set out on a walk to the nearby lake. It had been one month since they had moved to the tower in Pando, where Richard had taken a job as the summer fire lookout after the devastating wildfires of 1975–1976. Richard and Donna let Tessa walk ahead of them on the well-established trail, but they hadn't gone far when the little girl vanished from sight. After calling out to her and looking along the trail, they used the fire lookout radio to ask for help.

When search and rescue arrived, the mystery deepened. The ground around the lookout and in the woods was wet and muddy after a storm the previous night, and footprints were abundant on the trail. However, it didn't take long to discover that the vast majority of tracks belonged to Richard and Donna, while Tessa's tracks stopped in the middle of the trail only a tenth of a mile from the lookout tower. There was no evidence that she had left the trail to walk through the underbrush, and no other footprints or tracks were ever discovered in the vicinity.

The first—and only—break in the case came after three days, when one of the volunteers from town found several items of clothing eight miles away from the lookout. These were confirmed to be Tessa's, though they yielded no clue to her condition or what had happened to her.

"We're grateful for the sheriff's department, the search and rescue team, and the volunteers who have prayed and cried with us over the past month," Richard Shaw said. "We know that Tessa has touched the hearts of many people."

Chase's breathing was shallow by the time she finished reading. She was back in that night six months ago. She could hear her family's panicked voices calling to Guthrie, see the lines of flashlights bobbing through the trees, the flat, empty expression in Guthrie's eyes when Dad had carried her out. Gus had only been gone four hours. Chase couldn't imagine trying to exist in that place of unknowing dread for a month.

Not just a month. Over forty years, she corrected herself.

She closed her eyes and forced herself to draw in a deep breath, holding it until her ears rang and her head spun. Guthrie was just across the room from her, safe in her bed.

Shuffling through the papers, she found an "ask me anything" thread that had been posted five years earlier on a conspiracy theory message board.

→ **mulder99:** TLDR; my grandfather found tessa shaw's clothing AMA

→ **mulder99:** my grandfather was a sar volunteer for over forty years in central utah. he joined the search for tessa after the first twenty-four hours. like all the stories say, her footprints stoppe din the middle of the trail like she had been snatched up by something from the sky. the sar team followed protocol walking in formation through the woods but never found any trace of her once her footprints stopped. after three days my grandfather was searching in another area a few miles away. he was walking up a hill when he saw something bright purple in the bushes. it was a sweatshirt that he recognized from the desccription tessa's parents had given. the weird thing was that it was folded up nice and neat and when he picked it up it smelle dlike it had just come out o the laundry. it was perfectly clean, no dirt or tears or anything. it was set on top a pair of sneakers that were also perfectly clean. the laces were still tied. tessa's parents confirmed that all items of clothing belonged to their daughter

→ → **xXtheyxXwalkxXamongxXusxX:** the clothing was reportedly found over eight miles away. Why was your grandfather in that area? It wasn't part of the original search grid

→ → → **mulder99:** @xXtheyxXwalkxXamongxXusxX he just had a feeling that he should go that way.

→ → → → **xXtheyxXwalkxXamongxXusxX:** @mulder99 no offense but that seems really suspicious like did he have something to do with it

→ → → → → **mulder99:** @xXtheyxXwalkxXamongxXusxX stfu he was out of town the day she disappeared

→ → **little_green_dick:** did he see any tracks or signs of her where he found her clothes

→ → → **mulder99:** @little_green_dick nope

→ → **look0verth3re:** @mulder99 what laundry detergent did the clothes smell like?

→ → → **mulder99:** @look0verth3re: tide and he could never stand the smell again. my grandma had to switch to cheer

→ → → → **look0verth3re:** @mulder99 that sucks

Other articles and posts also mentioned the clothes, all of them agreeing that they were clean and fresh, not what you would expect after three days in the woods and an eight-mile trek. After the clothes were found, the search grid expanded, but just like at the lookout, there was no trace of a trail. It was like Tessa Shaw had just vanished.

Even though the official SAR operation ended after a month, Tessa's parents rallied volunteers to search a few times a year over the next decade. Ten years after the disappearance, Donna Shaw died of an aneurysm, leaving Richard the sole surviving member of the Shaw family. There was a photo of him laying flowers on his family's graves a year later—a double headstone for him and his wife flanked by two smaller ones, one for Tessa and one for the unnamed older daughter the first article had mentioned. Chase shivered at the macabre picture, aware that when the photo was taken, two of the four graves were still empty.

There was a resurgence of interest in the case after the windstorm uncovered Tessa's body in the lookout's clearing. The internet was full of conspiracies about the original disappearance: claims that Tessa had been part of a super-secret CIA experiment, that she had been abducted by aliens, that she had run afoul of Bigfoot or a similar creature. Chase rolled her eyes and set these articles to the side.

All of the posts about Tessa's remains mentioned the odd appearance of her bones. The roots in Pando were widespread and prolific, and they had wrapped around the body, cradling it like a mother holding her baby. Shoots sent out by the mature trees filled the skull cavity and twined among her vertebrae. Postmortem calcium deposits left bulging growths that reached for sunlight like saplings, and her femurs were described as spiraling, as though they had been growing in a twist.

Chase grimaced at the descriptions of the body. No wonder there were so many rumors. The problem was, each claim was as outlandish as the next. It would be impossible to sort out the ones that might actually have a kernel of truth on her own. What she needed was someone who had firsthand knowledge of the discovery of the body, someone who hadn't just read about it on conspiracy theory message boards.

Someone like Wilder.

Chapter Eighteen

Reading about Tessa when the lookout was dark and everyone else was asleep turned out to be a mistake. Chase was awake for hours, her skin crawling as she thought of Tessa dead in the woods, cradled in the roots of the trees.

And now Chase was lying in her old bed.

When she finally slipped into sleep, it was one filled with insidious dreams where Chase followed Guthrie through forests of grasping roots and bones sprouted from the ground like saplings. She tried to call out, but her voice was just a muffled vibration in her throat. When she ran her hands over her face, she felt no mouth, only smooth, papery bark, and her eyes were black knotholes, weeping, weeping . . .

She woke up strangling a scream, hands clasped over her mouth. Her chapped lips curled over teeth that felt as sharp as shards of stone. The dream didn't fade away, staying as vivid in her mind as the leaves that fluttered outside the lookout.

Guthrie was already awake, eating a bowl of cereal at the table. The shower was running; Chase could hear Dad's off-key singing over the water. She winced at it as she got out of bed and pulled on a fresh T-shirt.

"How'd you sleep?" Mom asked, climbing down the ladder with a book tucked under her arm.

Chase grunted. "Ugh. Did you and Dad talk about . . . you know. That thing I showed you yesterday?"

Mom's face tightened. Guthrie slurped the milk out of her bowl, oblivious. "We will today."

"Good," Chase muttered. "I'm going to Spruces. I told Wilder I would help him with something." She piled her hair on top of her head in a messy bun.

Half an hour later, she stood outside the small bus. The door was cranked open, and she could hear someone moving inside. A muffled curse was followed by a *thud*, and Wilder came floundering out, clutching his thumb. He kicked an empty five-gallon bucket and then froze when he saw Chase.

"Everything going all right in there?" Chase asked, not bothering to fight back a smirk.

Wilder gestured aimlessly at a pile of tools visible through the open door. "Yeah, yeah, everything's great. I've almost got all the seats out."

"Are they fighting back?"

Wilder snorted. "Okay, so there are a few bolts that are tighter than I would like," he admitted.

Chase climbed the steps into the bus. The air was stale and smelled like dust, decades-old sweat, and chewing gum. The seats Wilder had managed to remove were piled against the emergency exit door in the back, and the floor was littered with rusty bolts and discarded wrenches. She tried to open one of the windows, but it was stuck fast.

Wilder leaned over her and banged his fist against the frame, loosening the window enough that she could ease it down.

"I didn't think you'd come," he said. "I really appreciate this."

"Mm-hmm." She ducked away from him and examined the driver's seat. Yellowing foam poked out through a tear in the cover. It looked like it had been nibbled on by a mouse. "Maybe I can tell you what I know . . . if you do the same for me."

Wilder straightened up, wiping a bead of sweat off his forehead. "What do you mean?"

She pulled the sheaf of pages about Tessa Shaw out of her backpack and passed them to him. He took one look before shoving them back, his face going white under his sunburn.

"No. No way. I am not going to let that shit derail my family again."

"There are some wild theories. I just want to know what you think about them."

"Chase," he said flatly. "What could I possibly tell you that armchair detectives on the internet haven't already posted on a million forums?"

She ignored the edge of sarcasm in his voice. "You were here. You remember it, don't you? When . . . they found her?"

"When *he* found her," Wilder said. "If you already know about Tessa Shaw, then you must know my dad is the one who found her body. Don't patronize me by pretending that's not why you're here."

Chase flushed. He was right; she had thought using the anonymous "they" would put some distance between them and what his father had found, but for Wilder, there would never be any distance. It was disrespectful to pretend there ever could be.

"You were here when *he* found her. You can answer my questions, tell me if any of these"—she indicated the packet of papers—"have any merit."

Wilder's jaw tightened, eyes drifting past Chase and through the front windshield at the white trees marching up the hill. The lookout loomed over the camp, and even though Chase couldn't see it from here, she felt the blank, staring eyes of the tree where Guthrie liked to play. Their weight was suffocating. Her stomach twisted as she realized that Wilder lived under the weight of eyes, too, but instead of the unseeing knotholes in the trees, it was the entire town watching him and his father.

"Look," she started, but Wilder interrupted her.

"You can't say anything about this to my dad. Okay? He was really messed up for a while after he found Tessa Shaw. He said the woods were liars, that the things he saw there were trying to trick him, making promises they couldn't keep. He even started sleepwalking. I used to find him at the window, bumping against it like he was trying to get out. He—" Wilder shook his head without finishing the thought. He dropped back to his knees, grabbing a wrench and going back to trying to loosen the bolts. Chase got the feeling it had more to do with avoiding looking at her then anything else. "He can't have any idea that we're talking about Tessa Shaw."

"Of course," she agreed hastily, kneeling next to him. "I won't say anything to him."

Wilder sighed. "So what exactly do you want to know?"

"Um . . ." She wanted to know what his father had said after finding the remains, but there was no way she could ask that—not now. "Did you know that a girl had gone missing from the lookout before the body was uncovered?"

"No. I doubt my dad did, either, because it happened before he was even born."

"What about after he found her?" Chase asked. "Was it a big deal around here?"

"It's the only thing anyone wanted to talk about," Wilder said, enunciating each word crisply. "There were articles in the paper about the original search, and some of the people who were involved in it spoke at a memorial. Mr. Shaw wanted to thank my father, but—" He clamped his teeth together, sucking in a sharp breath. "Dad wasn't able to be there."

Chase chewed her lip. This was harder than she'd thought, getting information while avoiding the uncomfortable truth of Michael's reaction. She decided to switch tacks and ask about the details of Tessa's disappearance.

"Did you know that there are other cases like Tessa's where people have gone missing while hiking or camping under similar circumstances?" She rustled through the papers, pulling out a stack that was paperclipped together. "It's called Missing 411. They just vanish—no trail, no sign they were ever there. Sometimes the people who were with them see it happen. They blink, and they're gone."

Wilder tilted his head to the side, his mouth pressed into a doubtful line. "Those are all just exaggerations. People get in their heads and think that it happened right in front of their eyes, but that's just, like, their guilt speaking."

Chase blinked at this insight. She hadn't ever considered how guilt might color memories or change perceptions. The Missing 411 cases had wormed their way into her brain last night, disappearances of children Guthrie's age in places like the South Dakota campground. She had been especially intrigued by the firsthand accounts of witnesses—parents, grandparents, even perfect strangers—who claimed to have been watching until the moment of disappearance. The scoutmaster who had watched a twelve-year-old boy as he hugged the shore of the lake and crawled into his own tent, only to never be seen again. The grandfather who handed his three-year-old granddaughter a piece of candy and looked on as she walked back to her parents, ten feet away, somehow never making it.

If someone could disappear like that, with the people who loved them within eyesight . . . well, that would make that night a little easier to think about.

"So what are the theories?" Wilder asked, dropping the wrench and leaning back against the stubborn seat.

"Um . . ." Chase had sorted the articles and posts by

category, and she flipped through them now. "Well, a lot of people think the disappearance is linked to a cryptid."

"I've lived in Fitzgerald my whole life, and spent every summer here for as long as I can remember. I've seen moose, elk, coyotes, deer, cougars, and one bear. But no Bigfoot or chupacabras or anything else. Next."

"Aliens."

Wilder shrugged. "It's possible, I guess. But it doesn't explain how her body ended up in the tree roots. And I've never heard anyone in town talk about UFOs or lights in the sky or anything. What else?"

Chase shuffled through her papers. "There's government conspiracy."

"Like MKUltra? Officially, that program ended in 1973. Unofficially, who knows. The government *does* have a history of testing secret weapons and shit in Utah, and her dad was a fire lookout, so technically he worked for the government."

"That's comforting," Chase deadpanned.

"That's the truth," Wilder argued.

"So I'll put this one in the maybe pile," Chase said. "Okay . . . vortexes."

Wilder sat up straight, eyebrows drawn together over his glasses. "Let me see that."

Chase handed him the papers. The unfamiliar term had conjured up vague images of dust devils and whirlpools, and since she knew that Tessa's body had been uncovered after a windstorm, she assumed *vortex* referred to some kind of low-grade tornado.

"I've heard about this," Wilder muttered. "Willow's ex-girlfriend Sasha went on and on about vortexes for a while."

"What is it? Some kind of weather phenomenon?"

"No, not physical vortexes. *Energy* vortexes."

This did not help. Chase waited for Wilder to elaborate, but he didn't say anything else.

"Well, what does that mean?" she burst out.

Wilder shrugged, flipping through the pages. "I'm not really sure. Something about portals of energy. I kind of tuned her out."

"Does she live in Fitzgerald?"

Wilder nodded. "She works at Mystic Hot Springs."

"Maybe I can get her phone number from Willow," Chase mused.

"Or we can just go to the hot springs tonight and talk to her," he suggested. "Willow is home for the weekend, so I bet she would meet us there. She still talks about Sasha all the time even though they broke up, like, six months ago. And it'll feel good to soak after working all day." He groaned, rolling his shoulders so that the bones in his neck crackled.

"I don't know . . . how much does something like that cost?" Chase had barely ever touched her savings account, but the thought of withdrawing even five dollars made her toes curl.

"Don't worry about it. Dad has a stash of free admission passes in the office that he gives out to counselors. I'll get you one."

"Thanks." She gathered her papers into a neat stack, then scooted next to him, clasping her knees with her arms.

"So why is this stuff such a big deal to you? Tessa Shaw, I mean?" Wilder asked.

Chase hesitated. It would be easy to just tell him about the name carved by her bed, use that and Willow's story as excuses for her interest in the case, but she hadn't forgotten the vulnerability on Wilder's face when he talked about his dad. He had opened up to her, even though it was hard for him. She owed him a better explanation than Tessa's name.

"Guthrie had a bad experience in the woods a few months ago," she said. "I just want to make sure she's safe here."

Wilder's eyebrows knit together. "A bad experience? What happened?"

"It doesn't matter," Chase said quickly. "But it was bad. Bad enough that she stopped talking."

"Why did your family come here, then?" he asked. "If Guthrie had some traumatic experience in the woods, why would they move to a lookout tower surrounded by nothing but trees?"

"Because they're selfish," Chase snapped. "Because my dad thinks the only way to fix anything is to disappear into the wilderness and 'find yourself.'" She hooked her fingers into sarcastic air quotes. "Have you ever read *Walden*?"

"Never heard of it."

"'We need the tonic of wildness. At the same time that we are earnest to explore and learn all things, we require that all things be mysterious and unexplorable, that land and sea be indefinitely wild, unsurveyed and unfathomed by us because unfathomable. We can never have enough of nature,'" Chase quoted. "Henry David Thoreau."

Wilder blinked at her. "Um . . . what?"

"It's my dad's whole philosophy. We had a framed copy of that quote hanging over the door on our skoolie. He thinks it means everyone should embrace their wild side and go back to living off the land, communing with nature." Chase made a face.

"I kind of get it." Wilder laughed a little, holding up his hands in defense at Chase's instant scowl. "Living your whole life in a small town might seem nice, but sometimes it sucks. You can never reinvent yourself. You are who you are, no matter how much you change. No one will ever see you any other way."

"Hm." Chase considered this.

Michael had a kind of breakdown.

Everyone knows about—

No wonder Wilder was so desperate to leave.

She glanced around at the scattered tools and discarded

bolts; the lone remaining seat that they were leaning against. "Maybe you should just leave this here."

"What?"

"This seat. Look, you could use it as one side of a booth." She jumped up. "Install one of the other bus seats right behind the driver seat, facing backward, then add a table between them. Then you don't have to worry about taking this one out."

Wilder straightened up, following Chase as she paced out the dimensions on the bus floor. "That's not a bad idea," he said. "But I wanted to have a couch where people can sit. I was just going to use folding TV trays for a table."

Chase shook her head. "No way. That's such a pain, believe me. You want an actual table. Instead of having a couch here, why don't you do a futon along the back? It can double as a couch and your bed." She pointed at the door side of the bus. "That leaves room for the kitchen and a desk here."

"See, I knew you'd have great ideas." Wilder grinned at her. "Will you help me draw a floor plan?"

Chase blew out a long breath. "I'm going to get roped into helping you with this whole project, aren't I?"

"Yep." Wilder passed her a pencil and a pad of paper.

Chapter Nineteen

They spent the rest of the afternoon taking measurements and sketching out different floor plans. The one they settled on utilized the existing seat in a booth setup, like Chase had suggested, with a small kitchenette across from it: sink, propane stove, and mini fridge. The bathroom, a tiled wet room with a showerhead and composting toilet, would be tucked into a small closet behind the kitchenette. Wilder's bed would run across the back of the bus, folding into a couch during the day. Chase left a few feet of space at the back of the bus with the original emergency exit door.

"What's that for?" Wilder asked, leaning over her shoulder as she sketched.

"This," she said, "is your garage. We'll put a wall across the back, here, with your bed against it. On the other side is storage space that you can access from the emergency exit door. For stuff like bike helmets, rock-climbing gear, life jackets. Dirty shoes. Sports equipment. All the stuff people normally store in their garages."

Wilder whistled under his breath. "That's brilliant."

"Yep." She glanced at him. "I think that's enough for today. We can't start the build until after we clean everything really well, so that's the next step."

"I can work on that in the evenings during the week. Then maybe we can start building next weekend," Wilder said. He shifted, pushing his glasses up his nose. "So . . . do you still want to go to the hot springs tonight?"

An anxious tingle ran up Chase's spine. "Definitely. I want to meet Sasha and find out what she knows."

Wilder glanced at his phone. "Okay, give me an hour to shower, and then I'll come pick you up at the lookout. We can grab burgers or something in town. My treat. But not as a date," he assured her, holding up his hands mockingly. "Just two platonic friends who worked all day together and happened to get hungry at the same time."

Chase made a face. "Haha."

They left the bus and headed in opposite directions: Wilder toward the office, Chase into the woods. The ache in her muscles was forgotten as she imagined what Sasha might tell her in just a few hours, but she felt herself tense again when she got back to the lookout and found Guthrie playing alone in the clearing.

"Gus! What are you doing?" she snapped.

Guthrie cocked her head to the side, motioning at the twigs she was twining together with braided grass, forming a circlet that looked like it belonged to a wood nymph.

"Bring that upstairs. You can't be down here by yourself."

Guthrie rolled her eyes, pointing at the deck where Dad stood at his easel. Even if he wasn't staring at the canvas, he had his back to them; not exactly keeping an eye on her.

"Uh-uh. Come on, let's go." The twigs on Guthrie's lap scattered as Chase yanked her to her feet, dragging her up the five flights of stairs. At the top, Guthrie broke free from Chase's grasp, letting the screen door slam behind her as she stormed inside.

"What's going on?" Dad said mildly without taking his eyes off his easel.

"Didn't you and Mom talk to Guthrie about Tessa Shaw?" Chase hissed under her breath.

That got Dad's attention. He put his paintbrush down and turned to her, frowning. "Why would we do that?"

"Why would you not? Why would you hide what happened from her?" she shot back.

The door creaked open as Mom slipped out. She looked bemused. "Everything okay, Chase? Gus just threw her pillow at your bed."

"You said you were going to talk to her." Chase didn't elaborate; Mom knew what she meant.

Mom pressed her lips together. "No, I said Dad and I would talk about it," she corrected. "We decided that it's best not to bring it up. It happened a long time ago, and it has nothing to do with us."

"Nothing to do with us?" Chase sputtered. "What about the fact that she went through basically the same thing six months ago?"

"That's exactly why we shouldn't tell her. She would be scared to death if she knew about Tessa Shaw," Dad said, wiping his hands on his shirt. "She's just starting to act like her old self. You don't want her to start having night terrors again, do you?"

"I want her to be safe," Chase said. "And what do you mean, her old self? She never used to collect bones or talk to the trees."

"She's not scared anymore. She's happy again. Her eyes have lost that dull look they had before we came here." Dad ticked each point off on his fingers.

"And she is safe," Mom said, each word as brittle as splintering ice. "Part of her feeling that way is avoiding conversations that will only upset her."

Of course Mom and Dad thought that. Avoiding hard conversations was practically their only family tradition.

Shaking her head, Chase stomped inside. Guthrie stuck out her tongue and jerked her curtains closed when she saw her coming. Chase made a face back, skin rippling with irritation. But as bratty as Guthrie could be sometimes, keeping the truth from her wasn't right. She wasn't going to gamble with her sister's safety just because her parents were too blind to see the risk all around them.

Huffing out a frustrated breath, she crossed the room to Guthrie's bed, rapping on the wall next to the bed before crawling through the gap in the curtains. Guthrie was curled on her side, knees pulled to her chest. She stared out the window, ignoring Chase, but Chase didn't waste time apologizing.

"Look—you can be pissed at me if you want, but I need to tell you something. The woods aren't safe. You can't wander around out there by yourself. A girl named Tessa went missing here a long time ago."

Guthrie turned her head just enough to look at Chase, chewing on her lip as she listened.

"They didn't find her body for years. She died, Guthrie. Do you get that? It's like what happened to you in South Dakota, only they didn't find her." The words burned like poison in her throat. She hadn't mentioned that night to Guthrie since it had happened. "Not for a long, long time. So I'm not just being a bossy older sister. I'm trying to keep you safe. Please, please promise me that you won't go into the woods by yourself. Okay?"

Guthrie's eyes had grown larger and larger as Chase spoke. Now they were like dark pools of water that rippled when she nodded.

Chase sat back. "Okay."

Mystic Hot Springs looked like a cross between a junkyard and Woodstock. Graffitied buses and Volkswagen camper vans dotted the campground next to the parking lot. Chase even saw a double-decker bus painted in swirls of blue and silver like Van Gogh's *Starry Night*.

"Check it out." Wilder pointed at a bus with a couple people sitting in folding chairs on a rooftop deck. "I want to do that on Georgia Pie."

"That piece of junk you're always messing with?" Willow called, crossing the parking lot from the sidewalk.

"Just wait until I'm done," Wilder shot back. "Chase is helping me, and she's a genius."

Willow glanced between the two of them, the corner of her mouth pulling into a smile. "Oh yeah?"

"I have a few ideas," Chase said. She clutched her towel. "Did you walk here?"

"My house is just a block away," Willow said. "So Wilder said you want to ask Sasha about vortexes?"

Chase nodded. "You think she'll talk to me about them?"

"Definitely. She loves that kind of stuff," Willow said. She glanced at her reflection in the dark window of Wilder's truck, smoothing her hair behind her ears. "Come on. I texted her to tell her we were coming. Plus, I brought a special treat for all of us." Giggling, she opened her hand to reveal a joint, then led them into a small gift shop.

The gift shop was crowded and dim, the only light the pinkish glow cast by Himalayan salt lamps. Tables laden with crystals—from tiny spires that hung on chains, to chunks as big as Chase's head—lined every wall. Chase's eyes immediately started to prickle at the pungent, herby scent of incense that filled the room. At first, she thought her ears were ringing, but then she saw a woman crouched over a large brass bowl in the corner. The woman's long, straggly hair fell over her face as she ran her fingers along the edge of the bowl, deepening the sound's resonance.

"Whoa," Chase breathed out.

"They don't call this place *mystic* for nothing," Willow said, grinning.

A girl their age was leaning against the counter, arms crossed over her chest. Her blue hair was cut short around her ears and swept back from her forehead. Chase could see a tattooed vine twining around one ear. Her mouth drew into a slow smile when she saw Willow.

"Hi." Her voice was low and musical, almost the same timbre as the musical bowl that was still ringing through the air.

"Hi," Willow said. "It's good to see you. I like the new tattoo."

The girl tilted her head to the side to show it off, and Willow stepped forward to run her fingers over the curling vine. They seemed oblivious to Chase and Wilder until Wilder rolled his eyes and cleared his throat.

"Oh." Willow's hand fell. "Sasha, you remember Wilder. And this is my new friend Chase. She lives in the Fitzgerald Fire Lookout." She put a slight emphasis on the words *fire lookout*, and Sasha's eyebrows rose in response.

"Really?" She leaned closer. "What's the energy like up there in Pando?"

"Energy?" Chase repeated.

"Do you ever feel brain fog or lethargy? Sometimes negative vortexes can drain inspiration."

"So Pando *is* a vortex," Chase said.

"Oh yeah." Sasha nodded. "An especially strong one."

"That's why we came tonight," Wilder explained. "We were hoping you could answer some of our questions."

"I'll do my best. But of course, vortexes are inherently unknowable. Unfathomed because unfathomable."

Chase's shoulders tensed at the familiar quote. If she had any doubts that Pando was a vortex, that vanquished them. Thoreau's words, so often repeated by her father, perfectly captured the feeling she had when she was surrounded by the aspen trees.

Sasha looked around. "Let's go out to the springs where we can talk more freely. Jeff can handle everything here." She nodded at her coworker, a man with a wild red beard and bushy eyebrows.

She led them through a door at the back of the shop and down a gravel path that wound through clumps of sagebrush. There were no lights behind the gift shop, and the night was inky black and scented with sage and creosote. Railroad-tie steps were set into the hillside, and the path turned to dirt as they climbed, then to mud that squished between Chase's toes. Rivulets of warm water trickled through the red dirt.

At the top of the hill, the muddy path branched in several directions, disappearing into the desert. Chase and Wilder followed Willow and Sasha down the middle fork to a pair of claw-foot bathtubs tucked under a rock formation. Rusty pipes emerged from the ochre rock, filling the tubs with water from the spring.

"How did they get the tubs wedged into the rock like this?" Chase asked. Willow and Sasha splashed into one of the tubs in a tangle of limbs, leaving the other for Chase and Wilder. She slipped in hesitantly, hugging her knees to her chest. The rock that wrapped around the tub was slick with water that seeped out of the spring.

"It's not rock," Wilder said, sliding into the other end so that the warm water lapped against the knots in Chase's shoulders. "It's minerals. Like a stalagmite in a cave. These tubs were freestanding years ago, but the minerals in the water built up into these formations. There used to be more tubs, but the mineral formations kind of swallowed a few of them."

"Like the deer in the tree," Chase said. It reminded her of

the way she'd felt standing in the clearing at the base of the lookout for the first time.

Like the forest was going to consume them all.

"So." Sasha folded her arms over the side of her tub and leaned toward Chase, steam rising around her face. "What do you already know about vortexes?"

"Absolutely nothing."

"Okay. So we'll start with the basics," Sasha said. "Vortexes are natural phenomena that occur all over the earth. They're places where energy either spirals out of the earth in a positive vortex"—she made a twirling, upward motion with one hand—"or *into* the earth in a negative one." She reversed the motion of her hand, spinning tight circles toward the ground. "Positive vortexes are often found at sacred sites, like Machu Picchu and Stonehenge, so there's a misconception that they are *created* by humans. Really, the opposite is true—humans were led to those places because of the positive energy they release. But humans *are* responsible for negative vortexes. Those form by an imbalance in nature due to human interference. The fire lookout opened the year after Pando was almost destroyed by a wildfire set by a couple kids from town, and the damage created an exceptionally strong vortex."

"So what's the difference between a positive and a negative vortex?" Wilder asked.

"A positive vortex can open your mind. You might gain clarity about something you've been questioning. You might come away feeling cleansed or enlightened. People often describe feeling light or buoyant at positive vortexes. Negative vortexes, though . . ." Sasha trailed off, and her eyes flashed dark and glassy before snapping back to Chase. "They can be disorienting, make you feel unbalanced or drained. Lethargic. Everything feels heavy. Oppressive."

She was silent for a moment, then cleared her throat. "But

it's more complicated than just affecting you physically. Our minds are powerful things, and vortexes can tap into that. That's how positive vortexes help you gain clarity. Often, we already know the answers to our questions; the positive vortexes just help us recognize them. But negative vortexes can also access parts of our minds, and that isn't always a good thing. Sometimes negative vortexes can bring up manifestations of fears or memories that our psyches have tried to bury for good reason, to protect us from pain. Negative vortexes can be especially unsettling if you have any kind of unresolved trauma."

Chase clenched her hands into tight fists, half-moon nails digging into her palms. What had happened to Guthrie in South Dakota was the definition of *unresolved.*

"Could the negative vortex in Pando be responsible for Tessa Shaw's disappearance?" Chase asked, fighting to steady her voice.

Sasha lifted one pierced eyebrow. "I don't see how. Vortexes aren't physical things. I suppose it could have had an impact on the search—made it difficult for the volunteers to think clearly. That might explain why she wasn't found for so long."

"Right," Chase said vaguely.

"If you're interested in feeling the difference between a positive and negative vortex, there's another one nearby," Sasha said. "At Sun Tunnels."

"I've heard of that place," Chase said. "It's a—what do they call it?—land art installation."

Sasha nodded. "They're huge cement tubes that line up with the sunset on the solstices. That's when the energy is strongest, but it's always noticeable. Well . . . to me at least." She looked at Chase appraisingly, as though she wasn't sure Chase was sensitive enough to discern the difference. "Lots of people make it a point to go every year. It's kind of a pilgrimage. My mom's friend Ren will be there. She's the one who first taught me about vortexes."

"That's in two weeks. We should go!" Willow said, straightening up with a splash. "We could camp in Wilder's bus!"

Wilder glanced at Chase, one eyebrow cocked. "Think it could be ready by then?"

"Mostly," Chase said. "Especially if Willow pitches in."

"I could help, too," Sasha offered. "Last year, I had to sleep in a tent, and it got full of sand." She made a face.

Willow bent over the joint, her hand cupping a tiny flame as she lit it. She took a puff and passed it to Sasha. The conversation pivoted away from vortexes as they discussed what still needed to be done for the bus. Chase leaned over the edge of the tub with her chin resting on her arms, her mind drifting.

The buzz of anticipation she had felt at talking to Sasha was gone. She wasn't sure what she had expected to hear, but she had hoped there would be something measurable about vortexes, something rooted in science that might explain what had happened to Tessa.

Something that would help her keep it from happening to Guthrie.

After a moment, Willow reached across the space between the tubs to hand them the joint. Wilder shook his head, passing it to Chase instead, who sucked in a slow breath.

On the other side of the desert valley, the mountains stood outlined against the inky black horizon. She traced their silhouette until she found a tiny twinkling light near the top: the lookout.

Even when she left, even when she tried to escape it, the lookout was there, lurking in the background, watching, judging.

Couldn't she have one night—just one fucking night—

with her friends without the lookout and everything it meant looming over her?

The light winked at her. It might as well have been one of the twinkling stars above them. Part of a constellation, part of a story. *Cassiopeia*, a voice whispered in her ear. Her grandfather, sitting in the open doorway of their house in Boone, showing her pictures in the sky with her grandmother wreathed in flickering, dancing light at the top of the stairs behind them.

Chase blinked. The joint was gone, nothing but its earthy scent lingering in the air. The stars had moved overhead. They were unknown and anonymous now; Chase couldn't name a constellation if she tried. And one of them was missing.

"The lookout!" she cried, straightening up so fast that water spilled over the side of the tub.

"What about it?" Wilder asked.

"I don't see the light anymore," she said.

"They must have gone to bed," Willow said, holding up one bone-thin hand and examining it against the velvet sky.

"I guess," Chase said. Her head was clearing as the last effects of the joint slipped away. Of course they had just gone to bed. With all the windows that ringed the lookout tower, it was impossible to sleep with the deck light on. "It just took me by surprise. I was looking at it, and it was like it winked out all of a sudden."

Sasha laughed. "You get paranoid when you're high, don't you?"

"It's late," Wilder said, standing up so that water ran down his body. "We should go. I have to take Chase back to the lookout."

Chase dried off with the rest of them, squishing her muddy feet back into her sandals, but she couldn't help looking back toward the lookout, waiting for the light to turn back on, like it was signaling to her.

Chapter Twenty

Chase shivered as Wilder's hand brushed her leg. "Sorry," he said, glancing at her and putting the truck into gear. Willow and Sasha were crowded into the truck cab with them, though it was hardly big enough for two.

"I can't drive like this," he complained, pulling out of the parking lot. "Why couldn't you guys walk home? It would have taken like three minutes."

"Because it's freezing out there," Willow said. "And it's barely out of your way."

Wilder rolled his eyes. "It's June. It's not freezing."

But Willow had a point. All the hairs on Chase's arms were standing up—though maybe that had to do more with being pressed against Wilder from hip to knee than with the cool night air against her damp skin.

"Oh, Wilder, can't you see we're trying to do you a favor?" Sasha said cryptically. Chase concentrated on holding her body stiff so she didn't slide into Wilder as he turned onto a side street. He slowed to a stop in front of a small house with a pitched roof and Willow and Sasha tumbled out of the truck.

"Huh?" Wilder asked. Willow and Sasha exchanged a glance, giggling, then Willow leaned back into the truck, hissing a lewd suggestion before slamming the door and disappearing into the house.

Chase watched them go without saying anything, blushing

when she realized she was still pressed against Wilder. She blinked and slid a few inches across the seat.

"So," Wilder said. "Willow thinks that you and I should—"

"Yes, I heard her proposal," Chase said.

"Sorry. She just thinks she's funny because I've never actually had a girlfriend." He pulled away from the curb, staring straight ahead at the road that led through the town and back toward the mountains.

"Come on, a cute guy like you? There hasn't ever been some other girl?"

"It's hard when you grow up with the same twenty kids in your class every year."

"Yeah, I guess."

Wilder stopped at Fitzgerald's only traffic light, blinking red because it was after eleven p.m. "What about you?" His eyes darted toward her, then back at the road as he pulled through the intersection.

There had been someone, almost a year ago. A boy she had slipped away with at a campground while her parents were distracted and Guthrie was playing. When it was over, they had pulled their clothes on without talking, and she knew by the way he wouldn't look at her that sex had seemed overrated to him, too.

"No one I cared about," she said. "No one I wanted to be with."

They left the town and climbed into the hills. Wilder handed Chase the aux cord and she pulled up a Spotify playlist. The familiar jangly opening chords of "Strangers" by the Kinks filled the car.

"I love this song," Wilder said, turning it up. He drove with one hand on the steering wheel and the other draped out the window. The wind ruffled his hair, and every now and then he mouthed the words to the song without singing aloud.

Pando was just ahead of them, the branches reaching to

blot out the stars scattered across the indigo sky. Chase felt the familiar deadening of the air as they crossed into the forest. It was like passing through a bubble to a place where sound was muffled and the air was thicker. Definitely a wild place.

The headlights bounced across the endless ranks of white trees, flashing over knothole eyes and tangled branches. Wilder turned onto the dirt track that led to the lookout. It was so narrow that the trees seemed to sidestep out of the way, closing in again behind them as the car crept forward.

Gravel crunched under the tires as they slowed to a stop below the dark lookout. Chase could hear Wilder breathing, slow and steady, in the seat next to her. His face was hidden in the shadows, but she felt him looking at her.

A loud creaking noise echoed across the clearing. Chase jumped, the fluttering of her heart speeding into an anxious gallop. "What was that?"

The stairs that climbed the face of the lookout trembled as something moved down them, footsteps slapping hollowly against the worn wood.

"Someone's on the stairs," Wilder whispered. "Your parents?"

Someone. Something. Chase's mind spun as she imagined mournful black eyes in a paper-white face, fingers like twigs trying to draw her into the woods. She held her breath until her lungs shriveled. Dark spots began to dance across her vision just as a small girl in a baggy white T-shirt came into view on the second-to-last landing. She had a messy cap of dark curls, but her eyes were soft and wide. Chase let out her lungful of air in a whoosh of relief and sagged against the seat.

"It's Guthrie," she said. "Just Guthrie." She flung the car door open and dashed up the stairs to her sister. The staircase swayed as Wilder followed her.

"What are you doing out here?" Chase scolded. "You can't get out of bed and wander around at night, Gus! Didn't you listen to anything I said to you today?"

Guthrie smiled, pointing toward Wilder's car in the clearing.

"You saw us pull into the clearing, huh? God, you scared me to death!"

"I better get back," Wilder said. "You okay?" He seemed slightly amused by her reaction, and she remembered Sasha's observations at the hot springs: *You get paranoid when you're high, don't you?*

That's all it is, Chase thought, taking Guthrie's hand. *I'm still just a little high.*

"We're fine," she said. "I'll see you on Monday."

He smiled crookedly. "See you Monday."

Guthrie was already outside when Chase woke up the next morning. The windows were thrown wide to let in the cool morning air, and Chase could hear her humming and talking to herself out on the deck. Usually she wanted to drowse in Guthrie's voice, wrap herself in it like it was a plush blanket, but the memory of her sister standing on the stairs in the dark still rankled.

Chase stretched until she heard her spine crackle, then rolled out of bed.

"You were out late," Mom said from the kitchen table. "Did you have a good time?"

"Yeah. It was fun."

Mom cocked an eyebrow, waiting for details, but Chase's thoughts were preoccupied. "You do know that Gus came down the stairs in the middle of the night looking for me, right?"

"What? She wouldn't—"

"She did," Chase said. The tiny flame in her chest flickered into something bigger. "She saw the car pull up and came out to find me. She could have fallen down the stairs in the dark, or—or—" *or wandered away into the woods*, she finished in her head. "You have to watch her better."

"We were asleep," Mom protested. "We didn't hear her go out."

"Maybe you need to put a bell on the door," Chase said. She was only half joking.

"I'll talk to her."

"Really? Because you—"

"I said I'll talk to her," Mom snapped.

Chase recoiled. "Yikes, okay. I just don't want her wandering off in the middle of the night."

Mom pressed her hands to her temples like she had a headache. She wasn't wearing any of her usual rings. "You're right. I'm sorry." Her voice was strained, and when she dropped her hands, there were new lines on her face and a dullness in her eyes that Chase didn't recognize.

"Um . . . are you okay?"

"Ugh. Just feeling a little . . . well, I guess FOMO is the best expression for it." Mom made a face. "Today is the first day of the skoolie meetup in the Ozarks. First year we haven't been there since we left Boone."

"Oh." Chase felt a twinge of shame that she hadn't thought about this before. Maybe she wasn't the only one who hadn't wanted to come to the lookout. Mom loved the semiannual skoolie meetups, where she and her friends from the online skoolie community could visit in person. And not only was she missing the meetup by moving here, but she couldn't even keep up with her friends on social media because there was no service at the lookout. "I'm sorry, Mom. I didn't think about what moving here was like for you."

Mom waved one hand, batting away Chase's apology. "Oh, it's fine. This is where we need to be right now."

"Mom . . . seriously? You can't really believe that."

"Why not?" She looked genuinely surprised by Chase's attitude.

Chase gave a short laugh. "Guthrie still won't talk to anyone. Dad hasn't painted all week. You miss your friends. And I never wanted to come here in the first place."

"Hmm . . . I guess what I see is that Guthrie is no longer afraid when one of us leaves the room. She's talking more and more, and I know eventually it will be to us. You're making friends and saving money for college, which is important to you. And Dad has had this kind of painter's block before. When he's able to break through it, his work will be better than ever. And I have my garden."

"But is this *really* what you wanted out of your life?" Chase pressed.

"I wanted . . ." Mom settled her chin on her hand. "I wanted something different for you girls. Not the overscheduled, frantic childhood that I had. When I was a kid, I had an activity every day after school, plus homework. And I don't mean in high school, I mean as a little kid. Some days I was gone for twelve hours straight. We ate dinner in the car almost every night. There was no time to play. No time to explore. By the time I was your age, I was just burned out."

"Why didn't you stop?"

Mom shrugged. "I didn't know any better. It's how everyone around me lived. And there was just so much pressure to keep up. So when you were born, Dad and I decided to do things differently. We wanted to live a simpler kind of life. A more intentional kind of life." She sighed. "I always thought we would settle down somewhere on a homestead, like the Warners. It seemed like the natural next step after we spent a few years traveling. This is a good compromise."

Chase tugged at her hair. "I'll help you in the garden later today," she promised. "And . . . what if we got chickens? Then we would never have to worry about running out of eggs between trips to town."

"I love that idea." Mom squeezed Chase's hands. "We could build our own coop."

"Give all the chickens old lady names like Ethel and Pearl."

Mom laughed. "So what are your plans today?"

"Nothing. I just want to lie in the hammock all day and read until my eyes fall out of my skull."

"Sounds nice. Dad and Gus are already out there, and I'll come out soon."

"Okay."

The sun was just cresting the mountains when Chase stepped outside. She held up one hand to block the flat white light, peering at the painting on Dad's easel. The mountain was still a shapeless lump in the background, and he hadn't added the leaves yet so the trees were bare white skeletons. Out of the corner of her eye, she thought she could see the figure of a young girl hidden in the brushstrokes. But when she looked closer, she saw that the dark curls were just the tangle of branches; the black eyes, just knotholes. Like an optical illusion that creates a face from other shapes, Dad had painted Guthrie into the trees that surrounded the lookout.

Was *this* how Dad was dealing with the trauma of finding Guthrie that night? Maybe, like Chase, he worried that a part of Guthrie had never left the woods.

It made her wonder what else he was hiding in his paintings.

She went down to the clearing: to the turned soil of the garden, to the faint paths worn through the swaying grass. Guthrie looked up from her secret games as Chase settled into the hammock with her book.

"Where's Dad?" Chase called to her.

Guthrie gestured at the trees.

In the woods? That was strange. He spent almost all of his time up on the deck. She wasn't sure she had ever seen him in the woods, despite Mom's hopes for a family hike. And what was he doing going off and leaving Guthrie alone?

"Why didn't you go with him?"

Guthrie frowned and pointed at herself and then firmly at the ground. Her meaning was clear: Dad had told her to stay here.

Well, that was something.

The morning drifted along. Mom came outside to work in the garden, and Chase knelt with her in the soft dirt, clearing the weeds and watering the newly sprouted plants before the sun rose too high while Guthrie played.

They were pacing out the dimensions of a chicken coop when Dad appeared at the edge of the woods. Chase frowned. She had assumed he had gone for a walk on the trail, but here he was breaking through the underbrush.

She watched as he said something to Guthrie. Guthrie's eyes flicked to Chase. She looked down quickly, but not before Chase caught the stricken expression on her face. She looked like she had just been caught sneaking candy before dinner. Dad said something else and Guthrie nodded, standing up and reaching for his left hand. He winced, offering her his right instead, then steered her across the clearing to Mom and Chase.

"What were you doing out there?" Chase asked, but Dad didn't answer. His face was pinched, and he flexed the hand that Guthrie wasn't holding.

"We need to talk. Gus, you go upstairs so Mom and I can have a conversation with Chase."

Chase's heart seized. Her first irrational thought was that he had seen something in the woods, some malignant, creeping thing that would explain the sense of aliveness that pervaded Pando. Not the simple natural lives of the trees, but a sentience that was far older than any of them.

Dad waited for Guthrie to disappear up the first flight of stairs before turning on Chase. "You told her about Tessa Shaw."

It was a statement, not a question, and it was the truth, so she didn't bother to lie. "Yes."

"Chase, why?" Mom looked like she had been slapped, and Chase felt a brief ripple of shame. "We asked you not to."

"She needs to know to be careful. It's better for her to be a little scared and stay out of the woods than to wander off. How did you know I told her, anyway?" she shot at Dad.

"I heard her talking to that tree she likes," Dad said. "She called it Tessa. She said something about Tessa going home when she was lost. I asked her where she heard that story, and she looked right at you. And you know Guthrie. Her face doesn't lie."

Now *Chase* felt like she had been slapped. She staggered back, gut clenching as she remembered looking out at the woods on a silver-lit night, watching a girl with weeping black knotholes for eyes untangle herself from the trees. Maybe Tessa's body wasn't the only thing that the roots had held onto. Maybe a part of her—her spirit, her soul—still existed in Pando.

"So now are you going to take this seriously? Not only is she talking to the trees, but she's calling them by the name of a girl who went missing *from here*." Chase's voice shook. "That's sick."

"It *is* sick," Mom agreed. "It's sick that she knows anything about it, which is why we didn't want to tell her. But it's too late for that now. You took that decision from us." She squeezed her eyes closed, pressing her hands to her temples. "Look, Chase, I know you've always valued being in control, but you need to back off. Let me and Dad worry about Guthrie. You just worry about being a teenager."

Chase's nostrils flared. So maybe she was a little controlling. Why wouldn't she be? For the past nine years, her life had been chaotic, unpredictable, insecure. Anything could disappear without warning—her grandparents, her home, her possessions. The view out the window of her bunk in the bus. The friends she made at campgrounds and RV parks. So she had learned long ago to wrest control of the few things she could, to grasp some semblance of autonomy in her life.

"That's convenient. You want me to 'just worry about being a teenager—'" She twisted her fingers into sarcastic air quotes. "—when it works for you, but the rest of the time, I have to worry about things like whether we have enough gas to make it through the desert without getting stranded."

"That happened one time, and someone came along eventually," Dad protested.

Chase crossed her arms. "You can't have it both ways. If you don't want me to be so controlling, you could put a little effort into making my life more predictable. And if you don't want me to be overprotective of Guthrie, show me that I don't need to be."

Mom and Dad exchanged a bewildered look. Her outburst seemed to have stunned them into silence. Finally, Dad drew in a slow breath.

"I think that's a good point," he said.

Chase blinked in surprise. "You do?"

"So do I," Mom said. "We lead an unconventional life, so it makes sense that you have an unconventional relationship with your sister. It's not fair of us to change our expectations without discussing it with you. So let's discuss it right now. What can we do to make you feel more secure in Guthrie's safety?"

"Just freaking watch her." The words escaped like a hiss of steam. "Don't let her play down here by herself. And standing at your easel on the deck doesn't count," she shot at Dad. "We all know how you get when you're working." The world could burn down all around them, and he wouldn't look up from his paints.

"Another good point," Dad admitted.

"So if we are more attentive to what Guthrie is doing during the day—"

"And at night," Chase added, remembering last night.

"—do you think you can take a step back and let us parent her?"

"Yes." Chase exhaled, tension leaking from her shoulders. It would be nice to let go of some of the pressure she put on herself to watch over Guthrie.

"Okay," Mom said. "This is good."

Chase stood, brushing the dirt from her knees. Chalky mud was caked under her fingernails. "I'm going to head up. Gus probably thinks I'm mad at her for ratting me out."

She started up the stairs, but she didn't have to go far before she found her sister. Guthrie was perched like a bird at the edge of the first landing. She sprang up, eyes darting away from Chase.

"You heard all that?" Chase asked. Guthrie clasped her hands together and nodded, still without meeting her eyes.

"I'm not mad at you for telling Dad where you heard about Tessa," Chase promised. Guthrie chanced a look up, relief written all over her face. "But I'm a little creeped out about what he heard you saying. It's one thing to talk to the trees and pretend they're your friends. I already told you I used to have an imaginary friend. But Gus . . . *is* Tessa just an imaginary friend? Or is she something more?" Something with bloated, unnatural eyes, something that comes creeping out of the woods at night. "Does she talk back to you?"

Guthrie's eyes darted to Chase's face, and she quickly shook her head. *Not Tessa.*

The knot in Chase's stomach unclenched. Okay. Not the spirit of a long-dead girl trapped in the tree. Just an imaginary friend with an unfortunate name. She could handle that.

"It's really creepy to use the name Tessa now that we know she was a real person who lived here," Chase said. "You need to choose a different one."

Gus lifted one thin shoulder in a shrug, her nose wrinkling like she smelled something rancid. It was reluctant, but it was an agreement.

Chapter Twenty-One

Dad was standing at his easel on the deck when Chase left for Spruces the following morning. He stared out over the sea of silver-green leaves, not looking up even when Chase let the screen door slam behind her.

"You okay, Dad?" she asked. His eyes were muddy and far away, then he blinked. His pupils shrunk down to pinpoints as he focused on her.

"Hi, sweetie," he said.

"How's the painting going?" she asked.

"Slow," Dad grunted, dipping his brush into his paints and mixing carefully. Chase waited to see what he would add, but he just looked at the canvas as though it were a static-filled TV, the paint dripping from his brush back to the palette.

Brain fog or lethargy . . . drain inspiration . . .

Maybe the vortex *was* having an effect on someone at the lookout.

Dad clenched his hand, wincing as he straightened his fingers. His palm was swathed in gauze.

"What happened to your hand?" Chase asked.

"Oh. Blisters," Dad said. "They just popped out yesterday. Too much painting, I guess."

Chase raised her eyebrows doubtfully, glancing at the unfinished painting, but didn't argue. "Well, have a good day."

"You, too."

Willow was waiting for Chase at Morning Welcome. She squealed and linked her arm through Chase's. "So. Did you and Wilder hook up the other night? Because Sasha and I totally did."

Chase wasn't surprised in the least, but she pretended to be for Willow's sake. "No way! That's great."

"Yeah, I don't know why we broke up in the first place. We have such good chemistry." She sighed. "And speaking of chemistry . . . what about you and Wilder?"

Chase laughed, not because Willow was wrong, but because she was so right about what could be between them that it almost hurt. "Wilder and I are just friends."

"Why? I see the way he looks at you."

He was looking at her now from across the clearing. His ears turned red when their eyes met, like he knew what Willow was saying.

"It just doesn't make sense," Chase said. "I mean, he wants to go on the road, I want to go to college. What's the point of starting something now?"

Willow looked at her sideways, a grin creeping across her face. "Does there have to be a point besides a good—"

"Hey, Wilder," Chase said loudly, elbowing Willow in the side as he crossed the clearing toward them. Willow giggled but didn't finish her sentence.

"Hey." He glanced between them. "What are you guys talking about?"

"Willow and Sasha are back together," Chase said before Willow could jump in.

Wilder rolled his eyes. "What is this, like, the fifth time? Why do you bother breaking up?"

"Because getting back together is *so* much fun," Willow said.

The bell rang to start Morning Welcome. Chase tried to pay attention as Michael welcomed a new group of campers to Spruces, but her mind kept going back to what Willow had said. Why *was* she so hung up on her future—or lack thereof—with Wilder? It hadn't stopped her before, that time with the boy at the campground. That encounter had been almost clinical in its detachment. It hadn't met any of her needs—not physical, not emotional. Just like checking something off a list.

But Wilder . . . there was something else there. Something that made her think it would be different with him. Better.

And that scared her, because she didn't know how to be vulnerable enough for the kind of connection she felt every time their eyes met. Like something in her soul recognized him.

She cleaned up slowly after her last art class, then lingered by the boathouse while Wilder climbed down from the lifeguard stand. The back of his neck was red from sunburn.

"Hey," he said, gathering life jackets off the dock. "Are you headed back to the lookout?"

Mom's words echoed in her mind: *Let me and Dad worry about Guthrie. You just worry about being a teenager.*

In that case . . .

Chase shrugged. "Maybe I'll hang around for a bit."

His mouth curved into a smile. "Cool. I'll grab a couple sodas. Meet me by Georgia Pie?"

That first afternoon, she couldn't stop herself from glancing up at the lookout every few minutes, wondering what Guthrie was doing. But each evening Mom promised that she hadn't let Guthrie out of her sight, and after a few days, Chase started to relax. She and Wilder fell into an easy routine: sodas and a few hours spent working on the bus every afternoon. When the bus interior was fully cleaned and stripped—besides the one seat they couldn't budge—Wilder went to the hardware store in Fitzgerald and came back with a truckful of lumber so they could frame the bathroom, the back wall, and the futon. Willow's mother had just remodeled her kitchen, and she gave Wilder a few old cabinets that they screwed into place to form his kitchenette.

Watching the bus start to take shape over that week was like watching her father when he painted. Worlds created from previously empty space. Endless possibilities created from nothing.

By Thursday, those possibilities—*im*possibilities, really, because Chase was going to Boone and Wilder was chasing whatever it was that drew people to life on the road—filled her mind constantly. When Wilder's fingers brushed hers as they passed tools back and forth, she imagined his hands lingering on other parts of her body. When he shoved his glasses back up his nose, his tongue poking out between his lips in concentration, she imagined slipping the glasses off his face and setting them aside as he bent toward her.

"Chase," Wilder said.

And when he said her name, she imagined him whispering it against her neck—

"Chase!"

She blinked. "What?"

"Did you hear me?" Wilder was leaning in the doorway of the bus, his mouth drawn into a crooked grin. It felt like a forest fire when he smiled at her: hot, dangerous, and too easily spreading out of control. She tamped down the sparks in her chest and reminded herself of the resigned look in Mom's eyes when she'd said Pando was the right place for their family. Chase wasn't going to be like that—wasn't going to give up all her dreams just so someone else could follow theirs. She might feel like Wilder was the moon and she was the tides, but there could never be anything real between them.

"I guess I zoned out," Chase said.

"You ready to head back? I can walk you halfway," Wilder offered.

"Sure." She gathered her water bottle and backpack, then followed him out of the bus.

He shuffled his feet as they walked along the edge of the lake, hands shoved in his pockets. "Willow and Sasha are planning on helping us paint on Saturday if you still think we're ready."

"We are," Chase said, her shoulders aching from the hours they had spent buffing off patches of rust with wire brushes. "What color did you choose?"

"It's this kind of pale pinkish beige called Frosty Peach. Because Georgia is known for peaches, get it?"

"Nice," Chase said. "Our skoolie was light blue." An image of it flickered through her mind for the first time in weeks. They had put it in long-term storage on the outskirts of Las Vegas when they moved to Pando, taking the twenty-year-old Toyota that was usually towed behind the bus to the lookout instead. She hadn't given much thought to the bunk where she had slept for the past nine years, or the sagging, overstuffed couch where she and Gus had watched the world pass by since they had left it behind. But now the thought made her feel strangely lonely.

Almost homesick.

She didn't know why she was being sentimental. That was a trait she had never had the luxury to develop. With everything she owned confined to one storage bin and the shelves over her bed, she had become adept at letting things go.

The path wound into the woods. When the trees closed over them, it was like slipping through a curtain. On one side was the camp and the laughter echoing over the lake, but on the other, in the woods, she heard only the soft sound of the leaves whispering secrets and the trees growing, growing, growing, tangled together under the earth.

Wilder left her at Skully, the bones weirdly green in the

diluted sunlight. Memories of their last nine years on the skoolie chased her back toward the lookout: lying in her bunk and listening to her parents' soft voices drifting out of their bedroom at the back of the bus, tracing designs in the condensation that gathered on the inside of the windows when it rained. The memories were sweet, like pictures out of a storybook about woodland creatures bundled snug in their burrow, but they turned sour as Chase dug deeper. How could thinking about the skoolie make her feel both safe and insecure, nostalgic and bitter at the same time? It was like remembering a childhood that had never really existed.

She stumbled over a twisted root rising out of the dirt and fell against one of the trees. The bark was smooth as skin. It was so easy to imagine the roots breaking through the dirt, catching her in their grip and holding her tight until she didn't know where she ended and the trees began.

She shivered, looking up from the path. The air just ahead of her shifted like it was something alive, creeping through the underbrush. The sun flashed on a sleek, gleaming slope of wood, honey oak instead of the paper-white bark of the aspens. A faint scent of oranges and oil drifted through the trees. *Furniture polish. The kind you spray on a rag and rub into wood*, Chase thought as the shimmering air settled into something that was both fantastic and impossible . . . unbelievable and yet inevitable.

It was the staircase from her grandparents' house in Boone, brambles and flowers creeping up the elaborately turned spindles of the banister, standing there like it had been there for years.

Chase froze. The blood in her veins slowed, and her heart stuttered to a stop. There was nothing else except for her and the staircase—no Guthrie lost in the woods, no lookout where her parents were indifferent. The only thing that mattered was the staircase with its oak balusters and soft runner carpet, pale yellow with pink flowers worked into the deep nap.

Her fingers curled as she remembered plunging them into the thick plush of the carpet. Other snippets of memory came back to her, like birds flitting through the trees: polishing the banister for a dime per spindle when she was four, her grandfather showing her how to slide down the banister when she was six and making her promise not to tell her grandmother. The glamour of this place showed her things that she couldn't possibly remember. She was one year old, wrinkling her nose and pretending to smell the pink flowers in the carpet to make her parents laugh. She was two, crawling up the stairs like they were a mountain. They were so high, and she was so small. If she could just lay her head down on the soft carpet and rest . . .

Chase fell to her knees like she was worshiping at an altar. The air filled with ringing, a high, wavering sound that seemed to come from the very molecules around her. Every bit of her was drawn toward the staircase like a compass seeking north. She felt it in the marrow of her bones; she felt it in the pulse of her arteries.

The trees whispered in her grandparents' voices. *Chase*, they said. *Come home.* Twin silhouettes flickered at the top of the staircase, indistinct and winking like the shimmer of water at the end of the road on a hot day. Chase knew that her chance to go home was just as fleeting. If she hesitated, if she even looked away, there would be nothing left.

She stretched one hand forward, letting it hover over the pink and yellow carpet. Something engrained deep within her soul reached for the promise that waited at the top of the stairs, the answers to everything she had always wondered: what Dad was looking for, and if he would ever find it, and why their family—why she—wouldn't ever be enough.

The ringing in the air sharpened, wild music that she

almost recognized. The scream of a falling airplane, the roar of atoms colliding. A song playing on another frequency, one that made her teeth go loose in her gums until the taste of blood filled her mouth. It filled up her chest, intensifying into a bone-deep ache until she felt like she was going to crawl out of her skin.

There was a sudden, violent *crack* behind her. Chase rocked back on her knees, ears ringing and popping from the sudden shift in the air. It felt like a bubble of pressure had burst in her head. She was disoriented, like she was spinning in free fall, so she closed her eyes and put both hands on the ground in front of her, sinking her fingers into the loamy soil to steady herself.

The staircase was gone.

She knew it without looking. The atmosphere was different, lighter somehow. Her lungs didn't have to work as hard to draw breath, or her heart to pump blood.

When she no longer felt like she was tumbling end over end, she opened her eyes.

She was a few inches away from a clump of wild sage. The clean, earthy scent was nothing like the artificial citrus that had shrouded the staircase. And there was no other sign that it had ever been there—no crushed underbrush, no disturbed soil.

Her heart pounded, raw and erratic, like a rabbit caught in a snare. Had she imagined it? It had seemed so real . . .

Her thoughts spun as she walked back to the lookout. She grasped at the memories that had come back to her as she knelt at the staircase, but the tighter she tried to hold on, to try to draw out some kind of meaning, the faster they drifted apart. Like bits of a dream that only lingered long enough for her to know she was forgetting something.

Her shadow stretched across the clearing at an odd angle when she finally stepped out of the woods. It was the kind of afternoon where everything was edged in gold: earth, sky, hill, tree.

She winced as she climbed the stairs to the lookout. She thought she had gotten used to the climb, but today her back ached and her knees were stiff and every step was a battle.

Mom was standing at the stove, sautéing onions with garlic. "Dinner's almost ready." Her voice was muffled, like she was swaddled in cotton. Chase shook her head to clear the ringing in her ears, but it just intensified.

"Dinner?" she repeated through thick lips. "Why are we eating so early?"

"It's past seven," Mom said. "You must have lost track of time hanging out with Wilder."

Seven o'clock? That didn't make any sense, but when Chase pawed her phone out of her pocket, she saw that Mom was right. Over three hours had passed since she had left Spruces . . .

Since she had stumbled across a staircase that had seemingly been lifted from her grandparents' house and deposited in the middle of Pando.

Chase's stomach dropped as she imagined the scene from a bird's eye view: her kneeling before the staircase, motionless and staring, for hours. If that cracking sound—whatever it was—hadn't broken through, how long would she have knelt there?

Or would she eventually have gone up the stairs?

"Are you bleeding?" Mom asked. Her eyebrows drew together as she reached to brush Chase's hair out of the way. Chase stumbled back, hands probing gently at her ears. They came away sticky with blood.

She stumbled over an explanation. "Mosquito bites. I must have scratched them open."

"Oh." Mom frowned. "Mosquitos haven't bothered me

at all here. But there's some hydrocortisone cream in the bathroom to help with the itching."

"Thanks." Chase paused. "Did you guys hear a loud noise a few minutes ago? Like a sonic boom?"

"I didn't notice anything." Mom turned back to the onions. "Maybe a branch broke off a tree in the woods."

"That's probably it," Chase said faintly.

In the bathroom, she turned her head this way and that, pulling back her hair and peering at her ears in the mirror. A thin trickle of drying blood ran out of each one, and they were tender and sore, like a shot had been fired next to her head.

Come home, the trees had sung in her grandparents' voices. And Chase had wanted to. She remembered the feeling of being drawn forward, the magnetic pull, the promise that if she climbed the stairs, she would somehow find everything she had spent her life looking for: belonging and community and a sense of connection. She would finally understand what her dad was chasing.

But Dad was like the Thoreau quote that had become their family mantra, unfathomed because unfathomable. She would never understand him. And whatever was waiting for her at the top of the stairs could only leave her empty and disappointed like he did.

Our minds are powerful things, and vortexes can tap into that.

Sasha's words rang through Chase's mind for the rest of the evening. If they were true, it made sense why Pando had shown her the staircase. It represented the stability she had longed for since her family had left Boone—the stability that had always been out of reach.

Her skin prickled as she remembered the soul-ache she had felt kneeling at the base of the stairs. The guarantee of everything she had been looking for her entire life if she would only climb. And then the sickening spin of reality when it disappeared. It was as though Pando was making a promise it couldn't keep—which was exactly how Wilder said his father had described it.

Chapter Twenty-Two

Chase teetered at the start of the path to Spruces the next morning, wondering with a shiver of trepidation what else the vortex might show her. Last night she had lain awake for hours, flipping through the disconnected images like a photo album of forgotten memories. She still wasn't sure which were long-buried memories that had surfaced like the bones Guthrie plucked from the dirt, and which were simply lies that the vortex had manipulated her into seeing.

The threat of further manipulation, further unfulfilled promises, locked her knees and froze her limbs, keeping her stiff on the edge of the clearing until she reminded herself that someone else had seen something in the woods, too—someone who would understand, someone who could relate to the sudden emptiness in her chest. If she wanted to talk to Michael about the staircase, she had to go back into the woods.

Heart tightening, she stepped onto the path to go to Spruces. She felt off balance as she walked, like she was suddenly aware of Earth spinning beneath her feet. Her muscles tensed into tight, ropey knots. Every twist of trail, every shift of light, could be the molecules rearranging themselves into another half-remembered vision from her childhood. Every knothole gaze could be the empty eyes of the girl she had seen slipping out of the trees—Tessa, the girl who had disappeared into a place in these woods where no one could reach her.

Because she couldn't deny it any longer. No amount of logical explanations—physiological responses to the eyes on the trees, internalized trauma from that night—could delude her into continuing to believe that this was all in her head. The three hours she had lost yesterday afternoon, her eardrums left bleeding by a sound no one else had heard, was indisputable proof that there was more to Pando than just trees . . . more to the vortex than just energy.

By the time she reached the rocky shore of the lake, her shoulders were stiff and her fingers cramped from being clenched in fists, but she hadn't seen anything out of the ordinary on the trail.

She headed straight for the office without looking for Wilder. She knew he would be in the bus, but today she was here to talk to Michael.

Unfortunately, the office was empty.

Frowning, she crept past the desk and put her ear against the door that separated the office from the small apartment where Michael and Wilder stayed during the summer. Maybe he was—

"What are you doing here?"

Chase jumped, heart thundering in her ears. Wilder stood in the office doorway, head tilted to the side in confusion.

"Are you looking for me?" he asked, coming inside and shutting the door. "I saw you walking past the bus. We're not painting until tomorrow."

"I was actually looking for your dad." Her voice came out thin and insubstantial.

"Oh." He pushed his glasses up his nose. "What's up? Is everything okay?"

Was he suspicious, or did she just think that because of the chemical burn of guilt she suddenly felt when she remembered that Wilder didn't want his dad to know they were talking about Tessa?

She shifted, biting her lip and trying to rationalize talking to Michael about this. It wasn't *exactly* about Tessa Shaw—it was just about the things he claimed to have seen after finding her.

Something told her Wilder wouldn't see it that way.

"I was going to ask him for my paycheck," she said. "He said he would have them at the end of the week, right?"

"Right." Wilder slipped behind the desk, opening a drawer and shuffling through a stack of envelopes inside. He pulled out one with her name written in blocky letters and handed it to her. "Here it is."

"Thanks." She fingered the sealed flap, glancing at the closed apartment door one last time. She couldn't think of any other reason she would need to talk to Michael. "I better get back to the lookout, or my mom will leave for Fitzgerald without me."

"I'm actually going into town today, too," Wilder said. "To get the paint for tomorrow. You could ride with me if you want."

"Thanks," Chase said again. Her cheeks flooded with heat.

"We could go now and stop by the lookout so you can tell her, if you want."

"Th—" She stopped herself from repeating the word a third time. She couldn't tell if her brain fog was a result of the vortex or the butterflies she felt every time they were together.

Wilder looked at her sideways as they went out to the truck. "You okay? You're acting a little . . . off."

"Um." Chase fiddled with the paycheck. "Just tired. I couldn't fall asleep last night."

Even though Spruces and the lookout were only half a mile apart through the woods, it took almost twenty minutes to make it there by car. Wilder filled the silence with his ideas for the bus. He had found plans online for a rooftop deck that would be welded on after they painted, and he hoped the deck would be ready for their camping trip to Sun Tunnels next week.

Wilder waited in the truck while Chase jogged up the lookout stairs. Inside, Mom was unwrapping the bandage on Dad's hand. The blisters were getting worse, and Chase had overheard them arguing about it more than once.

"I think you need to see a doctor," Mom said, wincing at the raw skin. "Are you sure this is just blisters? It almost looks like a burn."

"It's fine," Dad snapped, jerking away. "It'll heal on its own."

"Why don't you come to Fitzgerald with us? We can ask the pharmacist—"

"No." He squirted some antibiotic ointment on his palm and rewrapped his hand before going back outside to his easel on the deck.

Mom sighed as the screen door slammed behind him. "Well, I tried."

"Why bother? Dad doesn't listen to anyone," Chase said. "Hey, I'm going to town with Wilder today. He needs to get something at the hardware store. I'll see you later, okay?"

"Oh . . . okay," Mom said. "Do you two want to meet us for pancakes?"

"Maybe," Chase called as she ran back down the stairs to Wilder's truck.

In town, Wilder stopped at the hardware store for a five-gallon bucket of Frosty Peach paint, while Chase deposited her paycheck, poring over the bank statement that the teller handed her. Nine years on a skoolie hadn't presented many opportunities to earn money, but she had saved every birthday check, every twenty-five-dollar scratcher, and every handful of change she had scrounged up, and the account finally had a couple thousand dollars in it. With financial aid, she should have enough to pay for the first year of college by next year.

When they were done with their errands, Wilder took her through the drive-through of a burger joint with sun-faded posters in the window, then drove into the mountains. Instead of following the road into Pando, he turned into a dirt parking lot surrounded by meadows of sage and scrub-oak trees.

"I want to show you something," he said, grabbing the bag with their French fries and a folded blanket from the back seat.

A narrow path curved into the meadow. Chase slurped at the melting top of her chocolate peanut butter shake and followed him past clumps of silver-green sage interspersed with sunshine-yellow wildflowers. The only trees were blackened skeletons that reached into the air with twisted branches, and tiny saplings, maybe as tall as Guthrie, bright with new growth.

"When did this fire happen?" Chase asked, huffing for breath as the path rose steeply to the edge of a plateau. She wasn't used to the undiluted strength of the sun on her neck.

"Couple of years ago," Wilder said. "It was relatively small, as far as wildfires go. The kind that clears out deadfall and old, diseased trees to make space for healthy ones. And"—he reached the top of the hill and turned, offering her a hand to pull her up the last few feet—"the kind that allows seeds to spread so we get places like this: the poppy fields."

The plateau was covered in the crepe-paper blooms of wild poppies, each flower as large as Chase's cupped palms and as red as fresh blood. A maze of twisting paths ran through the waist-deep bushes.

"Oh—" Chase drew in a breath. With the rich sky overhead and the sun warming everything to molten gold, the scene looked like one of her father's paintings.

"Come on." Wilder pulled her forward into the field, following a footpath to a small clearing just large enough for his picnic blanket. He spread it over the trampled poppies and flopped down. Chase settled herself next to him, leaning back on her elbows. The poppy bushes were thick and tall enough that she felt hidden from the world. Even the sun, already moving toward the western horizon, couldn't reach them there.

"This is beautiful," Chase said.

"Yeah," Wilder said, looking at her. "They only bloom for a few weeks. I wasn't sure they would be ready now, but we got lucky." He passed her the carton of fries. "Do you want fry sauce?"

"Fry sauce?"

He reached into the bag for a small container of pink sauce, and pulled off the lid. "It's a Utah thing. Just ketchup and mayo mixed together."

Chase wrinkled her nose. "That sounds disgusting."

"Trust me. I can't eat fries without it," Wilder promised.

She cocked an eyebrow and dipped one of her fries into the sauce. It was the perfect mix of salty and sweet. "Okay, you're right, that's delicious."

"Told you." Wilder grinned, leaning back on his elbows. He was so open and soft. Every time he looked at her, her heart thrummed a little faster. There was nothing disingenuous about Wilder—no guile hidden in those gold-flecked eyes, no hint of insincerity—and Chase's stomach suddenly knotted with guilt. How could she sit here with him, passing the fries back and forth like they had shared food for years, and pretend that she hadn't planned on betraying his trust just a few hours earlier?

"I lied to you," she blurted out. "Earlier today, when I was in the office, I wasn't just going to ask your dad for my paycheck. I was going to ask him something else."

"What?"

She drew in a slow breath. "I was going to ask him about what he saw after finding Tessa Shaw."

Wilder tensed beside her. "You were—"

"But I didn't," she said in a rush. "I mean, I won't. I know you don't want me to. It's just . . ." Her voice trailed off as she tried to make sense of what she had seen in the woods. Here in the poppy fields, with Wilder warm beside her, yesterday seemed like something she had read in a book. But it had been real, and if she didn't give voice to it soon, she thought it might consume her.

"You saw something, didn't you?" Wilder said, pulling the petals off a blossom without looking at her. "In the woods. I know you did."

Chase felt like he had caught her in free fall. The uncontrollable spin in her chest slowed. "How do you know?"

He let out a long breath, still studying the flower. "Because I saw something, too, once. It was years ago, but I remember it like yesterday." He dropped the shredded petals and looked at her with eyes open and deep. "A door. Black, with a bronze handle and doorknocker, just standing in the middle of a clearing without walls or anything to hold it up, cracked open enough that I could see light coming from the other side. Not sunlight. Not forest light. It was a different light." He swallowed. "It was like something on the other side was trying to draw me through. I took a step forward, and then—"

He put his hand to his temple, then looked at his fingers like he expected them to be covered in blood.

"Something hit me," he said. "In the side of the head. A bird. It flew right into me, hard enough for me to see stars. And when I looked back for the door, it was gone. Like it had never even been there."

"There was a noise," Chase mused. "That's what—snapped me out of it, or woke me up, or whatever you want to say. Some kind of sonic boom . . ."

"I've always wondered where I would have ended up if I had gone through that door," Wilder said. "I think there must have been something on the other side. Something that takes people away from you. Because the door I saw in the woods was the one my mother went through when she walked out on my family eight years ago."

Chase's stomach dropped like the floor had fallen out from under her as Wilder continued. "She's in Georgia. At least, that's where she was the last time Dad heard from her. But that was two years ago, so she could have moved on now. Letting us know where she is doesn't seem to be her top priority." He exhaled roughly. "I know that *she* wasn't on the other side of that door in the woods. I just meant . . . it felt like . . ."

"Like there was something on the other side," Chase supplied. "Something big. Something important."

"Yeah."

She was silent for a moment, wrapped up in the memory of the implicit promises she had felt while crouching before the stairs. She knew exactly what Wilder meant when he said he felt like something was trying to draw him forward. It wasn't the kind of thing she would ever forget. So why hadn't he mentioned it when she had first asked him about Tessa Shaw?

Wilder seemed to anticipate her question. "I'm sorry I didn't tell you earlier. It's just . . ." His face was twisted, bitter. "I remember how people looked at my dad when he talked about seeing things in the woods. And I didn't want you to look at me like that." His jaw was locked so tight that Chase could see the outline of the bone under his skin. "My dad was really messed up after he found Tessa Shaw. My mom couldn't handle it. But why did she leave me, too? I was just a little kid."

Chase choked back the words that she knew she couldn't say: *I won't leave you.* That wasn't a promise she could make, not if she wanted to go to Boone. Instead, she put her hand on his wrist, fingers brushing the back of his hand. He turned his hand over and twined their fingers together. Holding Wilder's hand felt right in the same way that hearing birds on a summer afternoon felt right.

Chapter Twenty-Three

Chase could still feel the ghost of Wilder's hand in hers when he dropped her off at the lookout an hour later, like he had left his thumbprint as a scar on the inside of her wrist. An ache ran through her veins as she climbed the stairs to the lookout, spreading from his touch to her heart and reminding her that as much as she liked him, she wanted to go home and be part of a real community, and that was what he was trying to escape. The two things were incompatible.

She understood why he wanted to leave. Fitzgerald and Spruces were full of painful memories, and Wilder had spent half his life knowing that the rest of the town had watched his family fall apart. But a part of her still stung with jealousy. She didn't even know details about how her grandparents had died. Mom and Dad had told her there had been an accident and they had died instantly, but never elaborated on their injuries or the circumstances.

That was why talking to Dad about what she had seen was not an option. He refused to have any conversation about his parents or their home in Boone. At best, he would rage at her about letting go of the past and leaving themselves unburdened in order to move on; at worst, he would shut down, disappearing into a fugue state that made his painter's block episodes look like a picnic in the park.

But maybe she could talk to Mom. After all, the injury to Dad's hand wasn't the only thing he and Mom had been arguing about lately. At night, the low, tense sounds of their voices sometimes drifted down from the cupola, and Chase could hear Mom telling Dad how much the isolation of the lookout was wearing on her.

"I just need you to spend more time with me during the day," she said. "I need social interaction."

"You agreed to come here," Dad rumbled. "What did you *think* it would be like?"

"I thought we would be spending time as a family, but lately you won't even talk to us."

The longer they were here, the more obvious it was that the vortex really *was* affecting them. Chase couldn't be the only one who felt it. First Dad's painter's block and now his sour mood and withdrawal from the family . . . Guthrie's new fascination with bones and talking to the trees . . . and of course, the staircase that the vortex had shown Chase, the impossible promise it had made . . .

If Mom was starting to see the changes in their family, maybe she would listen to Chase's explanation about the vortex.

"Have you ever heard of vortexes?" Chase asked Mom while they were weeding the garden later.

"Like the ones that are supposed to be in Sedona?"

"They're places where—" Chase stumbled over the explanation, surprised that Mom was familiar with the term. "Wait, you know what they are?"

"Don't you remember when we met Natalie and Joe in Sedona a few years ago?" Mom snorted at the memory. "Dad *hated* it. It's gorgeous, but it's full of tourists. Unless you're up before the sun, you can forget about hiking. You have to take a shuttle to the trailheads and walk in a line on the trails. Especially the vortex trails."

"Did *we* go to a vortex?" Chase furrowed her brow, trying to remember.

"Not after we saw what a scam the whole town is. You have to admit, it's a pretty brilliant ploy to bring in tourism. Vortexes are supposedly metaphysical, so there's no way to prove where they're located or if they exist at all. All you have to do is say, 'Oh my God, do you feel that energy? This must be a vortex!' and the power of suggestion takes care of the rest."

Chase's heart sank. Mom's derisive snort of laughter and mocking tone told Chase exactly how she would react if Chase started talking about a staircase in the woods.

"What made you wonder about vortexes?" Mom asked.

"Oh . . . Sasha, the girl I met at Mystic Hot Springs, said that Pando is a vortex."

Mom rolled her eyes. "I'm sure she did. Mystic Hot Springs sounds like the kind of place that would do twice as much business if tourists started pouring into Pando the way they do Sedona."

"But you and Dad are always going on about, like, the healing power of nature and other bullshit—"

"Language," Mom muttered, glancing across the clearing at Guthrie.

"—and that's what vortexes are, right? I don't understand how you can believe in one but not the other."

"Vortexes are a New Age hoax born of capitalism and cultural appropriation," Mom said. "We do believe in nature and living a sustainable, intentional life, but it should be simple. It should be instinctive. It should be something we're born knowing how to do. It *shouldn't* rely on spirit guides and expensive retreats."

Chase chewed her lip. What Mom said made sense, but nothing could explain away what she had seen in the woods, and that made her anxious to talk to Guthrie about the vortex. Warn her that Pando was different from other places, the dangers more uncertain.

Guthrie was so absorbed in her private game that she didn't notice Chase crossing the clearing. She stood at the edge of the forest, whispering and laughing, leaning toward her favorite tree.

"Gus," Chase finally said, falling into the hammock so that it swayed behind the trees. "Come here. I want to talk to you."

Guthrie glanced over her shoulder, curiosity written across her face. She trailed her hand over the smooth white bark of the tree she called Tessa, then climbed into the hammock beside Chase.

"Have you been staying close to the lookout like I asked you to?"

Chase felt Guthrie stiffen next to her. She scowled and nodded, obviously still annoyed that she wasn't allowed to play by herself.

"Good. These woods are . . ." Chase tried out several words in her mind. Strange? Wrong? "Different. You feel it, too, don't you? I know you do."

A hesitant nod.

"It's called a vortex. It can take things out of your mind. Things you don't even realize you still remember. That's another reason you shouldn't go into the woods by yourself. It's dangerous because you could get lost, but also because you might think you see something that isn't really there."

Chase knew, in her bones, that what she had seen in the woods was nothing more than an illusion meant to catch her off-guard, draw her into a place she might never escape.

"Do you understand?"

Guthrie gazed into the trees without answering. Chase gripped her by the shoulder, maybe a little harder than she meant to. "Hey. Do you understand?"

This time when Guthrie nodded, she met Chase's eyes.

Chapter Twenty-Four

Wilder pried the lid off the five-gallon bucket of Frosty Peach paint and held it up with a flourish. "Ta-da!"

"You sure that's the look you want to go for? What about that black bus we saw on Pinterest?" Willow asked.

"Black is too hot," Chase said. "And this will look amazing."

"Thank you, Chase," Wilder said. "She sees my vision even if no one else does."

"So how do we start?" Sasha eyed the painting tools spread across a tarp. "Just grab a brush?"

"First we need to tape off all the windows," Wilder said. He tossed a roll of blue painters tape to Willow. "You guys take one side, and we'll do the other."

Chase climbed up the ladder while Wilder ripped off pieces of tape and handed them up. She glanced through the windows at the half-finished framing as she worked. "It's looking really good. It won't be completely finished by the solstice next week, but close."

"So are your parents cool with you camping? You know . . . with me?" Wilder asked. Their fingers brushed as he passed up a strip of tape.

"I haven't actually asked them yet," Chase admitted. "But they'll be fine with it. I mean—" She stretched to reach the top edge of the window frame. "They know we're just friends. And Willow and Sasha will be there, too."

She reached for another piece of tape, but Wilder didn't

put one in her hand until she looked down. His face was carefully blank, like he was trying very hard not to show his true feelings. He blinked, then hitched his mouth into a crooked smile.

"Hey, I'll finish the windows," he said. "You can start painting the other side with Willow and Sasha."

"Oh—you sure?" Chase tried to decipher the look in his eyes, but he kept his gaze fixed on the bus behind her. Her fingers twitched, remembering the thrum of his pulse against the inside of her wrist. It hadn't felt like they were just friends yesterday. She climbed down the ladder slowly. "Wilder, I didn't mean anything by that."

"It's fine," he said, grinning at her and moving the ladder a few feet so he could reach the rest of the windows. "Go on, it won't take me long to finish these."

There was a knot in her chest as she moved to the other side of the bus and poured the paint into the tray. She was just trying to keep them both from getting hurt.

Willow joined her while Sasha finished taping the windows on their side. The paint went on smoothly, covering the faded school bus orange, and by the time Sasha and Wilder were done taping the windows, the lower half of the bus already had one coat. Once all four of them started painting, it went quickly, and the entire bus was done by lunchtime.

"That was easy," Willow said, stretching so that her crop top rose up. She had a smeared pink handprint on her stomach.

"Yeah, it was easy because Chase and I already did all the backbreaking prep work." Wilder groaned, but Chase's shoulders loosened with relief at the casual way he said her name. "I'm going to be picking flakes of rust out of my hair for months."

"It looks good," Chase said, surveying their work. "Like a brand-new bus."

"Give us a tour of the inside," Sasha said. "What else do we have to do before next weekend?"

The four of them tramped inside. The scent of fresh lumber had replaced the musty smell, and Chase couldn't help but feel a warm bubble of pride as she looked around at what they had accomplished in just one week.

"Insulation is in, walls are framed, futon and bathroom are built," she said, ticking them off on her fingers. "We still need to tile the bathroom, but we can do that later this summer."

Willow glanced around. "What about, like, wiring for lights and stuff? Water? A stove?"

"We're going to keep it really simple," Chase said. "The stove will be a basic propane camping stove with a counter surround. Wilder will even be able to move it outside if he wants more space while cooking. The shower will have a propane tankless water heater, and we won't need a blackwater tank because we're using a composting toilet instead. That covers lights, water, and cooking. The only thing left is giving Wilder some power. Once we figure out a solar setup, we can put the panels on the roof at the front end of the bus, in front of the roof deck."

Willow and Sasha stared at her blankly.

Chase glanced at Wilder, then back at them. "What? You think we should do something different?"

"Uh—" Sasha laughed. "We have no idea what the hell you're talking about. How do you know all this stuff?"

"Oh." Chase's face warmed. "I mean, I spent half my life on a skoolie. You pick things up."

Wilder looked at Chase appreciatively. "This is why Chase is the best. It would have taken me a year to finish Georgia without her. And now look—she'll be ready to go before school starts. I wonder if Dad would let me homeschool myself from the road."

Willow snorted. "No fucking way. He might not let you go at all."

"Your dad doesn't want you to go?" Chase asked.

"He'll come around," Wilder insisted. "He just wants me to keep helping with the camp. But I'll be eighteen, so what's he going to do? He can't make me stay here forever. It's like he's worried I'll never come back." Wilder rolled his eyes, trying to play it off as a joke, but his jaw was tense.

Wilder's mom hadn't come back so Chase felt like his dad's worries weren't completely unfounded, but she didn't say this to Wilder. It would be like rubbing salt in a wound. Unease twisted in her stomach. This was why she hadn't wanted to get involved with the skoolie. She had spent her whole life resenting her father for disrupting his family's lives, and now she was helping Wilder do the same thing: break his family apart.

Chapter Twenty-Five

The day before their planned camping trip, Chase and Wilder did a final sweep of the bus. He had obviously been working on it without her, because besides the bathroom and the solar panels, everything was done.

"Well? What do you think?" he asked after they climbed the ladder on the back of the bus to the small rooftop deck.

"It looks great," Chase said honestly. She could imagine him sitting up here, the bus surrounded by the waving grass on a Nebraskan prairie, or the soaring red walls of a canyon in Arizona.

Anywhere but here, where the whole town watched and the trees whispered his secrets.

There were flowers strewn along the path when she walked back to the lookout. Chase could always tell when Mom and Guthrie had gone on walks, because Gus had a habit of picking wildflowers and discarding them as they went. But today the trail of flowers veered into the trees, marking Guthrie's path just as surely as her footprints would. Chase followed the flowers, gathering them into a bouquet that she would give to Guthrie when she got back to the lookout.

She didn't realize her mistake until, like Tessa Shaw's footprints, the trail of flowers abruptly stopped. Picking the last one up, she looked around, her skin prickling with the first hint of panic when she realized that she could no longer see the path. The trees all looked the same—anonymous and ranked in lines, each one fading into the next so that Chase could barely tell where one ended and the others began. *Of course*, she reminded herself, *they don't end. These trees are all connected, all a single organism.* It gave new meaning to the expression "can't see the forest for the trees."

She took one hesitant step forward, then stopped, head spinning. The atmosphere felt heavier suddenly—denser, more concentrated. When she moved, her limbs broke through the air like she was wading through water. She closed her eyes, dropping the bouquet so she could press her fists into her eye sockets. She heard each individual flower hit the ground, a volley of deep and muffled thumps like sound effects in a movie.

When she opened her eyes, she was crying. Something dark seeped down the bark of the trees all around her, dripping from the knotholes. Her stomach turned. It looked like tears trickling from the dark eyes of the trees—or the blood that had been left behind when the moth flew into her window. Her own tears rolled down her cheeks, hot and coppery. She swiped at them frantically, sure that her hands would come away covered in blood, but the tears were nothing more than water.

She turned in a slow circle, trying to get her bearings, eyes raking over her surroundings for something familiar, something that would point her in the right direction. The trees stretched higher and higher, white arms reaching into the blue sky, black knotholes distorting as the trees grew until Chase felt like she was huddled at the bottom of a well that was impossible to climb out of.

The sun hung motionless in the sky. The leaves fluttered in a breeze that felt endless. Time stood still with Chase trapped at the bottom, her past, her present, her future, flowing around her like a forest fire.

And then—

And then—

Movement bloomed out of the dark eyes that surrounded her. A bird, black as night, the sun flashing blue and green off its iridescent feathers. It crawled out of one of the knotholes, its beak moving in silent cries that Chase could hear with something deeper than her ears, something in her soul that recognized what the bird was offering her.

A way out.

She stepped toward the bird, hand extended to touch its glossy feathers. It moved just out of reach, disappearing into the bottomless knothole and then emerging out of another one on a tree a few feet away. Chase followed the bird this way for some time, her ears popping as the pressure in the atmosphere shifted, her tears drying as the rivers of red sap disappeared. The trees thinned and shrank, their bloated eyes ever watching but no longer empty holes that threatened to swallow her up.

She broke out of the woods and into the clearing all at once, a bubble of pressure popping in her ears and sending her stumbling to the ground. Her legs shook as she pushed herself up, blinking in the sun and looking around. The fire tower loomed over her, but there was something wrong with its now familiar shape. She felt off-balance, the same sick, swooping sense of unease that she felt when she saw a mirror image of her own face.

It's the other side, she realized. She had come out of the woods on the other side of the clearing and was looking at the tower from the back instead of the front.

She glanced over her shoulder, back into the woods, trying to work out how she had looped so far away from the path. The trees looked mournfully back at her, already closing their ranks and hiding their secrets.

Chase climbed the stairs slowly, all her senses still slow and dull. She half expected dinner to be ready and for Mom to ask her what had taken her so long to get back, but unlike last week when she saw the stairs, today no time at all seemed to have passed. Mom looked up from a notepad at the kitchen table, smiling and asking how her day was; Guthrie slid off her bed and padded across the room to hug her.

"We were just about to go outside," Mom said, putting her pencil down and holding up a paper so Chase could see what she had been sketching. "The deer and rabbits keep getting in my garden, so I'm going to try and build a cover to keep them out. I found some old chicken wire and lumber in the shed."

Chase looked longingly at her bed. Her bones ached from struggling through the heavy air, but it made her uncomfortable to think about Guthrie playing alone at the edge of the woods while Mom worked in the garden, so she grabbed a book and followed them down the stairs.

Guthrie dropped to her knees by the trees, already whispering to herself, as Chase rolled into the hammock and tried to shape her mind around her latest experience in the woods.

Either she was becoming more sensitive, or the vortex was getting stronger—maybe both. As uneasy as she was about being away from the lookout overnight, she was relieved that the solstice had finally arrived. She could only hope that someone at Sun Tunnels would be able to tell her how to protect her family—and herself—from the effects of the vortex.

She glanced over the edge of the hammock at Guthrie, who had something white tangled in her hair. Wild white lilac, or maybe aspen twigs woven together. But then Guthrie tilted her head to the side, a curtain of dark hair fell over one eye, and the ringlet of bone that crowned her head slipped.

Chase's mouth went sour as she scrambled out of the hammock.

"What is that?" she cried, reaching for the crown of bone. Guthrie stepped back, grabbing it in both hands to keep it from falling off her head. A circlet of vertebrae: all smooth, round knobs and gaping spaces between the bones. It was linked together by a hank of rough rope, threaded through the gaps in the bones and formed into a circle just the right size to rest on Guthrie's curls. "Where did you get that? Did you find it in the woods today with Mom?"

Guthrie's eyes darted away, and the truth hit Chase with a sickening slap. "Oh my God. You were out there by yourself, weren't you?"

For once, Guthrie's silence was as much of a response as if she had shouted. Chase's stomach clenched as she thought about the trail of flowers and how they had lured her off the path, the sickening panic she had felt when she realized that she couldn't find her way back.

How had Guthrie found her way back?

Her hands locked around Guthrie's thin wrist, and she yanked her away from the tree, scattering flower petals as they went. Guthrie dragged her feet, making low, harsh noises in her throat.

"Mom!" Chase shouted. "Come here!"

Mom dropped the roll of chicken wire she was struggling with and raced across the clearing to meet them in the middle. "What is it? What's wrong?"

"Look—" Chase swiped at the bones in Guthrie's hair again, and Gus darted back. "Look what she's wearing."

"What is that?" Mom said in a low voice. "Guthrie, hold still and let me see."

Guthrie froze, glowering at Chase, and let Mom lift the crown from her head. Mom's face twisted as she examined the ring of vertebrae. "Is this . . ."

"Bone," Chase said. "Ask her where she found it."

Mom's eyes dropped from the crown to Guthrie. "Gus?" she said softly.

Guthrie shot a look of pure loathing at Chase, then pointed into the woods.

"But we didn't go for a walk today."

"She was in the woods by herself," Chase hissed. "I found flowers on the way back from Spruces. She didn't even stay on the trail."

"Guthrie." Mom's voice dropped in disappointment. "You know you aren't supposed to go out there without telling me first."

"She shouldn't go out there alone at all!" Chase said. "And look at this thing, it's so creepy. The bird skull and her bone collection are bad enough, but you can't let her keep this."

Guthrie let out a moan of protest, scrambling for the crown of bone, but Mom held it out of her reach. "Chase is right. This is too much. You still have your necklace, but we're going to get rid of this."

Mom ignored Guthrie's angry sobs all the way back to the lookout steps, where she opened the lid of the bear-proof trash can and dropped the ring of vertebrae inside.

Chapter Twenty-Six

Guthrie still hadn't even looked at Chase by the time Wilder, Willow, and Sasha arrived in Georgia Pie to pick her up the next morning for their camping trip.

Chase paused before leaving. The curtains were still closed around Guthrie's bed, but she could feel her sister's simmering resentment all the same.

"Are you sure you'll be okay?" she asked Mom, biting her lip. "I can stay if—"

"Go. We'll be fine." Mom followed Chase's anxious gaze to Guthrie's bed. "I'm not letting her anywhere near the woods without me, after yesterday. And by the time you get home, she'll be over this."

Chase nodded. She hated leaving her sister like this. It was so rare that they fought, but Guthrie had to start being more careful.

"Bye, Gus," she called, waiting in vain for a response.

In the bus, Willow and Sasha bounced on one of the bench seats. "I'm so ready for this!" Willow squealed as Wilder pulled away.

The aspen grove was littered with black rocks patterned with lichen, sage that scented the air with its clean, sweet smell, and bunches of mustard-yellow weeds that grew like flowers. Chase caught glimpses of the sky through the shifting silver leaves; it was so blue that it hurt her eyes. It got bigger as the trees thinned and the road opened up into a sloping valley cradled between the mountains. Pando fell away behind them.

The landscape changed as they passed through Fitzgerald and left the mountains behind, the trees turning from aspens and pine to stunted scrub oak and pinyon-juniper. They drove on a cracked two-lane highway, the asphalt shimmering in heat mirages, passing rusted farm equipment, broken-down barns, and road signs peppered with bullet holes. The rocky outcroppings and narrow canyons flattened until Chase thought she could see to the edge of the world.

"Look at that." Chase pointed at a mailbox held by a ten-foot sculpture of a robot that was pieced together with scraps of rusty metal.

"Love it," Willow said. "Taking things that have been discarded to make something new. Plus the contrast of creating something and then leaving it to be reclaimed by the elements. Nothing lasts long out here. It's like the desert is the last place that humans can't control."

"I didn't know you were so interested in art," Chase said.

Willow shrugged. "I'm not really—I just like stuff like this."

They passed other installations: an arch made out of glass Coke bottles, a circle of fence posts topped with the heads of rubber dolls, a vaguely dinosaur-shaped sculpture covered in license plates.

It was a kind of art that Chase had never been exposed to, completely different from her father's paintings. Those asked nothing of the viewer but to be admired. But these installations were, in a word, weird. They could mean anything or nothing, and it didn't matter if Wilder or Willow or Sasha—or even her father—saw something different. The meaning belonged just to her.

For the first time, she thought she understood what her father meant when he talked about chasing everything that was wild. She had always taken it to mean the things that he complained about: the overdevelopment of rural areas, the crowded national parks, the wilderness slipping away into suburbs. But now the quote shifted, changing meaning.

Maybe Dad wasn't looking for the last wild places; maybe he was looking for the wild part of himself. The part that was untamed and unknowable—or, like Henry David Thoreau had described it, unfathomed by people because unfathomable. Maybe the death of everything that was wild meant giving away all of herself without holding anything back just for her.

After an hour, Wilder pulled into the dirt parking lot of a dingy gas station. Rolling his shoulders, he stretched before cranking the door open and standing up. "Last call for a toilet that flushes until we come back this way tomorrow morning."

Chase, Willow, and Sasha took turns in the bathroom and then joined Wilder in the tiny convenience store. He had an armful of snacks.

"We brought plenty of food," Chase pointed out, surveying the junk food that Wilder wanted to get.

"But road trip snacks just hit different," he said, dropping it all on the counter. "Plus you never know when you might get stranded out here. Better to be overprepared." He frowned at the pile of food and then added two gallon jugs of water.

After the gas station, even the sage disappeared, and the ground turned a pure white that sparkled in the sun like desert snow. There wasn't a hint of life anywhere. Nothing could grow through the thick salty crust.

"The salt flats," Sasha said. "You definitely don't want to get stuck out here without water. That's what slowed the Donner party down."

Wilder took one hand off the wheel and hefted one of the gallon jugs that he had just bought. "See, Chase? Overprepared."

She rolled her eyes.

Chapter Twenty-Seven

Sage and dirt reappeared after five miles of blinding, desolate salt, and the sun flashed off the windshields of a dozen or so cars in the distance. They were parked in a circle around something that rose out of the dirt, something unnaturally round in this land of flat planes.

As they got closer, Chase was able to make out four large concrete tubes, like the ones used in construction to run culverts under roads. They were arranged in a cross and were tall enough to walk through. In fact, as Wilder parked, she watched several people step into one of the tubes.

"Ren!" Sasha shouted out the open window. A woman with a long dark braid shot through with strands of silver waved back. Sasha pulled Willow out of the bus and ran across the dirt clearing to throw her arms around the woman as Wilder and Chase set up the propane stove and unpacked the cooler. The hairs on Chase's arms stood up in the harsh wind blowing from the east. Sasha said that positive vortexes sometimes felt like tingling, but Chase was pretty sure she was just shivering because it was colder here than she had expected.

"I brought an extra sweatshirt," Wilder said. "Here—" He rummaged through his backpack and tossed her a red University of Utah hoodie. She pulled it on, tucking her hair into the hood. It smelled like him, and she never wanted to take it off.

"Hey, guys, this is my mom's friend Ren and her partner

CJ," Sasha said, leading the dark-haired woman and a person with a thin, pointed face over to Georgia. "Ren's an amazing practitioner of energy healing."

Chase immediately imagined Mom's reaction to this introduction. It must have showed on her face because Ren's eyes wrinkled at the corners, and she said, not unkindly, "I can see you're a skeptic. Don't worry, energy healing isn't nearly as kooky as most people think."

"I wasn't—I mean, no, I—" Chase stumbled over her explanation. "What I mean is, I used to be a skeptic. But I'm not so sure anymore."

"What changed your mind?" CJ asked. They had a slow, steady voice that reminded Chase of hot tea and honey.

Chase exchanged a wry look with Wilder before looking back at Ren and CJ. "Have you heard of Pando?"

Ren's eyebrows rose so high that they disappeared under her bangs. "Oh my. Yes, if you've been to Pando, that's enough to change anyone's mind."

"Yeah," Chase deadpanned. "The thing is, I haven't just been there. I actually *live* there."

She explained about the fire lookout while Willow and Sasha started dinner, telling Ren about the changes she had seen in Guthrie, the weight of the air when it settled over her like water, the sense that she was always being watched. How Guthrie had changed after having a traumatic experience in the woods six months ago, and how she was changing again in Pando.

The only thing she left out was the way her grandparents' stairs had appeared right in front of her.

She wasn't sure why she skipped over that. She had no doubt that the others would believe her. But something in her chest twisted around those words, drawing them in where she could hold them tight and greedy against her heart. The stairs were hers.

"Pando is a particularly strong negative vortex," Ren said when Chase was finished. "It's not surprising that you can feel it."

"But it's just, like, bad energy, right?" Chase said. "It's not dangerous or anything?"

Ren's mouth pulled into a sympathetic frown. "Oh, but it can be. Like anything else in our minds, it can be easy to fall in too deep. Difficult to climb out of."

"What does that mean?" Chase pressed. "Is that what happened to Tessa Shaw?"

"No one knows what happened to Tessa Shaw," Ren said. "But if I had to guess . . . I would say yes, it's possible that the vortex was too much for her. She may have become trapped in her own mind."

"I don't understand." Chase balled her fists. "The mind isn't a physical thing that you can drown in. How can something that only exists in your mind be dangerous?"

"It's metaphysical," Ren corrected. "It creates its own reality. And in that sense, anything it creates is very, very real. And that makes it dangerous."

"So what can we do?" Wilder said in a low voice. "How can Chase stop that from happening to her or her sister?"

"Being aware of the vortex's power helps," Ren said. "Find ways to ground yourself, whether through your senses or through relationships with your community."

Chase felt like she was wilting. Easy for Ren to talk about community, surrounded by hers here in the middle of the western desert. But Chase didn't have that. Her family didn't have anyone to rely on.

Wilder shifted next to her, moving just a breath closer. She could feel him like a burn, radiant heat that would consume her from the inside out if she let it.

"Dinner's ready," Willow said. "Ren and CJ, will you eat with us?"

They ate beef stew and crusty bread with their backs to the wind, trying to shield the food from the blowing sand and dirt. By the time they were done and the dishes put away, another dozen cars, buses, and campers were scattered around the dirt clearing. People were setting up camp chairs facing one of the tubes. Chase and Wilder wandered over, standing together at the back of the crowd and watching as the sun sank lower. She blinked to keep the blowing sand out of her eyes, envious of Wilder's glasses. Even though it was the end of June, the western desert was cold and the temperature fell with the sun. She shivered through Wilder's sweatshirt, wondering why so many people had made the trek to this barren, godforsaken part of the state just to watch the sunset. The sky was a blinding blue-white without any clouds to reflect the color of the setting sun, so it wasn't even particularly pretty.

But then the sun met the edge of the earth and the concrete tube filled with light, a perfect halo that flashed like phosphenes. Chase's hand found its way into Wilder's almost unconsciously as the light swept through her. And that moment, with its perfect alignment of nature and art, was like the time at Delicate Arch when she had come together with strangers to witness something sanctified and ancient. Bigger than themselves.

The light faded as the sun disappeared beyond the horizon. Chase let out her breath all in a rush. She felt like her heart had just started beating for the first time.

"Uh—" Wilder glanced down at their interlocked hands.

"Sorry," Chase said automatically, but she didn't let go. She realized that she *wanted* to hold his hand. This moment was perfect, and she wanted to share it with him.

"Wait." She tightened her hand on his as he started to pull free. Her legs trembled as she moved closer. His glasses slid down his nose as he looked at her, and then he was just a breath away and all she had to do was rise up onto her toes and—

When she kissed him, he was like a burst of light on the insides of her eyelids, a firework only she could see.

His breath fluttered against her mouth in surprise, but then he took a step forward, pressing their bodies together. His lips moved with hers. He tasted like salt and cherry Chapstick and sunshine after a rainstorm. They ignored Willow's and Sasha's catcalls, kissing until Chase was dizzy and she had to pull back to catch her breath.

"*Finally*," Willow called at them, grinning.

A drum circle was forming in the middle of the four concrete tubes, rhythmic music already echoing around the campsite. Willow and Sasha joined the dancers, but Chase and Wilder hung back.

"Not a dancer?" Wilder said into her hair, his voice a low rumble that she could barely hear over the music.

She laughed and shook her head. "Definitely not. There aren't a lot of opportunities to dance growing up in a skoolie."

"Me neither." His gaze darted to Georgia Pie. "Want to go talk?"

They held hands as they ran toward the bus, their legs and faces peppered by sand blowing in the wind. Inside, it was warm and dim, and then his mouth was on hers and her hands were tangled in his hair and they were falling onto the futon. It amazed her how they responded to each other without any conscious thought, almost like they were connected by something deeper than touch.

His lips moved against hers in a whisper. "I thought we were just friends."

"Are you saying we should stop?" She kissed the corner of his mouth, then pulled back, shrugging. "Okay, if that's what you want."

"No, no, I didn't say that—" Wilder grabbed her and hauled her onto his lap, making her giggle.

There was a shriek of laughter from outside the bus. "If the bus is a-rockin', don't come a-knockin'!" Willow shouted, hammering her fist against the door. "Let us in!"

Wilder grimaced, and Chase rolled her eyes, sliding off his lap to open the door. "It's unlocked, you ignorant potato."

"Just trying to give you fair warning," Willow said, holding up her hands innocently. "Everyone decent here? Wilder? Do you need a minute?"

"No, Willow," Wilder said loudly. He sighed. "Just get in here."

"I expect details tomorrow," Willow whispered to Chase as she and Sasha climbed in, cranking the door shut behind them.

Wilder passed around snacks and set up his laptop to play a Syfy original movie about a solar flare wreaking havoc on a small town in the Midwest. The acting was so bad and the dialogue so predictable that Chase got a stitch in her side from laughing in the first fifteen minutes. It didn't help that Wilder had seen it so many times that he had long portions of the script memorized, and he kept saying the lines along with the actors, exaggerating everything they said.

"Oh, come on, this is a classic!" he said over mixed laughter and groans after another one-liner fell flat. "They don't make movies like this in Hollywood."

By the end of the movie, Willow and Sasha were sprawled across the futon, curled together like cats, leaving just a corner of the lumpy mattress for Chase. She prodded at them, trying to make them roll over, but her only answer was a rasping snore.

"I give up," she said, dropping her sleeping bag and a pillow onto the floor next to Wilder. "I guess I'm on the floor, too."

"Here—" He tugged a thick foam pad out from under his

sleeping bag, offering it to her, but she shook her head and tried to hand it back.

"No way, it's yours. I should have brought my own."

"I don't need it, I swear. I like sleeping on firm surfaces better, anyway."

She smiled and accepted, rolling out her sleeping bag on top of it and crawling inside. Wilder turned out the light, and in the dark, all the sounds suddenly seemed much more pronounced: the slither of nylon and rasp of a zipper as he lay down beside her, the soft rush of Willow's and Sasha's breathing, the cry of the wind that buffeted the bus.

"Are you warm enough?" Wilder whispered. They were lying on their sides, facing each other, knees bent and pressed together. He cupped her cheek with one hand like he was afraid she would drift away.

"Yeah."

They were quiet for a moment, and then Wilder asked, "How are you feeling about what Ren said?"

The sense of creeping disquiet from her conversation with Ren had faded during the sunset, but now it came flooding back, and she wanted to scream at how helpless she was. A physical threat was something she could protect Guthrie from—run, or hide, or fight. She would put herself between her sister and danger without a second thought. But if the threat was something inside Gus's own head? She didn't know Guthrie's thoughts or fears or dreams. She didn't know what Guthrie ached for. All she knew was that six months ago, Guthrie had shut her out. Nothing she had done since could make up for leaving Guthrie in the woods that night.

Chapter Twenty-Eight

When she woke, there was a soft quality to the darkness that Chase recognized as early morning. Wilder's eyes were on her face. He flushed slightly when she caught him looking at her.

"Hey." He smiled at her slow and lazy, one curl twisting in the opposite direction than it usually did. Without his glasses, his eyes looked bigger, the flecks of gold more pronounced against the hazel. "How did you sleep?

Chase was still wearing his sweatshirt from last night. Outside, the wind moaned as it passed through the cement tubes, and every once in a while, a strong gust rocked the bus on its springs.

It felt like home.

"Good," she said. "How about you? How long have you been awake?"

"A while," he admitted. "I couldn't stop thinking about last night." He swallowed. "So, uh . . . what are the odds you don't completely regret kissing me?"

Last night. Chase's stomach flipped as she remembered the press of his mouth against hers, the give and take of their lips moving together. She should regret it, shouldn't she? Getting involved with Wilder wasn't like the time with the boy at the campground, when she had felt nothing but hot curiosity tempered by the fact that they would both be gone the next day. There hadn't been any personal connection to make their parting painful . . . but that also meant it hadn't been particularly meaningful.

This thing with Wilder was different. It could get messy. They would have a whole year together before their separate plans took them down opposite paths, but if Chase was being honest, it wasn't thoughts of their eventual goodbye that was holding her back. It was more the idea of choosing to know Wilder—choosing to let him know her—in a way she had never experienced before that made her feel weak and panicky. Her life had been full of surface level relationships, friendships that were more about convenience than connection.

She had never felt a connection with anyone the way she felt with Wilder, and that scared her.

But it also intrigued her.

"I don't regret it," she said. "At all. I might even want to do it again."

His face loosened into an easy smile and he ran his thumb along the curve of her jaw before leaning in to kiss her.

When Willow and Sasha woke up, they folded their blankets and sleeping bags and made oatmeal on the propane stove before going outside. At least half of the vehicles that had been there the night before were already gone, and the people who remained were milling around with steaming mugs of coffee.

"We should say goodbye to Ren and CJ before they leave," Sasha said, pointing.

CJ was taking down their rooftop tent on the other side of the campsite. They called hello as Chase and the others approached, and Ren poked her head out of the back of the station wagon where she was rolling up sleeping bags.

"You guys heading out?" Sasha asked. "I'll tell my mom I saw you. She'll be so jealous."

"You do that. And tell her it's her turn to come visit me." Ren pecked Sasha on both cheeks. "Goodbye, sweet girl. And you, and you—" She hugged Willow and Wilder in turn. When she got to Chase, she whispered in her ear, "Remember what I said. Hold on tight to the people around you. They'll help keep you safe."

Chase nodded, though she still wasn't sure how. Wilder couldn't forge his way into her mind any more than she could Guthrie's.

When Chase entered the lookout, Mom and Guthrie looked up from a puzzle spread across the kitchen table. "Hi! How was camping?" Mom asked.

Chase struggled to sweep the dorky grin off her face, make it blank and inexpressive, but she couldn't stop smiling. She dropped her backpack on her bed and tried to appear very busy unpacking. "Camping was fine," she said with her back to the rest of the room.

The chair creaked as Mom leaned back. "Fine, hmm?" Chase could practically hear the smirk in her voice. "Do you have something you want to tell us?"

"Like what?"

"Like did a certain Spruces lifeguard just kiss you goodbye when he dropped you off, or is your sister trying to pull a prank on me?"

Chase froze halfway through unfolding the sweatshirt she had borrowed from Wilder, then spun around. "You little spy! Were you watching us?"

Guthrie laughed and dodged the sweatshirt as Chase hurled it at her.

"I'll take that as a yes," Mom said.

Chase threw up her hands. "Yes! Wilder and I kissed. But wait—how did you know? Did Guthrie tell you—did Guthrie *talk* to you?" Her heart pounded at the thought of hearing her sister's voice directed at them again instead of the trees.

"She got her point across without having to," Mom said, and behind her back, Guthrie made a sloppy, exaggerated kissy face at Chase that made her giddy with relief. So Mom was right—Guthrie had gotten over her anger at Chase. "So . . . are you happy?"

The helpless grin was back. Chase's chest bubbled like it was a soda bottle all shaken up. "Don't get too excited. This is just a casual thing." She was trying to convince herself just as much as Mom. "But yeah, I am happy."

"Happy about what?" Dad grunted, climbing down from the cupola. His hands were smeared with yellow, pink, and green.

"Just . . . happy in general," Chase said vaguely.

"I'm glad someone is," he said, turning on the kitchen sink to scrub the paint off his hands.

Guthrie's smile faded; Mom's jaw went tight. Chase glanced between them, gauging the tension that had descended the ladder with Dad. It was thick and ripe, bloated, like it would split open if anyone addressed it.

"Anyone want to go for a walk?" she suggested carefully. Guthrie wilted in relief, pulling on her shoes.

Mom glanced at Dad as he slammed the faucet off. "Sounds nice. Tom, want to come? It might be good for you to—"

"I have to work," he said shortly, heading back to the ladder. "Not everyone can . . ." His voice trailed off as he climbed, but Mom winced all the same.

Chase waited until they had made it all the way down to the clearing and Gus was distracted by a flurry of fat bumble bees crawling over the wildflowers. "What's wrong?" she asked Mom in a low voice.

Mom sighed and pressed the back of her hand to her forehead. "He's stressed. He says nothing is turning out how he really sees it. Yesterday, he came storming in and moved all his stuff into the cupola. He said he was getting too distracted outside."

Chase frowned. Why would Dad set up his easel in that cramped, airless room instead of on the deck? He was the one who always went on and on about fresh air and turning your face to the sky like a sunflower. Not to mention the lack of a view from the cupola. She didn't understand how he could paint landscapes when all he could see was the circle of sky through the skylight.

"That's . . . weird. He talked so much about the 'endless views' and 'sun-soaked vistas' when we first got here," Chase said, bracketing the words and rolling her eyes.

Mom shrugged. "I'm sure he'll get over whatever it is. He always does."

And as another week passed, he did manage to break through his painter's block. Chase could hear the steady *thwack-thwack-thwack* of his brush against the canvas when she got up in the morning and when she went to bed at night. The sound was familiar since earliest childhood, but she didn't find it comforting here. Maybe because he had never moved his paints or easel back out to the deck. Chase was used to Dad being right in the middle of things, completely zoned out in front of his work, no matter how chaotic his surroundings were—he had always said he worked best with a little bit of background noise. Now that he wasn't underfoot, it felt unnatural for him to be holed up in the cupola.

When he did come down for breaks or meals, he was different: quieter, less likely to sing Arcade Fire loud and off-key. He didn't even tease Chase about Wilder, which concerned her more than she wanted to admit. What had happened to her father, the man who had no boundaries and wanted to know everything she was thinking?

Dad's lack of interest actually bothered her so much that

she avoided introducing Wilder to the rest of the family, as though that would make it less real—both the changes in her father and her deepening relationship.

Wilder walked her back to the lookout after camp most days. Chase always made up an excuse of why he couldn't come upstairs until one day a week after the camping trip when the sky was dark with threatening clouds, black with edges tinged green like a week-old bruise.

"I think it's going to rain," he commented. There was a quick whiff of ozone as lightning flickered along the horizon.

"You better get going then," she said cheekily, prodding at his chest.

He scoffed. "Come on, you won't really make me walk back in this storm. Let me come upstairs and meet your parents."

"Meet my parents?" She looked at him doubtfully. "I don't know . . ."

"I don't mean it like, *Oooh, let me meet your parents*," he argued. "Just like . . . let me meet them. You know *my* dad."

"I *work* for your dad. And my dad has been so stressed lately. He's no fun. Believe me." The first few raindrops started to fall, smearing his glasses. She groaned. "Okay, fine, but don't say I didn't warn you if he says something weird."

They dodged the raindrops as they hurried up the steps and burst through the door just as the storm broke. Not the soft mist of early spring; this was the machine-gun drumming of a summer storm, sudden and violent.

Inside, it was dim and quiet, but the atmosphere was charged, the air almost buzzing. Prickles of energy raced across Chase's skin.

"Hello?" she called. "Mom? Gus? Are you home? Dad?"

There was no answer.

She shrugged. "Huh. Mom must have actually been able to talk Dad into going somewhere with her and Gus."

"Do you mean"—Wilder moved against her, tipping his

head down to hers so that his breath tickled her face—"we're all alone?"

She giggled and tugged him toward the sagging couch in the middle of the room.

A splinter of lightning showed the dim room in silhouettes: the kitchen sink still filled with the dishes from breakfast, the puzzle pieces strewn across the table, the slight figure crouched in the corner—

Guthrie.

Chase stopped breathing long enough for her lungs to revolt and the blood to throb in her temples, long enough for the crash of thunder that came after the lightning to rattle the windows in their frames. Guthrie didn't move—didn't smile her crooked-teeth smile, didn't throw her arms around Chase's waist. She was slumped on the floor next to Dad's favorite armchair, her thin shoulders rounded and her head with its halo of curls bowed, as still as she was silent.

"Guthrie, what are you doing?" Chase tried to make her voice casual, but the words came out strangled. She pulled away from Wilder, crossing the room to crouch next to her sister. She had never seen Guthrie like this—hollow and empty like a living doll. She reached for Guthrie's arms, which unfolded at her touch, but otherwise she didn't move.

"What's wrong?" Wilder appeared over Chase's shoulder.

"I don't know. Stop messing around, Gus."

Another flash of lightning. The hair on Chase's arms stood up, though whether from the electrical charge in the air or from fear, she wasn't sure. She brushed Guthrie's tangled hair off her face to reveal blank and unseeing eyes. The pupils were just pinpricks against brown irises. Empty. Her face was slack, her lips loose and turned down at the corners. She breathed through her mouth, wet little exhales that reminded Chase of the way she had smacked her lips as she slept when she was a baby.

Guthrie's head lolled on her neck, rolling bonelessly up so that her eyes found Chase's. The pupils swelled, dilating until her eyes were like dark moons in her face.

"Chase," Guthrie said. Her voice was low and hoarse, like her throat was full of dirt.

"What's wrong with her?" Chase cried. Her lungs shriveled, her breathing turning fast and shallow. She used to think that she would do anything to hear her name on her sister's lips again—but this? This was worse than the silence.

She clutched at Guthrie's hands, but the only response was the clatter of a tiny skull falling out of Guthrie's hand as her fist opened. Chase moaned, trying to yank her to her feet. "Gus, please—"

"Let me." Wilder stooped and gathered Guthrie in his arms; her head lolled against his shoulder. He eased her against the threadbare cushions of the couch. "Guthrie? Can you hear me?"

The soft baby deer eyes looked through him, like Guthrie could see something that Chase couldn't. They made her think of the knotholes on the trees outside: empty and black. Soulless. She could hardly breathe around the lump in her throat, and her vision blurred as anxious tears flooded her eyes. Wilder snapped his fingers in front of Guthrie's face, but she didn't blink. Instead, her eyes darted from side to side, rolling and twitching without stopping. One slowed so that they were looking in slightly different directions.

The pounding of the rain stopped as quickly as it had begun, and now Chase could hear the familiar, monotonous *thwack-thwack-thwack* of Dad's paintbrush coming from the cupola. He must have been there all along, oblivious to Chase and Wilder coming in or to whatever had happened to Guthrie while he drifted in his own world.

Chase sprang to her feet and darted to the ladder. "Dad!"

she screamed through the trapdoor. “Something’s wrong with Guthrie!”

A shadow appeared on the ladder and Dad clambered down, a smear of paint across his cheek. “What?”

“She was on the floor next to the chair and now she won’t answer me,” Chase said. She took hold of Guthrie’s hand again as Dad knelt next to her, running his hands over her body like he was looking for an injury.

“Guthrie? Gus?” he said, leaning closer to her. Her eyes rolled, passing over his face without recognition.

“Should I call the doctor?” Chase asked. “Maybe she’s having a seizure—”

But before she could finish speaking, something changed: Guthrie’s hands relaxed, and her face sagged. Her blank, staring eyes closed, long eyelashes laid against her cheek like delicate spiderwebs. She settled her full weight into the couch, her chest rising and falling in slow, steady breaths.

“She’s asleep,” Wilder said suddenly. “My baby cousin used to sleep with his eyes open, and it looked just like that.”

“She must have been sleepwalking,” Dad said. “Look, here’s her book.” He pulled a dog-eared copy of *Matilda* out from under the couch. “I bet she fell asleep reading. She’ll wake up soon.”

“Sleepwalking?” Chase said doubtfully, clinging to Guthrie’s limp hand. “She’s never done that before.”

“She’ll be okay,” Dad promised. “I’m sure it was scary to find her like that, but sleepwalking isn’t that unusual.”

He was right; it only took a few more minutes for Guthrie to wake up. Her eyelids fluttered, and then she sat up, rubbing at her eyes and looking confused at the way the others were hovering over her.

“Gus,” Dad said. “Did you fall asleep? What was going on?”

Guthrie shook her head, then yawned and rubbed her eyes. She shrugged. *No. Maybe. I don’t know.*

"You scared me," Chase said in a harsh whisper. Her heart was thumping so hard that it hurt, each beat like a concussion in her chest. "You wouldn't answer me."

Guthrie never answered her, not in words at least, but this had been different. Her blank, staring eyes—

"We think you were sleepwalking," Dad explained. Gus's eyes went round and her eyebrows shot up: *Who, me?* "Yes, you. But it's not a big deal. Plenty of people sleepwalk."

"Were you dreaming about something?" Chase pressed, still wondering what had spurred the incident. She had never wished more that she knew what was in Guthrie's head, that Gus's thoughts would open for her like a moth's wings spreading to show their hidden eyes.

Guthrie's gaze darkened, and she looked away without answering. Her meaning couldn't be clearer: She didn't want to talk about what she had been dreaming.

Maybe in her dreams, somewhere inside her mind, she was still alone in the woods.

Maybe she always would be.

Dad straightened up at the sound of gravel crunching down below as a car pulled into the clearing. "Mom's home. I'll go help her bring up the groceries." He glanced at Wilder while he pulled his shoes on. "I'm Tom, by the way. You must be the boy monopolizing all my daughter's time lately."

Six months ago, he would have said it like a joke, winking to make Chase blush; but now his voice was flat and gruff and it came out more like a threat.

Wilder stuck out his hand. "I'm Wilder. Chase has been a huge help with my skoolie build. I'd love for you to come down and see it if you ever get the chance."

Dad's lips twisted into a frown as he glanced sideways at Chase. "Has she? That's . . . surprising. I'll make sure to come check it out soon."

Guthrie moved as though to follow him outside, but Chase

tightened her grip, fingers clenching so hard that Gus winced and tried to pull away. "You should stay in here."

A hand on her shoulder, warm and steady. "It's okay," Wilder said. "Here—" He put his hand on hers, slowly easing her fingers loose. She let go reluctantly. Guthrie scrambled away and went outside after Dad.

Chase's heart was still pounding as she climbed onto the couch where Gus had just been lying. She leaned forward with her elbows on her knees and her head in her hands. "Oh my God," she murmured. The couch springs groaned as Wilder settled down next to her. "That was like a nightmare."

"I know." Wilder rubbed her back until Chase leaned in, tucking herself under his arm.

"Thank you for being here," she said. "If I had been alone when I found her like that—" Her heart hitched a little at the memory of Guthrie's rolling, blank eyes.

"It looked scarier than it really was," Wilder said.

"But Ren said that sometimes people fall in too deep. What if that's happening to Guthrie?" she said, then blew out a sharp breath as something else occurred to her. "Your dad started sleepwalking after he found Tessa Shaw, right? Maybe he—"

"No." Wilder took his arm from her shoulder. "I know what you're thinking, and the answer is no. We agreed not to talk to him about this."

"Please, Wilder." She couldn't keep the note of desperation out of her voice as she ran her fingers up his spine, twining her hand in the loose curls at the back of his neck. "Don't you want to help me, especially now?"

He pulled away just enough that she felt his absence like a wound. "What's that supposed to mean? 'Especially now'?"

"Um, especially now that we just found Guthrie sleepwalking." She stared at him, her anxiety about her sister giving way to something new: something she hadn't felt between them, something cold and flinty. "What did you think I meant?"

The door swung open before he could answer, and Mom came staggering in with an armful of reusable grocery bags. She beamed as Wilder sprang to his feet and took the bags from her. "You're Wilder!" she cried. "It's so nice to finally meet you."

"You, too. Are there more groceries to bring up?" Wilder said.

"No, Tom and Guthrie are getting the rest." Mom started unpacking the bags. "Would you like to stay for dinner?"

"I need to get back to Spruces," Wilder said. "Thank you, though. It was good to meet you." He pulled the door open, holding it for Guthrie, who had both arms wrapped around a gallon of milk. Chase followed him out, reaching to stop him before he went down the stairs.

"Wait. What did you think I meant?"

Wilder turned to her, raking his hand through his hair. "I thought maybe you meant now that we're together. Like maybe all this"—He gestured between them and her hand tightened on his sleeve—"was just to get me to let you talk to my dad."

Chase felt his accusation like a burn, stinging, spreading, until her entire chest was open and raw. "Nice."

He shrugged. "I mean, you were pretty adamant about us just being friends. Why would you change your mind?" His jaw was tight, but there was just the slightest quaver to his voice, and she realized that he was really asking her. He really thought that she didn't want to be with him.

I've never actually had a girlfriend.

Why did she leave me too?

Chase wanted to run her fingers along the line of fuzz on

his jaw and cup his cheek in her hand. She wanted to put her head on his shoulder and hold him until his eyes lost that broken look.

"*This*"—she tugged him closer—"has nothing to do with me wanting to talk to your dad about Tessa Shaw."

His arms crept around her. She could feel the steady rhythm of his heartbeat against her chest, marking the moments that they were together. She would have stopped their hearts if it meant she could stay in his arms forever. "Really?" he murmured into her hair.

"Really."

He sighed. "It's not that I don't want to help you and Guthrie. I just don't think that's the right way to do it."

Guilt twisted in her belly. The right way to help Guthrie was to stay with her, and Chase had already failed at that once. But it was so easy to let go of all her fears when she was in Wilder's arms. The flood of endorphins that his touch sent racing through her body drove everything else away. So she nodded, kissed him goodbye, and watched him disappear into the woods, hoping as always that Wilder's knowledge of the vortex would be enough to keep him safe.

Chapter Twenty-Nine

"Everything okay?" Mom asked when Chase came back in.

"Yep." Chase rubbed her temples absently. "I'm just glad he was here when I found Guthrie. I would have completely freaked out if I had been alone."

Mom looked up sharply. "Found Guthrie? What does that mean?"

"You didn't tell her?" Chase scowled at Dad, who was just coming in with the last of the groceries.

"I haven't had a chance yet."

"Tell me what? Did something happen to Gus?" Mom prodded at Guthrie as though looking for an injury. Guthrie squirmed and pulled away, folding her arms across her chest.

"When I got home, she was completely unresponsive," Chase said.

"She was sleepwalking," Dad explained. "She had her eyes open. It scared Chase."

Mom's eyes darted between Chase and Dad as they told her about the incident. "Sleepwalking, huh? What was that like, Gus?"

Guthrie held up her hands, lips pressed into a tight line, and shook her head.

"She doesn't remember doing anything," Dad said. "Most sleepwalkers don't. It's really not a big deal. Odds are she won't ever do it again."

Chase chewed her lip. She still wasn't sure what Ren had

meant about falling too deep into the vortex, but she couldn't shake the uneasy feeling that it might look like sleepwalking. "I met a lady at Sun Tunnels who told me that Pando is a negative vortex."

Mom and Dad exchanged a look, and by the way they rolled their eyes in unison, Chase knew Mom had told Dad about their earlier conversation about vortexes.

"I know you think vortexes are bullshit—"

"Your sister is *right here*," Mom hissed.

"—but you have to admit that there's something different about this place. Don't you feel it? It's dangerous. Ren said it can take things from our minds, twist them, and make us think they're really there."

"Enough." Dad held up his hand. "Chase, really? There's nothing in the woods but trees. I know you don't want to be here, but you have to just accept—"

"That's not what this is about!" Chase shouted. "I'm trying to keep Guthrie safe, since apparently neither of you will."

Mom and Dad stared at her in silence; Guthrie looked confused, like she wasn't sure if they were still upset about her sleepwalking, or if this was something else entirely.

Finally, Mom cleared her throat. "We keep Guthrie safe. We're her parents. Not you."

We keep Guthrie safe.

Not you.

"Fine." Chase grabbed her backpack from where she had dropped it by the couch and flung it onto her mattress. "Ignore the vortex just like you ignore everything else."

She climbed in and jerked the curtains closed around the bed. She had never had a door to slam, but she was sure it must be more satisfying than the swish of curtains.

Chase stayed sequestered in her bed until the sun was down and the lookout quiet. She listened as her family took turns in the bathroom and her parents said goodnight to Guthrie; she waited for the creak of the ladder as Mom and Dad climbed into the cupola. Only then did she slip through the gap in the curtains to find something to eat, and came face-to-face with Mom at the kitchen table.

"Sit." Mom motioned to a chair and slid a mug to Chase.

Sighing, Chase slumped into the seat and wrapped her hands around the mug, breathing in the fragrant steam: lemon tea sweetened with honey.

Mom bobbed the teabag in her own mug up and down. "I'm worried about you, Chase," she said. She glanced at the curtains drawn around Guthrie's bed and lowered her voice. "You've got this fixation on Guthrie, and it isn't healthy for either of you. It's making you paranoid and anxious, and it's stopping Guthrie from healing completely. She'll never feel safe and secure if you're constantly telling her that she isn't."

"But she's *not* safe here," Chase hissed. "She's already gotten lost in the woods once, and I don't think we should downplay what happened to Tessa Shaw just because it was a long time ago. The vortex—"

"Isn't real," Mom cut in. "It isn't real, Chase. You've latched on to it because it's a danger you can name, rather than just the vague fear of something happening to Guthrie. But you need to work on letting go of that fear, and that starts with this idea of a vortex. No more. Okay?"

Chase pressed her lips together. There was no use arguing anymore; Mom and Dad were brushing off the vortex, just like they had brushed off Tessa Shaw and Guthrie's selective mutism. She nodded and handed the tea brusquely back to Mom, her appetite gone, then went back to bed.

In the middle of the night, Chase woke to a muffled thumping sound that was familiar in the same way stranger's faces are familiar in dreams. She sat up, rubbing her eyes and trying to blink herself back to reality, glancing automatically at the window expecting to see a moth fluttering there, listening for the heartbeat flutter of its wings.

It was only when she drew her curtains that she saw the true source of the sound.

Guthrie stood at the front door, the dark glass reflecting glazed and empty eyes. As Chase watched, she took a step forward, bumping against the door over and over like she was trying to escape something.

Chase slid out of bed, padding across the room to her sister's side. Her heart almost stopped at the blank expression on Guthrie's face. What did Guthrie see with those vacant, roving eyes?

"Come back to bed," she murmured. Guthrie went limp as Chase helped her back to bed, her bare feet scuffing across the bleached wood floor. Chase slid in beside her, wrapping her arms around Guthrie's thin shoulders and trying to ignore her staring eyes.

She woke up the next morning to the shrill sound of birds squabbling outside her window. The trees along the edge of the clearing were crowded with magpies, their glossy black-and-blue feathers flashing in the sun like the inverse of the silver-and-green leaves.

There was another squabble going on in the cupola. Chase

could hear her parents' tense voices as she poured a bowl of cereal and ate at the kitchen table.

"I can help you move everything back downstairs, if that's the problem."

"Put that back—I have everything right where I want it."

A muffled curse. "Tom, *please*, it isn't good for you to be closed up here. You'll get heatstroke, for God's sake. Not to mention you barely talk to the girls anymore. I'm worried about you."

"I can't concentrate down there. There's too much to see. Just leave me alone, Sadie. Go."

Mom's bare feet came into view one rung at a time. She didn't bother to try to hide her red-rimmed eyes from Chase.

"I guess you heard that," she mumbled. "I was just trying to convince Dad to bring his stuff back down here."

"Is he okay?" Chase asked.

Mom shrugged. "I haven't ever seen him like this . . . usually when he's working, he's so happy. But whatever he's painting up there has got him so tense."

It's the vortex! Chase screamed in her head, but she didn't bother saying it out loud. If Mom and Dad were determined not to believe in the vortex, then they could just suffer with its effects.

Chapter Thirty

Wilder was waiting for her by the lake on Monday morning.

"Hi." He rubbed the back of his neck in an unconscious gesture Chase had come to recognize as a sign that he was nervous. "I, uh—I wanted to apologize about the other day. That wasn't fair of me to accuse you of using me."

She sighed. "It wasn't fair of *me* to ask about talking to your dad. I know how strongly you feel about that."

"It's not just that, though." The words tumbled out in a rush, like he was forcing himself to say them before he lost his nerve. "Chase, I really like you. Like, a lot. I don't want this to just be a casual thing, but I can feel you holding back."

Her heart fluttered. "I like you a lot, too."

"Then what is this?" he pressed. "Are you my girlfriend? Are we just friends who kiss? Because as much as I'm enjoying that, I want us to be more than friends with benefits." He reached for her, stroking his thumb down the inside of her wrist before twining their fingers together. "I want to be with you. For real."

"I want to be with you, too," she whispered. "But I'm not ready for anything serious."

"Why not?"

"I just . . ." She bit her lip. "I can't get distracted."

It wasn't even saving for college that she was worried about, but she didn't know how else to articulate her fears about getting closer to Wilder. It all felt like too much—the vulnerability, the emotional intimacy that came from the kind of relationship he wanted. She didn't know how to give herself to someone like that.

Maybe she never would.

They walked along the shore of the lake in silence for a moment. Wilder was still holding her hand, but it felt perfunctory. Her stomach sank as she took in the expression on his face: disappointment. Resignation. She could already feel him drawing away from her, steeling himself to let her go because that's what he thought she wanted.

"Look," she said, pulling him to a stop. "I don't know exactly what we are, but I've done the no-strings-attached thing before, and trust me when I tell you that this is different. This is more." She looked up into his eyes, willing him to hear what she didn't know how to say. "Can that just be enough for now?"

He drew in a slow breath, his face softening as he bent to kiss her. "Yeah," he murmured against her mouth. "That's enough."

The mood was lighter as they broke apart and continued on their way, swinging their clasped hands. The excited babble of campers greeted them from the clearing with its log-hewn benches in the middle of the camp.

"How's Gus?" Wilder asked as they joined the rest of the staff.

Chase yawned, pressing one hand over her mouth. "She sleepwalked every night this weekend."

Wilder's jaw tightened. "No shit?"

"I spent half the night holding her in bed, trying to keep her from wandering away. That night you brought me home from Mystic Hot Springs and she was outside . . . do you think she was sleepwalking then?"

"Maybe," Wilder said reluctantly. "But don't worry. I have an idea."

"What?"

"Let me look through the tool shed first," he said. "I'll show you at lunch."

When she and Willow walked into the kitchen a few hours later, he was there, holding out a few inches of chain. "Here ya go."

Chase took it, letting the tarnished links run through her fingers. "A chain lock! Wilder, you're a genius."

He grinned. "Put it at the very top out of Guthrie's reach. If she tries to drag a chair over to stand on, it'll wake you up."

"What's going on?" Willow asked.

"My sister has started sleepwalking," Chase explained. "I'm afraid she's going to go outside and fall down the stairs or something."

Willow grimaced. "Yeesh. That would be quite a fall."

"I can walk you home and install it today, if you want," Wilder offered.

"Sure." Then, because Willow was smirking with a knowing glint in her eye, Chase said, "Do you want to come, too, Wills? You haven't seen the lookout yet, have you?"

Willow shuddered. "No way. That place still creeps me out." She caught Wilder's eye and added quickly, "For totally normal reasons."

"Come on," Chase wheedled. "My mom would love to meet you. And you can stay for dinner. I'm sure whatever she's making will be better than camp food."

"She has a point," Wilder said.

"Ugh, fine. But only because I'm sick of eating frozen pizza and meatloaf."

Willow was predictably horrified by Skully later that afternoon, squealing and covering her eyes as soon as the pitted skull came into view. "How do you walk past this monstrosity every day, Chase?"

"You should have been here the first time she saw it," Wilder snickered. "She thought it was talking to her."

Chase threw a handful of berries at him. "You almost gave me a heart attack that day."

"Awww, it's like the creepiest meet-cute ever," Willow said.

This time, Chase and Wilder both threw berries, but Chase's heart twinged all the same.

Guthrie looked up from her tree when she saw them coming, then scurried across the clearing to Mom. Her eyes were wide and anxious—almost like the empty eyes Chase was already too familiar with when she sleepwalked.

"Chase! You brought some friends home," Mom said, straightening up and pulling off her gardening gloves. "Wilder, and if I had to guess, you must be Willow."

Willow beamed. "I am! I work with Chase at Spruces. I already got to meet Guthrie once, so I'm happy to meet you now, too."

Guthrie edged out from behind Mom, looking sideways at Willow as though she were trying to place her.

"I run the ropes course at Spruces," Willow said to her. "The day you came, that girl Madison said she didn't need help crossing the bridge, and then she fell in the mud puddle, remember?"

Guthrie giggled.

"Can Wilder and Willow stay for dinner?" Chase asked Mom.

"Sure, but it's nothing fancy tonight. Just spaghetti, garlic knots, and fresh veggies."

"That sounds amazing," Wilder assured her.

"Thanks," Chase added. "We're going to show Willow the lookout."

"Guthrie, do you want to come up with us? You can show me where you sleep." Willow offered her hand, and Guthrie actually took it.

"Wow," Chase muttered to Wilder as they followed Willow and Guthrie upstairs. "This is a whole side of Willow that I haven't seen before. I thought she was mostly . . ." She trailed off instead of saying what she was really thinking: shallow. Ditzy.

"I know what you mean. But she's great with kids," Wilder said.

It was more than that; she was great with *Guthrie*. Instead of asking Chase questions, she directed them at Guthrie, and she had an intuitive knack for understanding Gus's nonverbal responses. She treated her like she did any other kid. After months of people acting like Guthrie was invisible as well as silent, it was refreshing to see how Willow interacted with her. Chase's chest warmed with a new appreciation for her friend.

It didn't take long for Wilder to install the chain lock. He slid the chain into the mechanism and showed Guthrie how it kept the door from opening more than a few inches. Guthrie stretched to reach it, but even on her tiptoes, she was too short.

"See?" Chase said. "This way if you keep sleepwalking, we don't have to worry about you hurting yourself."

Guthrie ducked her head, her cheeks flushing at the mention of her sleepwalking.

"Hey, walking in your sleep is no big deal," Wilder reassured her. "My dad used to do it."

Willow looked up sharply, but she didn't say anything. Chase remembered their first conversation about Tessa Shaw: *Michael had a kind of breakdown.*

"Should we play a game or something?" Chase suggested. "Guthrie is an Uno master."

"Sure," Wilder said. "But only if she promises to go easy on me. It's been a while."

Guthrie smirked and got out the cards.

She did not go easy on any of them. She ruthlessly played so many draw-four and skip cards that Wilder finally accused her of cheating. Giggling, she was offering to show him her cards when Mom tried to open the door, walking right into when the chain caught it.

"Ow!" she cried, rubbing her nose. "What the—"

"I'm sorry!" Wilder leapt to his feet and closed the door so he could unfasten the chain. "I was showing Guthrie how it worked, and I must have forgotten to take it off."

Mom looked at the newly installed chain lock. "Why do we need this?" she asked, bemused.

"It's so Guthrie can't open the door at night if she sleepwalks," Chase said, handing her a bag of frozen peas to put on her nose.

"That won't happen again," Mom protested.

"Uh, it's been happening every night," Chase said. "I barely slept at all this weekend because I was so afraid she'd wander away."

Mom frowned. "Oh. Really?"

"Yes, really," Chase snapped. "I told you guys—"

"Oooh, are those from your garden?" Willow said, pointing at a bowl of snap peas on the counter. "They look great. How can I help with dinner?"

Mom set Willow to work washing and slicing the vegetables while she started the spaghetti. Soon the scent of simmering tomato sauce, redolent with Mom's homegrown herbs, filled the small room.

"Do you think your dad will come down for dinner?" Wilder asked Chase, glancing at the ladder. The faint, raspy sound of his paintbrush drifted down through the trapdoor. "I didn't get a chance to talk to him about skoolies the other day, after everything that happened with Guthrie."

"Oh, right," Chase said. "I'll go see."

She climbed the ladder to the cupola, calling out to Dad

when she was halfway up. There was a clatter as Dad dropped something, then he was kneeling at the top of the trapdoor, blocking her access.

"Hey," she said. "My friends are here. Wilder wants to tell you about his skoolie."

Dad blinked. His pupils were dilated, and they shrank back down to their normal size slowly. "Don't come up here. There's not enough room while I'm working."

"I'm not." Chase frowned. "I want *you* to come down. To talk to Wilder. Plus, dinner is almost ready."

"Right," Dad said vaguely. "Dinner." He turned and started lumbering down the ladder so fast that Chase jumped the last few rungs to get out of his way.

With two extra bodies in the lookout, the room felt smaller and cramped. No matter where Wilder moved, he was underfoot, his lanky limbs bumping against the furniture or walls. Chase took a step back so Mom could open the oven, backing directly into Wilder. He grunted as she trod on his foot but grabbed her by the arm so she didn't fall. She looked up at him, rolling her eyes. "This is what life is like in three hundred square feet. You sure you can handle it?"

"There won't be six people in Georgia Pie," he pointed out. "Just me." His thumb moved in absent circles on her elbow where he was still gripping her. "Unless I can convince you to come with me, of course."

"Not likely," she said, but a little voice inside her head whispered, *Convince me.*

After dinner, they went out to the deck and sat under the faded sky. Chase propped her head on her hand and listened to Wilder gush over Georgia Pie to Dad, telling him every detail of the bus's history and all his ideas for life on the road. Dad's eyes gradually cleared, and he looked more like himself than he had in days; he even laughed once or twice.

"This is good for him," Mom murmured in a low voice. "He needs something to get him out of that cupola more. Maybe he can go down to Spruces and help Wilder sometime."

"Maybe," Chase said.

"So what made you decide to move into your skoolie full-time?" Wilder was asking Dad. "Was there—"

But he was interrupted by Dad standing up so quickly that his chair toppled over.

"What's that?" Dad said sharply, gripping the splintered railing so tightly that his knuckles turned white.

"What?" Chase rose to her feet as well. She looked out over the sea of trees, but the only thing she saw was the quaking of their silver-green leaves.

"I thought I saw—" He bit the words off, jaw snapping closed. "Do you see anything?"

Willow stood up, shading her eyes in the direction that Dad was staring. "I just see trees, Mr. Woolf. Was it smoke?"

Smoke!

The word was like an alarm bell. Chase's mouth immediately went dry, as though in anticipation of breathing in the phantom smoke. She felt like a bird that had suddenly forgotten how to fly, spinning helplessly through the air and struggling to remember the magic that had once kept her afloat, while the earth rose up, faster, faster, faster—

"No, it wasn't smoke," Dad said. "It wasn't anything. Forget about it."

Mom frowned. "Are you sure?"

"I'm sure." He gave his head a little shake and turned back to the door. "I have to get back to work." His eyes had already gone back to the muddy, dull expression he had been wearing for the past few weeks. Mom and Guthrie followed him in.

Chase's jaw ached from being clenched. She tried to force herself to breathe, but the tight knot of her lungs wouldn't relax enough to fill. The threat of fire hung over her like a dark cloud. Even after a month at the lookout, she had never fully internalized why they were there, or what would happen if they did see smoke on the horizon. And what if a fire sprang up too close to the lookout for them to escape, like a rogue wave sweeping over a lone ship on the water? The splintery wood of the tower was tinder, the perfect fuel for a fire to rage out of control.

"You okay?" Wilder said, peering at her from behind his glasses.

She swallowed. "Do *you* see anything?"

"No. But don't worry, I'm sure it was just a trick of the light. He wasn't *seeing* things." He gave a slight emphasis to the words that made it clear what he was thinking: that she was worried the vortex had shown her father something.

The things he saw there were trying to trick him . . .

But her fear of fire had been so all-consuming, so visceral, that she hadn't even considered the vortex.

Chapter Thirty-One

Now that it was July, the days were getting hotter. The temperature didn't reach as high in the mountains as it did in the valleys, but the sun was relentless. The art room was nothing more than a glorified shed retrofitted with a portable air conditioner that struggled to cool the air, and Chase was always damp with sweat by the end of the morning.

Still, it was better than the lookout. With its walls of windows high above the trees and any respite their shade offered, living in the lookout was like living in a magnifying glass. Mom and Guthrie spent most of their time in the clearing, where shade and the power of evaporation kept them cool.

Chase didn't know how Dad stood it in the cupola, but that was still where he insisted on working.

She flopped down under the tree where she, Wilder, and Willow had started eating lunch. It was Thursday, and she was dreading the next three days at the lookout, heavy with the heat and Dad's simmering frustration.

"Long day?" Willow asked.

"Just hot," she said. "But I guess I shouldn't complain about that to you guys. You're outside all day." She eyed Wilder's sunburned nose.

"At least I can jump in the lake to cool off," Wilder said. He picked up Chase's hand, playing with her fingers idly.

"Mmm, that sounds good," Willow said, stretching out

in the grass under the tree. She sat up suddenly. "Hey! We should have a lake day tomorrow. I bet Sasha could come."

"That's a great idea," Chase said, imagining the cool green water lapping against her skin. "I'll come down after lunch."

Wilder came to find her after her last art class. One of the kids had knocked over a gallon jug of glitter, and she was sweeping it into a dustbin and sneezing as the itchy flecks went up her nose.

"Oh my God, you're covered in glitter. It's like, embedded in your eyebrow," Wilder said, easing the door closed behind him. He snorted back a laugh as she straightened up.

"What, you don't like it? It's my new look." Chase waggled her eyebrows up and down. A few flecks of green fell out.

"Gorgeous," Wilder agreed. "Come here." She closed her eyes as he rubbed his thumbs over her eyelashes and eyebrows, brushing away the glitter. He kissed her while her eyes were still closed.

She moved closer, pressing into him as he slid his hand under her shirt, fingers spread against the soft skin of her back. The world spun behind her eyelids until Wilder was the only thing keeping her grounded.

There was a tap at the door, then Michael poked his head into the art room. "Wilder—"

He frowned, turning to face the corner as Wilder pulled away from Chase. Her cheeks flushed as she straightened her shirt. She could still feel his hands on her skin like a burn.

"Sorry," Michael muttered. "Wilder, I need you to help me with some paperwork in the office today. One of the campers coming next week just emailed to tell us about their food allergies, and we have to redo our whole shopping list."

"I'll be right there," Wilder promised.

"Now, please. Sorry, Chase, but we need to take care of this."

"Of course!" Chase chirped, trying to act like her boss

hadn't just caught her with his son's hands under her shirt. "I have to get back anyway. I, um, I'll see you Monday."

Michael nodded goodbye, disappearing out of the doorway. As soon as he was gone, Wilder collapsed in laughter, pressing his face into Chase's shoulder.

"Oh my God," she exclaimed. Her toes curled in embarrassment. "I can never show my face here again."

"Yes, you can," Wilder said. "He likes you. I'm the one who's going to get a lecture about keeping my hands to myself." He slid one hand back under her shirt, and she swatted him away.

"You better go, or he'll come looking again," Chase warned.

Wilder pulled away, groaning. "Okay. I'll see you tomorrow."

Outside, campers raced down gravel paths, leaping over the benches by the firepit and trying to avoid being tagged by a group of kids wearing blue bandanas. The last night of each session was always dedicated to a camp-wide game of tag with complicated rules that Chase didn't understand. She wove in and out of the running kids, smiling as half of them called hello and held up their wrists to show her the friendship bracelets she had helped them make. There was one girl this session who had the same wild curls as Guthrie. Chase spotted her ducking behind the boathouse with a couple other kids. She and Chase made eye contact, and the little girl grinned and held one finger to her lips.

With a pang, Chase nodded and returned the gesture, thinking of how easily that could have been Guthrie. If Guthrie had just tried, Chase knew she could have had fun at camp, even without talking. She could have made friends and come out of her shell a little, instead of spending all day playing by herself and talking to the trees.

The whoops and hollers of camp faded away as Chase entered the woods. She followed the path without thinking. By now, after weeks of walking back and forth each day, she knew every twist and turn, every root and hollow by heart.

The small clearing where Skully presided over Pando from his tree was just ahead when Chase heard a breathy laugh.

She froze, poised on the balls of her feet as she listened. The wind rustled through the trees; a twig snapped. And there was the laugh again, so quiet that it could almost be the quaking of the leaves overhead.

"Guthrie?" Chase called. The light had gone a funny green, turning the trees the color of sour milk. Everything was green and silver and white, until she saw a flash of tawny brown.

Brown like dirt, brown like bark, brown like Guthrie's curls. Brown like the soft, spotted coat of the fawn that bounded away. There was something wrong with the way it moved, a humping stumble with one of the legs twisted and dragging underneath.

Where was the doe? The fawn was young enough to still have a spotted pelt, surely too young to be without its mother. Why was it alone in the woods?

Why was Guthrie? She had promised Chase that she wouldn't leave the little copse of trees where she played by the lookout.

Leaves rustled and twigs snapped as a small figure with a tangle of curls crashed through the underbrush after the fawn.

"Gus, get back here!" Chase shouted, bolting after them. The forest did something to her words—stole them, took them for its own—and they echoed all around her as she ran. The thunder of Chase's body—blood rushing, lungs gasping, muscles bounding—spread through the air until the woods were filled with a dull roar. The mindless hum of silence howled inside her head, a tangled cry of voices with Guthrie's rising out in a wail just ahead of her.

Guthrie stood at the edge of a clearing ringed with toadstools and wildflowers. Her mouth was open in a scream, but the rush of sound blotted it out the way a storm cloud does the afternoon sun. Chase stumbled to her side and yanked her close, her own mouth opening in a shout, but Guthrie raised one hand and pointed.

On the other side of the clearing, the fawn struggled to its feet at the base of a tree marked with blood. It staggered a little, its dragging foot tangled and useless, then hurled itself against the tree. Chase could hear its neck snap, a tiny *pop*, before Guthrie drew breath and screamed again.

The scream shattered the stillness, and discordant birdsong rose above them. A cloud of birds wheeled out of the trees; underbrush rustled as some small animal scurried away from the disturbance. Chase's breath whistled in and out of her chest, and Guthrie's ragged sobs filled the air as she crawled to the fawn's side.

Its eyes were still open, deep brown and soft. Guthrie cradled its head, loose and sagging, on her lap, and murmured as she stroked its spotted fur. Chase's ears popped as she swallowed. Her mouth was dry, and her throat felt like sandpaper. She closed her eyes, but in her mind, the desperate flight through the forest and the fawn's dazed expression began to play again like she had slipped into a nightmare.

Dropping to the ground, she knelt next to Guthrie and the fawn. Its foreleg was ragged and torn, the fur wet with blood and split to the bone. The injury was messy. Sharp teeth hadn't made this cut. A coyote or a cougar's bite would have punctured the hide neatly. Instead, the foreleg looked like something had gnawed on it—something that had no need of ripping flesh, something like the fawn's own large, flat teeth—

The fawn's mouth sagged open. Inside, its teeth were streaked with blood and its tongue matted with fur. Chase's stomach churned, but she gently cupped her hand over the fawn's face, closing its mouth and running her fingers over its eyelids.

"It was all alone in the woods," she said. She half expected her voice to fade away again, but it was there. Thin and reedy, but strong enough for Guthrie to look up with her trusting, soft brown eyes.

Baby deer eyes.

"Something must have happened to its mother. It didn't know how to survive on its own." The words tasted bitter in her mouth. An orphaned baby animal might not know how to avoid a predator or look for food, but she had never heard of a deer trying to chew its own leg off or breaking its neck on a tree trunk.

"Come on," Chase said, climbing to her feet and reaching down for Guthrie. "Let's go back." Suddenly all she wanted was to be at the top of the lookout, where she could stand above the trees, watching to be sure nothing was creeping up on them.

Guthrie shook her head and stroked the fawn's spotted hide. She had stopped crying and now had a determined set to her jaw that Chase barely recognized.

"We can't take it with us," Chase said. Her skin crawled at the thought of gathering the limp animal in her arms, the head lolling on its broken neck. "It's *dead*, Gus. We have to leave it here."

Guthrie reached for a chunk of rock with one hand, the other still curled protectively around the fawn, and began to scrape through layers of dirt and leaves, digging a shallow hole.

Chase sighed, but Guthrie was right—they couldn't leave the fawn there. She couldn't lie in bed at the lookout while the fawn rotted on its bed of dead leaves in the forest.

"Let's come back with a shovel," she said. "We'll bury it."

Guthrie kept her eyes locked on the fawn, but let it slip back to the ground as Chase pulled her to her feet. Chase glanced at the trees around them, trying to memorize the way they had run after leaving the path, but everything looked the same. Finally, she pulled a pair of scissors out of her backpack and used the sharp edge to carve arrows leading back to the clearing and the fawn.

Mom was weeding the raspberry patch at the base of the lookout when they burst out of the woods. "Oh good, you girls found each other. I was just—"

"Why weren't you watching her?" Chase hissed.

"She wanted to go play. I told her it would be okay if she stayed close."

An ember of rage flared to life in Chase's chest. *It would be okay?* That was even worse than if Guthrie had slipped away unseen. How could Mom actually let her go, watch her disappear among the trees, without gagging on the corrosive burn of battery acid like Chase did at the mere thought of her sister alone in the woods?

"You promised me you wouldn't let her play by herself," Chase said through gritted teeth. "It isn't safe."

Mom lifted one eyebrow. "Chase, I think you're overreacting. We talked about this. Guthrie has spent enough time in these woods by now to know her way back home."

"This isn't our home," Chase muttered, pushing past Mom toward the stairs.

Guthrie made a sound of protest low in her throat, tugging at Chase's hand. She pointed into the woods.

Dammit. The fawn. "We need a shovel," Chase said curtly to Mom. "We found a dead baby deer, and I told Guthrie we could bury it."

"Oh, how sad!" Mom brushed dirt off her hands and stood up. "I'll come with you. It'll feel good to move around. I'm stiff from kneeling over those bushes." She handed Chase a garden shovel with a splintered wood handle. The edge looked dull, but it would have to do.

Guthrie led the way down the path, glancing over her

shoulder every few minutes to be sure Mom and Chase were following. They passed Skully without comment. Chase slowed, studying the trees and looking for the arrows she had carved into the wood.

"It was right around here, wasn't it?" Chase asked Guthrie.

Guthrie glanced around and nodded. This was the place. So where were the marks that Chase had scratched into the trees?

Chase ventured off the trail in the direction they had fled, examining each tree for the jagged lines she had carved. The marks had stood out green and fresh against the paper white bark of the trees, easy to spot in a sea of dark knotholes. But now, no matter which direction she turned, they were gone.

Guthrie wandered past Chase, running her hands over the knotholes in the trees. Mom hesitated on the edge of the trail. "Is it nearby?"

"It's a little ways into the woods," Chase said. "I carved arrows on the trees to lead the way. But now I can't find them . . ."

They searched the trees along the edge of the path as the sun dropped in the sky and the light faded, but there was no sign of the arrows. It was as though Chase had never carved them at all.

But she had—she could see them in her head, remember the awkward feel of the scissors in her hand. The bark had peeled back like skin around a wound, exposing the slightly green flesh of the tree in rough, jagged lines.

She was still thinking about the missing arrows when they walked back into the clearing at the lookout, Guthrie sobbing in Mom's arms. Shadows crept across the grass. Inside the woods, twilight had already fallen. Chase was reminded, again, of THAT NIGHT when they had carried Guthrie out of the woods. But this time, Guthrie was crying because Mom wouldn't let her go back in.

It was only after dinner that she realized she had left her backpack in the clearing at the bottom of the lookout.

Groaning, Chase flicked on the porch light and started down the five flights of stairs. She shivered as the wind shifted, whispering against the back of her neck.

She was halfway back up with her backpack when she noticed the fresh carving in the wood of the stair rail.

A crude triangle at the end of a line. One of the arrows that Chase had carved to mark their path back to the fawn.

Chase swayed a bit on the step and had to put her hand on the railing to steady herself. It couldn't be the same arrow—she just hadn't noticed this one before.

But it stood out fresh and yellow against the weathered gray of the wood, with a little hitch at the end of the shaft where the scissors had slipped as she carved it . . .

Chase kept her hand on the railing as she began to climb, feeling for more carvings and finding one at each landing where the stairs changed direction. Arrows pointing up, leading the way to the lookout.

At the top of the stairs, the arrows circled the deck on the railing in both directions, converging at a single spot on the other side.

Under Guthrie's window.

Chase stood outside her sister's window, heart pounding and stomach churning. She felt like she was going to throw up. Images flashed through her mind every time she closed her eyes: the bones twisting their way out of the ground like fungus, the blank look in the fawn's eyes as its life drained away . . .

The fawn, with eyes like Guthrie's.

Chase had carved the arrows to lead their way back to the fawn, but now she wondered what she was leading to her sister. What might come out of the woods, creeping toward Guthrie?

Chapter Thirty-Two

Chase closed the door behind her. Hooking the chain lock didn't feel like enough, so she turned the deadbolt for the first time since they had come to the lookout. She felt exposed, like someone had posted a picture of her on social media that she didn't remember taking. With the windows uncovered and the lookout lit up like a torch, they must be visible for miles.

"Why are you locking the door?" Mom looked up from the couch, where she was curled up with an old paperback mystery.

Chase glanced at Guthrie. She was sprawled across her bed with a sketchbook and pack of colored pencils, off in her own world. Dad was in the cupola. She could hear the steady *thwack-thwack-thwack* of his brush on the canvas.

"I think something's out there," she said in a hoarse whisper, dropping onto the couch next to Mom. "Watching us."

Mom's face tightened, and she closed her book. "What do you mean?"

"There's something carved on the railing by Guthrie's window."

"Show me."

Chase didn't want to step back out into the night, didn't want to show herself to the trees with their gaping, watchful eyes. But she unlocked the door and slipped onto the deck, pointing out the arrows that circled the lookout and stopped under Guthrie's window. "See?"

Mom studied the carvings, tracing them with her thumb. Her mouth was pressed into a tight line, and when she finally looked at Chase, her eyes were flat. "Chase. Tell me the truth. Did you do this?"

Chase's mouth fell open. "Me? Are you serious? Of course I didn't."

"There's a pair of scissors sticking out of your pocket."

"Because I used them to mark the trees, to help us find our way back to the dead deer! This is why I couldn't find the arrows—something moved them, brought them here instead. It's like it's marking Guthrie's window."

Mom pressed one hand to her forehead. "Chase, that's impossible, and you know it. Why did you do this? I thought you would get over your anger about coming here. You're making friends, you have a job. You have Wilder. And Guthrie is doing so well. She's not afraid to be alone anymore, and she's playing and talking more—"

"She's talking to the *trees*, Mom! And to an imaginary friend that just happens to have the same name as the girl who disappeared here—in the woods where you let Guthrie play *alone*. I mean, we of all people should know not to let a kid wander around the woods by themselves. Aren't you worried that she'll get lost again? Or worse?"

Mom's face was blank. "No, *you* should know. You should have known not to leave your ten-year-old sister alone."

Chase reeled back like she had been slapped.

"There's a difference, Chase. Dad and I trust Guthrie to know her limits. We've been here for weeks, and she's gotten more and more comfortable because we're allowing her to push her boundaries. I understand that you're still upset about what happened in South Dakota, and I'm sorry to speak so bluntly. I'm not trying to make you feel bad. But you need to understand that even though we're handling things differently than you think we should, we're still taking it seriously. So these arrows, pretending that someone is watching us and targeting Guthrie just to get us to keep her out of the woods—" Mom's face twisted in distaste. "No more. It's sick. I just—" She shook her head, brushing a few tears away, and went back inside.

Chase sagged against the railing, stunned. Her entire body was numb, like novocaine was coursing through her veins. So they did blame her. After that night in South Dakota, Mom and Dad had cried with her and told her that everything was okay and Guthrie was safe. But now she realized that they had never actually said it wasn't her fault.

It hurt more than she had thought it would, knowing that they blamed her, too. After all, she had blamed herself every day since Guthrie had come out of the woods shaking and silent. It was why she had confronted them about getting Guthrie help; it was why she had hounded them about going back to Boone, where Guthrie could have stability and therapy and all the things she needed to be whole again. But after a while, it had gotten easier to focus on her parents and how they avoided dealing with Guthrie's trauma instead of facing the pain of what she had almost let happen.

Mom was upstairs in the cupola when Chase crept back inside. She didn't bother to lock the door this time. There was an ache deep inside her heart, like a fissure had opened in her chest. The curtains around Guthrie's bed were closed and her light was off, but Chase had to see her. Sleep was the only time Chase still recognized her.

She slid the curtains open. A corner of the picture Guthrie had been coloring poked out from under the pillow: red spattered across the page like spots of blood. Guthrie grunted and rolled over as Chase tugged the drawing out.

It was a staircase drawn in heavy, bold strokes. The railings were made of aspens and the carpet was deer hide flecked with blood. At the bottom stood a girl with knotholes for eyes. She tilted her head to the side in invitation.

Chase lay awake for hours watching for shooting stars, but tonight their only movement was from the rotation of the earth. Her head throbbed from trying to sleep. She groaned and sat up. Maybe a glass of water and some aspirin would ease her headache.

Slipping through the gap in the curtains around her bed, she stood, swaying slightly, waiting for her eyes to adjust to the dark.

Guthrie came into focus little by little. She was out of bed, standing at the window that overlooked her favorite grove of trees. Her shoulders slumped forward, and her head was bowed, hair covering her face. Chase tiptoed across the room to her, put her hand on her shoulder, and waited for Gus to look up at her with eyes full of stars.

Chapter Thirty-Three

Chase couldn't leave Guthrie for a full day, not after lying next to her, bathed in that blank gaze half the night.

Not after what Mom had said when she showed her the arrows: *You should have known not to leave your ten-year-old sister alone.*

So, in the morning, she got dressed and took a book down to the hammock instead of packing a bathing suit and towel to spend the day at the lake with her friends. She felt a little pang when she thought of Wilder waiting for her, but she had no way to contact him without walking to Spruces, and she wasn't willing to leave Guthrie for even that short amount of time. He would understand when she explained later.

Guthrie played by her favorite tree while Chase read. Mom glanced over at them from the garden once or twice, but Chase pretended not to notice. There wasn't anything to say. Mom blamed her for leaving Guthrie in the woods. Did it really matter if she also thought Chase had carved the arrows leading to Guthrie's window?

Besides, in a way she had. She had marked the trees, knowing that they watched with their knothole eyes.

After lunch, during the hottest part of the day, Mom tried to convince Dad to go to Fitzgerald with them. The drone of their voices drifted down through the trapdoor, an incessant buzzing that Chase could feel on her skin like the drops of sweat rolling down her neck.

Mom shook her head as she climbed down the ladder. "Not

today. But he does want us to bring him pancakes," she added brightly to Guthrie.

They spent the afternoon luxuriating in the air-conditioning at the library. When they got back to the lookout, Wilder was standing at the edge of the clearing. Chase's heart clenched as she took in the tight expression on his face.

"Is that Wilder?" Mom asked, helping Guthrie out of the car and handing her the Styrofoam box of Dad's pancakes.

"We were supposed to hang out earlier," Chase said.

"You were?" Mom frowned. "Why didn't you?"

She shrugged and started across the clearing. Now that he was here, all the anxiety she had felt last night when she found the arrows came flooding back. It was like she had wrapped it up tight and tucked it away, saving it for when she could collapse in his arms, trusting him to hold her up.

"Where were you?" Wilder said when she was a few feet away. "I waited all—oof." Chase walked into him hard enough to knock him off balance. He staggered back a step, wrapping his arms around her so that she could feel his heartbeat, strong and steady like a promise.

"What is it?" he said into her hair. "What's wrong?"

Chase let out a shaky laugh. "God, what *isn't* wrong? This place is just . . ." She shook her head, and Wilder tightened his grip on her. She could feel his breath against her neck, his fingers between the notches in her spine.

Sighing, she told him about hearing Guthrie in the woods and following the fawn; the arrows she had carved to lead them back and the way they had disappeared. How her stomach had twisted into a tight knot as she followed them up the stairs and to her sister's window.

"I showed my mom, but she—" Chase's belly squirmed with shame. She couldn't tell Wilder that her parents still blamed her for what had happened to Guthrie—and that they had every right to. "She thought *I* carved the arrows under

Guthrie's window and made up a story about someone—something—watching her, so that she and my dad would keep a closer eye on her."

"That's sick," Wilder said flatly. "You would never do something like that. Pretend that something was targeting your sister."

"I know. She says that they trust Guthrie to know her limits and push boundaries at her own pace—which sounds okay in theory, but here? This place takes things from our heads and warps them. Like the way sound sometimes changes. The odd way the animals behave. And the bones that Gus finds . . . so many of them are deformed. Twisted. It's like there's something mutating here. Like Pando is some kind of counterfeit nature that can't get all the details right."

It was happening now, as she spoke. The air was turning still and hushed, absorbing their voices like they were underwater. The light went colder, almost like the sun had drifted behind clouds, but the sky was still empty, soaring blue. There was something wrong with the sound of the birdsong that Chase couldn't identify. A dark cloud of birds swooped through the trees, rustling the branches and dropping leaves. They wheeled into the sky, circling overhead in a tight spiral.

"Do you hear that?" she asked. Her voice was almost drowned out by a swell of birdsong. The sound repeated with a high trill, and then died away. "That—" The song swelled again before falling silent. And again. And again.

Chase's lungs stopped drawing breath; her blood stilled in her veins. The birds wheeled overhead again, and her eyes tracked them through the sky: a counterclockwise circle that grew tighter and tighter as their repeating song grew to a discordant shriek. Wilder's mouth moved, but instead of words, all Chase heard was the unearthly sound of the birds, the birds, the birds in their death howl as they plunged toward the wall of windows on the lookout tower.

The glass splintered under the stream of birds, their limp bodies falling to the deck. Chase and Wilder stood frozen until the barrage ended. When it was over, the otherworldly sound of the repeating birdsong was replaced by shrieks from inside the lookout.

"What the fuck," Wilder breathed. "What the—"

But Chase had already left his side, running across the clearing to the wooden stairs. She took them two at a time for the first few flights, then climbed the rest as fast as she could. Dad stood on the deck, staring at the heap of dead birds under Guthrie's window.

"Dad!" Chase said. "What happened?"

"They just kept coming," he said, gesturing toward the bodies. "I've never seen anything like it."

Wilder came panting up the stairs. "Are you okay?"

Guthrie's sobs drifted through the open door. Chase pushed past her father into the lookout, where Mom and her sister sat huddled on Guthrie's bed. Guthrie's hands were clenched over her ears, and she hunched over Mom's lap, crying. The window above her was spiderwebbed with cracks and dotted with blood that trickled like the sap on the trees, like the blood from the moth that still marked Chase's window.

"Gus!" Chase flung herself onto the bed, wrapping her arms around her sister. "Oh, sis, it's okay, you're okay."

"She was sitting right here, looking out the window," Mom said. Her face was pale. "The birds just kept coming."

"Birds rely on the earth's magnetic fields to navigate," Dad said. "Maybe there was some kind of disturbance that caused them to lose their way."

"I was afraid they were going to break through," Mom said.

They did break through, Chase thought, but that didn't make sense, it was just a fragment of nonsense. "I'm so sorry," she said, planting a kiss on Guthrie's head.

"We can clean it up," Wilder said. "Do you have buckets and sponges? And maybe some rubber gloves?"

Mom gave Chase and Wilder the cleaning supplies, then led Guthrie to the couch so she wouldn't have to watch them sort through the broken bodies. Guthrie clutched the tiny skull around her neck. Her eyes were still rimmed with red, but she wasn't crying anymore.

There were over a dozen birds on the splintery deck, and Chase could pick out at least four different species. She frowned. She had never seen birds behave that way—different species flying together like that.

She had seen murmurations before—huge flocks of birds flying in seemingly synchronized patterns, the entire group turning at the same instant. They were connected in a way that science didn't fully understand, each bird a part of the larger whole, each one conscious of the others' movements. But murmurations were limited to groups of birds of the same species. That was where the saying "birds of a feather flock together" came from.

Some of the birds looked off to Chase, their bodies twisted in a way that was more than just from their snapped necks and broken wings. One was covered in bony growths that protruded through its glossy feathers; another had an overlarge beak that sagged open, revealing a second, smaller beak inside. Chase shuddered.

"There is something *wrong* with these birds," she said. "Like the bones Guthrie finds around here. They're all warped and twisted."

"Did you know that deformities in frogs are one of the first signs that something is wrong in the environment?" Wilder pulled on a pair of rubber gloves and started lifting the maimed bodies into a five-gallon bucket.

"What about birds?" Chase asked. "The ones around here are weird. Not just this—" She nudged one of the birds with a skeletal deformity with the toe of her sneaker. "But the way they sing."

"They were repeating," Wilder said.

A creeping sense of dread raised the hairs on Chase's arms as she remembered the sounds the birds had made, how the discordant noise had filled the air so that when Wilder opened his mouth to speak, only the twisted birdsong came out.

"And that's not the first time that I've seen them fly into something," she added. "The very first day we were here, a cardinal flew into a tree down there. Like, folded its wings and just hurled itself into the tree. It was like it was trying to escape something."

"Once I was in the woods looking for a walking stick to use on a hike," Wilder said. "I was cutting one off a tree when I got this really weird feeling. Like, sick to my stomach, dizzy, ears ringing. I felt like I was crawling out of my skin. I ended up dropping my knife and going back to camp, and as soon as I stepped out of the woods, everything"—he snapped his fingers—"snapped back into place. Like, just went back to normal. I could hear the birds singing, and that's when I figured out what had been wrong in the woods."

"What?"

"The birds had been singing *backwards*. Fucking swear it. I felt sick because everything was flipped around." He dropped his sponge in the bucket of soapy water and leaned closer to Chase. "I think here in Pando, the birds are like the frogs. They can sense when things aren't right."

"Things are never right in Pando," Chase said. She dipped a sponge in the bucket and wiped the blood from the window. The water turned pink and ran in rivulets, collecting in the grooves of the arrows. "I get that you don't want to upset your dad, but look at what just happened. These birds flew into Guthrie's window less than twenty-four hours after it was marked. What else might come for her?"

Wilder's jaw tightened. "We already discussed this, Chase."

"If I could just talk to him—"

"No. No fucking way. After he found Tessa Shaw, it's like he went somewhere else. My mom *gave up* on him. Do you get that? It was that bad. And me, what was I supposed to do? I was just here, waiting for him, hoping he would come back to me. Somehow he did, but it took a long time, and I'm not going to risk losing him again." He looked at her like she was a bruise he didn't remember getting. "Please don't ask me to do that."

He slumped to the deck, leaning against the wall. He was shaking. Chase sank down next to him. The splintery wood was rough against her back, pricking her through the thin fabric of her T-shirt like sandpaper. Her head spun, and there was a dull, pounding ache in her chest.

"I can't leave Guthrie alone anymore," Chase whispered. "I can't come back to Spruces."

Wilder pressed his hands to his temples. "Why does it have to come down to you? You act like you're the only one who cares about her."

Chase's stomach clenched. She knew she wasn't the only one who cared about Guthrie, but *she* was the one who had left her behind. Broken her. "You don't get it, Wilder. She—" Her breath hitched. "She needs me."

Tears poured down her cheeks, hot and angry. Her chest felt like it was about to crack wide open. She wasn't sure who she was most mad at—her parents or herself. Why had she ever left Guthrie alone in the woods?

"Guthrie's not the only one who needs someone," Wilder said, his voice low and husky. "God, I'm right here, Chase. Why won't you let me in?"

She couldn't speak around the lump in her throat. Every

time she breathed in, she felt the vice that had crushed her chest that night all over again. That was why she couldn't let him in; that was why she could never let anything take her from Guthrie.

Not Wilder.

Not even Boone.

It hit her like a blast of heat, forcing the air from her lungs. She couldn't leave Guthrie to go to Boone. The dream she had been chasing for most of her life had become an unrealistic delusion the second she left Guthrie alone that night. When she had walked away from her sister, she had also walked away from the possibility of home, of belonging, of community—and from any kind of future between her and Wilder. Because when it came down to it, she was willing to give everything up to protect Guthrie.

"I can't," she said in a small voice. "I can't risk letting something happen to her again."

Wilder shook his head. "Don't you see what you're doing? You're so stuck in your own head and so obsessed with whatever happened to Guthrie that you haven't even begun to unpack your trauma about it. It's like you'll do anything to avoid facing what happened and how it affected you."

You've got this fixation on Guthrie, and it isn't healthy for either of you.

Chase's heart shrank down until it felt like something hard and twisted, like one of the knobby bones that Guthrie found half-buried in the dirt. She wasn't avoiding her trauma. She had spent every moment since that night in the woods hovering over Guthrie, trying to make up for leaving her. "That's not true."

"It is true." He cleared his throat, and she realized that he was crying, too. "Chase, I love you—"

Her heart stopped at his words. It was like being in free fall—exhilarating, paralyzing.

"—but you have to decide if that's what you need from me." He brushed his hand over her tight fist, his touch as soft as moonlight. "Don't worry about work. We'll handle it."

Chase watched him go without breathing. The door creaked open as Mom let herself out on the deck. "Are you okay? I saw Wilder leave. He seemed upset."

The trees swayed, quaking leaves flashing silver-green in the breeze. It sounded like they were mocking her.

Chase shrugged. "I quit my job."

Chapter Thirty-Four

Chase was too numb to cry, and that was somehow worse. She lay on her bed, staring at the ceiling and waiting for the tears to come, but the only thing that happened was her eyes felt itchy and dry. There was a chasm inside her chest that got deeper every time she thought about Wilder. After a while, it would have been a relief to cry—maybe the tears could have filled the rift he had left behind when he walked away.

And he loved her.

She heard his voice saying the words over and over again in her head—*I love you, but* . . . It took her breath away every time, leaving her suffocating and gasping for air.

Saturday was endless.

She read until her eyes felt like they were going to fall out of her head. She weeded the raspberry patch with Mom and came out dripping blood from the thorns. She stood on the deck and watched Guthrie like a witness as she darted in and out of the woods.

She didn't see Dad at all—he spent the entire day in the cupola.

"What's he working on up there?" Chase asked one day. She kept her voice low enough that Dad wouldn't be able to hear her over the sound of his paintbrush.

Mom sighed. "I actually don't know. It's too hot to go up there during the day, and he puts everything away before bed. I haven't seen any of his work since he moved his stuff up there."

That wasn't like Dad at all. She had been tripping over his half-finished paintings for as long as she could remember. Why was he suddenly keeping them hidden?

"How are you holding up?" Mom asked, her voice sympathetic. She was elbow-deep in sticky bread dough.

Chase focused on her book so she wouldn't see Mom watching her with that patient, understanding look on her face, like she was just waiting for Chase to break down.

"Fine. I'm glad I get to spend more time with Guthrie." She glanced at her sister, who was kneeling on her bed, face pressed against the glass, staring out at the pale trees like she was looking for something. Her windowsill was filled with wilted wildflowers and the dried husk of a wasp nest, bits of bone and a handful of bird feathers tucked in a glass jar. Most of the feathers were drab browns and grays, but there were a few blue feathers and one bright red one that stood out like a spot of blood.

"Do you want to play Uno?" Chase asked, flopping onto the bed next to her. Guthrie didn't respond. Chase could see her eyes reflected against the glass, wide and somber. Without blinking, Gus took the red feather from the jar and used it to trace the thin line where the birds had hit.

"Hey—" Chase reached for Guthrie's hand, but Guthrie yanked it away, eyes flashing. She crushed the feather in her clenched fist. Chase held up her hands and leaned away. "Hey, Gus! Geez, I was just wondering if you're all right. I thought we could do something together."

All the fierce lines of Guthrie's face softened. She smiled, her eyes crinkling at the corners, and reached to put her feather back.

"Wait." Chase took the jar off the windowsill and shook it onto the bed, spreading the feathers out like a deck of cards.

"I have an idea. These are too pretty to be stuffed in a jar. We could make a garland to hang across your window, over the rest of your collection."

Guthrie clasped her hands under her chin and nodded. Chase's heart ached at the trusting look in her eyes. She still looked at Chase like she would follow her off a cliff.

"I have some twine in my backpack that we can use. Why don't you start laying the feathers out in the order you like?"

It didn't take long to tie each feather to the length of twine. Chase also had a handful of wooden beads from the Spruces art room, and Guthrie strung them on the ends of the garland. When it was done, Chase found a couple thumbtacks in the junk drawer in the kitchen and hung the garland across the window.

"Ta-da!" she said as Dad climbed down the ladder from the cupola. He had blue paint smeared across one cheek. "Look what me and Guthrie made."

"Nice," Dad said. "Did you collect all those feathers in the woods, Gus?"

Guthrie nodded. The feathers danced in the breeze that came in through the open windows, spinning over the collection of bones and bark and other forest things.

"Maybe the moving feathers will keep birds away from the window," Mom said, glancing over to admire their work.

"Yeah, maybe," Chase said. She hadn't considered the possibility in so many words, but a part of her felt better with the feathers strung across Guthrie's window. If the birds really were sensitive to Pando and its peculiarities, maybe the feathers would act as a token and keep her safe.

Sleep took Chase to a place where the white trees that surrounded the lookout were made of bones that twisted in cancerous lumps, splitting the soil like skin. Chase was on the path to Spruces, half a step behind Guthrie, who was gathering phalanges and clavicles into a wild bouquet. She broke off a delicate string of vertebrae, and the air filled with the sound of the bone snapping.

Chase's eyes flew open. The scratching sound had followed her out of the dream, but now she recognized it for what it was—not a bone breaking, but a match being struck.

The curtains around her bed were open, so she could see Guthrie standing at the kitchen sink, a tiny flame lighting her face from below. Her eyes were wide and blank, and her mouth sagged. The feather garland dangled from her hand.

Gus, Chase tried to cry out, but her lungs contracted, all the air sucked out of them by a vacuum. Her limbs were stiff and unyielding. She couldn't so much as twitch a pinkie. Terror settled on her chest like a weight. *What are you doing!* she screamed inside her head.

Dark spots danced across Chase's vision as she struggled against the force that held her motionless against the mattress. Guthrie touched the match to one of the feathers. It glowed as it caught, and she stood frozen, watching the flame devour the feather and race up the twine toward the next one.

And then, suddenly, the pressure on Chase's chest eased. She sucked in a breath that sent her head spinning and flung herself sideways, landing in a tangled heap of sheets and pillows on the floor. Scrambling up, she knocked into Guthrie just as the twine began to burn in earnest. Guthrie dropped it into the sink, shaking out her hand where the fire had singed her fingers. She blinked, bemused, as Chase leaned over and turned on the faucet. Water hissed as it hit the burning garland, and smoke and steam billowed up. Chase wrenched Guthrie's hand under the running water.

"Mom! Dad!" she screamed. Her heart was still racing from the dread that had pumped through her veins when she woke up and couldn't move.

There was a bump overhead as her parents stumbled out of bed and down the ladder.

"Oh my God. Oh my God," Mom said, flapping her hands. "What happened?"

"She was sleepwalking again," Chase hissed. "She almost burned down the lookout."

Dad grabbed Guthrie from Chase and pulled her onto his lap on the edge of her bed. She was blinking over and over, like she was trying to bring everything into focus, make the scene make sense.

"This is getting out of hand," Chase said. "You have to do something!"

"Like what?" Dad snapped. "How do you stop someone from sleepwalking?"

"You deal with the shit making them sleepwalk in the first place."

"Chase!" Mom looked like she was about to cry. "Don't talk like that."

"Guthrie just lit a match in her sleep, and you're worried about me saying *shit*?" Chase said. "Do you know what it's like to die in a house fire? It isn't pleasant."

Dad reeled back, all the color draining from his face until his skin was the same grayish-white as the aspen trees. He cradled Guthrie against his chest, wrapping his arms around her so tightly that she grunted. "Stop it. God, just stop it. Saying things like that won't help the situation."

"The only thing that will help this situation is getting the fuck out of here," Chase said. "Going somewhere where we can have a normal life with friends and a house and school. *Therapy*. It doesn't even have to be Boone, since you're so dead set against going back there, but somewhere. *Please*, Dad!" She choked on the words. "Please, let's just leave. Please, Mom." She turned beseechingly to Mom, who was holding her hands against her face.

Dad stood up, dropping Guthrie back on her bed. "We're all upset. There's nothing we can do tonight. I'll take the matches and—and the knives and anything else that could hurt her downstairs to the storage shed. Go back to sleep."

He rummaged through the kitchen drawers while Mom ran her hands over Guthrie like she was checking that she was still there. Guthrie's eyes were already closed again, her chest rising and falling slowly.

Chase stood by the sink, her hands balled into tight fists. Her breath was coming short and shallow, and her muscles and limbs were frozen, held just as tight by shock as they had been when she woke up and saw Guthrie with the matches. There was a chasm in her chest where her heart should be, and she could feel it growing by the minute, the edges crumbling away into nothing. She forced her legs to unlock and crawled back in bed, lying down on top of the rumpled sheets. She was vaguely aware of something crushed in her palm—something pulpy and small. She loosened her grip, and the pack of matches she had taken from Guthrie fell out, forgotten in her panic. Another flash of fear rushed through her body. If she hadn't woken up . . . if Gus had dropped the garland on the rug instead of into the sink . . . she didn't want to think about how quickly the lookout could have gone up in flames.

She stuffed the matchbox into the pocket of the sweatshirt draped over her bed frame. She would put it in the storage closet tomorrow.

But sleep still didn't come easily. Every time she closed her eyes, she saw that tiny flame again, heard the scrape of the match against sandpaper as Guthrie lit it. The last thing she saw before finally dropping into an uneasy sleep was the five flights of stairs that led to the lookout, wreathed in flames.

Chapter Thirty-Five

Chase's chest was tight with anxiety when she opened her eyes the next morning. A hint of bitter smoke still hung in the air. The stench made her stomach roll. Who knew burnt feathers could smell so bad? Dad should have taken them downstairs to the big bear-proof dumpster last night. Now they would never be able to get the smell out of the lookout.

She glanced across the room. The curtains around Guthrie's bed were drawn. Good, she probably needed the sleep. It was early enough that Chase might be able to fall back asleep, too—after she got rid of the stinking feather garland.

It was still in the kitchen sink in a soggy, charred heap. Wrinkling her nose, she prodded it into a grocery bag from the stash under the sink and crept across the room, easing the door open so she didn't wake Guthrie.

Outside, the sky was painted pink and blue, and the trees were limned in gold. Chase took in a deep breath, letting the fresh air fill her lungs, and held it until the taste of smoke was gone. Her head spun when she let it out. She dropped the knotted plastic bag over the railing, letting it fall next to the dumpster to throw away later, and went back into the lookout for a few more hours of sleep.

After the clean scent of mountain morning air outside, the lookout was sour and stuffy. Chase crept around the living room, opening the windows to let in fresh air. The sweet nectar of wildflowers swept in on the breeze. It was already starting to smell better.

She hesitated by Guthrie's bed. She didn't want to disturb her sister, but the burning-hair smell of the feather garland lingered in the curtains. Chase slid them apart, murmuring apologies for waking Guthrie—but the window was already open, and the bed was empty.

"Gus—" she breathed out in a hitching gasp. She crawled over the messy nest of blankets and clutched the window frame so tightly that her knuckles turned white.

Guthrie was outside, halfway down the smoldering staircase that had appeared outside her bedroom window. Her curls fluttered in the smoke that rose from the pink-and-yellow carpet, and her head cocked to the side like she could hear something Chase couldn't.

Chase moaned, thrusting her arms and head through the window and trying to wriggle her way out. The opening was too narrow for her shoulders. "Gus!" she screamed. "Come back!"

Guthrie paused, her head rolling limply on her neck until she was looking at Chase over her shoulder. Her eyes were blank and unseeing, pupils dilated like the knotholes that watched from the trees all around.

With her head still twisted around, Guthrie stumbled forward, plumes of floating ash rising with every footfall. She was almost at the bottom. From this angle, halfway out the window, Chase could see that the staircase ended right by the tree with the face—the one that Guthrie called Tessa. Chase knew that if Guthrie made it to the bottom, she would be gone.

Adrenaline roared in her veins, breaking the mind-numbing terror. She shook off all her fear and shock and shoved herself back inside, scraping the back of her neck on the rough aluminum window frame. Tangled in the curtains, she fell off the bed.

"Chase?" Mom called down the ladder. "What's wrong?"

"Guthrie's going into the woods!" Chase shouted, flinging off the curtains and racing out the front door. She felt a splinter pierce the skin between her toes as she skidded around the deck just in time to see her sister take the final step. Pain needled her skull as Guthrie reached the bottom of the staircase. Chase fell to her knees, clapping her hands over her eyes as light flared all around, hot and white like the flash of a nuclear bomb.

The staircase was gone.

It still burned against the backs of her eyelids, like an afterimage on a bright day. Chase blinked, rubbing her eyes with her fists to try and clear her vision, and scrambled to the edge of the deck. Peering over the railing, she searched the clearing for what remained—a depression in the dirt where it had rested, or flattened grass and weeds—but all signs of the staircase had vanished with it.

"Chase, what on earth is going on?" Dad's voice was gravelly from sleep. He and Mom were behind her, barefoot and sleep tousled.

She gulped in a ragged breath, but her lungs felt like they were filled with wet ash, sodden and useless. Panic overwhelmed her, her limbs going weak and loose. Her sister was gone. She had vanished somewhere that Chase didn't understand, swallowed up by the wild places of Pando.

"She's gone," she burst out. Her chest screamed as she forced herself to breathe. Every breath felt like shards of glass. "Into the woods."

"It's early, but she's probably just going out to—"

"*No*," Chase insisted, gasping. Now she was breathing too much, too fast, the air whooshing in and out of her lungs like the bellows for a fire. "No, she was sleepwalking again.

She came through the window and went down the stairs, but they're *gone* now, she's gone and the stairs are gone and—"

The world tilted on its side, and her cheek hit the rough planks of the deck. The grain of the wood was like waves on the ocean, graceful and delicate. She could see entire worlds in that wood grain, and she fell into them with a dizzying sense of relief.

". . . no sign of her." Dad's voice crawled into Chase's ear like a bug. Her head was still spinning, but she could breathe again. Someone had moved her inside to the couch. She pushed herself up to a sitting position, pain lancing at her temples at the movement.

"Mom?" she croaked.

Mom and Dad were huddled together by the kitchen sink. Dad had pulled on a pair of boots over his pajama pants. A few twigs stuck out of his hair. Mom's face was drawn, and she kept fiddling with the neck of her nightshirt.

"Chase," she said, hurrying to the couch. "You passed out. Here—" She thrust a glass of water into her hands.

Chase drank so fast that the water dribbled down her chin and her belly felt swollen. "Did you find her?"

"No," Dad grunted. "I went all around where she usually plays and didn't see anything. Not even footprints."

"Maybe she went to Spruces," Mom said.

"I'll go." Chase struggled off the couch, grabbing her shoes from the rack by the door. She knew that Guthrie wasn't at Spruces; she wasn't anywhere in the woods. She was somewhere else entirely, somewhere only Chase could follow. If she went into the woods, if she looked into those soulless black eyes on the trees, maybe she would find the way to Guthrie.

"Sadie, you stay here in case she comes back," Dad said to Mom. "I'll keep looking in the woods while Chase goes down to check Spruces."

The trail to Spruces unraveled like a ribbon under Chase's feet. She whipped her head around as she ran, searching for the staircase, straining to smell the chemical-fire scent of the burning banister. The birds passed messages overhead, bits of song that followed her all the way to the lake.

This was a nightmare; it must be. A post-traumatic stress response to what had happened in South Dakota. The terror that drove Chase into the woods, heedless of the thorns that raked her skin and tangled in her hair. The sour taste Guthrie's name left in her mouth as she shouted in increasing alarm. She could feel her panic spiraling in her chest tighter and tighter, winding itself into her heart and ribs like the roots of the trees that watched her search with weeping red eyes. She felt like one of the birds in their death spiral, so desperate to escape that they were willing to break themselves on the ground.

She burst out of the woods and onto the shore, stumbling as the rocks shifted underfoot. Wilder was bent over a canoe by the boathouse.

"Wilder!"

He looked up at her shout. His brow furrowed when he saw her, and he pushed himself to his feet. "Chase? What's wrong?"

"It's Guthrie," she whispered. "She's gone."

Chapter Thirty-Six

Dad had already called for help when Chase got back with Wilder, who insisted on staying with her after they swept through the camp. She felt like she had stepped to the side and was watching from outside her body as the county sheriff and a pair of deputies arrived at the lookout, herding everyone up the steps.

Her chest was hot and prickly. How many times had she gone to her parents to tell them she was concerned about Guthrie? If they had just listened to her—if they had taken things seriously when Guthrie first stopped talking—

If she hadn't left Guthrie alone in the woods that night.

By the time they sat shoulder to shoulder on the couch with the deputies flanking them, she was numb. Mom was weeping on one side of her. Wilder slid his hand into hers and squeezed. Chase stared down at their interlocked fingers, at his thumb moving in circles on the back of her hand, but she didn't feel anything. It was like Wilder was holding a stranger's hand.

Someone was taking pictures of Gus's bed and belongings, gently moving things aside with gloved hands, and putting the lumpy teddy bear that Gus slept with in a large Ziplock bag. Someone else was looking through the box of photographs that Mom had gotten out. Guthrie's face looked up from each print: wild curls, deep brown eyes, mouth turned up slightly in her shy smile.

"Shouldn't we be down there?" Dad said, his hands balled into fists, after trying to explain that though Guthrie didn't talk, she didn't have a developmental delay or diagnosis. In the clearing, more deputies and first responders were gathering and setting off to comb the woods.

"No, sir," the sheriff said. "The most important thing you can do right now is make sure we have all the information we need to find Guthrie. Has she been acting strange lately? Have you noticed anything off?"

Chase had filled Wilder in on the details of Guthrie's disappearance on their way back to the lookout. Now he twitched next to her, his sharp elbow catching her in the ribs, and she remembered what he had said about his dad.

He said the woods were liars.

He was really messed up for a while.

Everyone knows—

The sheriff's eyes drifted from Dad to Mom, and then across the couch to Chase and Wilder. His face was relaxed, placid, but there was something dark under the cool expression.

"Wilder?" he asked. "What about you?"

Chase still didn't know what Michael Nelson had said after he found Tessa Shaw's remains, but it was clear that the sheriff was expecting Wilder to bring it up. Expecting it—and maybe hoping for it. Urging Wilder to spout off the same kind of nonsense his father had nine years ago so the sheriff could go ahead and dismiss it and move on to the real investigation.

"She sleepwalks," Chase said. "That's new. And she's been talking to one of the trees like it's her imaginary friend. And the bones . . ." She shuddered, her voice trailing off as she remembered her dream from the night before.

"Bones?" The sheriff frowned. "What kind of bones?"

"Just animal bones," Dad said. "She finds them in the woods. Collects them." He gestured at the splintered skulls and vertebrae scattered on the floor next to Guthrie's bed, knocked to the ground during Chase's frantic attempts to follow Guthrie out the window.

"Oh." The sheriff's face loosened. "I thought you meant like what we found here before."

Wilder's hand tightened on Chase's at the mention of Tessa's remains.

The sheriff flipped his notebook closed. "Deputy Brown"—he pointed at a heavyset man in one of the armchairs—"will oversee the initial search here at the lookout and in the clearing of all the obvious places: the storage sheds, the woodpile. We'll then move on to a systematic search of the surrounding woods and trails before doing a thorough search using a grid system. I'm going to send Deputy Dawes here"—he nodded at the unsmiling woman standing next to Dad—"to Spruces with Wilder to interview the staff there. Tom, Sadie, and Chase, I'd like you all to come down to the station with me. I have some more questions for you."

The sheriff rose, and after a moment, Chase, Wilder, Mom, and Dad stood as well and followed him down to his patrol car in the clearing, where the search was already under way.

Chapter Thirty-Seven

By the time they got back from the station, it was late afternoon, and the driveway was crowded with search and rescue volunteers. A white tent had been set in the middle of the clearing next to a huge van with a satellite on the roof.

"What is all this stuff?" Chase asked the sheriff through numb lips as they walked past the van, glancing into the open back doors and seeing a bank of computer screens.

"This is a mobile command unit," the sheriff explained. "We use it for operations when we're too far from the station to use that as a base. It serves as a workspace so we can coordinate our search efforts and has everything we might need for a rescue operation: maps, satellite and heat signature imagery, radio, medical supplies. The sheriff's office is responsible for the operation, but we select experienced members of the search and rescue team to run the mobile command unit, and they're the ones who oversee the operation."

He gestured at the dozen or so people bustling around. "Our SAR team is made up entirely of volunteers. Between them, there are over a hundred years of experience. Your sister is in good hands."

Wilder and his father were waiting for them in the tent. Wilder hugged Chase against his chest. She closed her eyes briefly, breathing in his familiar scent, then pulled away.

"What happened while we were gone? Any . . ." She

struggled to find the right word, feeling ridiculously like a caricature in a police procedural. "Any leads?"

Wilder pressed his lips together. "Dad and I just came back about an hour ago, after they talked to everyone at Spruces, and they haven't given us any new information. I wanted to go out with them to search, but they said not yet. Right now it's just members of the SAR team. But tomorrow, they'll open it up to volunteers—if they don't find her tonight."

Tonight. It would be dark soon—even sooner in the woods. Chase bit her lip hard enough to draw blood, thinking about Guthrie alone in the dark.

"We're so sorry," Michael said, putting his hand on Dad's shoulder. "I've already canceled next week's session at Spruces so my staff will be available to volunteer in the search operation. All of the cabins are available for you if you need to get away and rest."

"Oh, no." Mom shook her head frantically. "No, I couldn't possibly leave. But Chase should go with you."

"No," Chase said sharply. "Mom, I don't want to go either. What if they find her?"

"You need sleep," Mom argued. "And it's going to be chaotic here all night. I don't want to have to worry about you, too."

She was right; Guthrie was the priority now. Still, Chase turned to implore her father. "Dad?"

He cleared his throat. "You should go, Chase."

"I have a radio," Michael said. "They'll call down with any new information, and I can bring you right back."

"Come on," Wilder said, drawing her back against him. She went limply, sagging against his side. "Let's go get your stuff."

Chase tried not to look at the corner where Guthrie slept when they got upstairs, but the bare mattress pulled her gaze. All the bedding and stuffed animals were packed away in plastic evidence bags in Fitzgerald. She stuffed pajamas and a change of clothes into her backpack and grabbed her toothbrush from the bathroom.

The sun was setting as they pulled away from the lookout, but the clearing stayed bright with spotlights that cast harsh shadows far into the trees. Chase leaned against the window as the car bumped along the rutted road, searching the ranks of white trees for any sign of her sister. Did those blank, unseeing eyes know where Guthrie was? If they did, they were keeping her secrets.

Michael pulled into the parking lot at Spruces twenty minutes later, parking in front of the office. By then it was full dark, but Chase could see the lookout on the hill, lit up like a beacon. Maybe the light would draw Guthrie back.

Like a moth to a flame.

"I'll take the couch so you can have my bed," Wilder said as they got out of the truck.

"Thanks." The word came out in a croak. Chase cleared her throat and tried again. "Thank you."

"Can I get you anything?" Michael said, unlocking the office door. "Tea, hot chocolate? Something to eat?"

The only thing Chase was hungry for was answers, and it occurred to her that now was her chance to get them. Wilder couldn't possibly protest—not now, not with Guthrie gone. She thrust out her chin, daring him to stop her, and said, "Actually, I have some questions I think you can answer."

Wilder stiffened, but he didn't object. His eyes met hers, those sparks of light escaping their endless fire. He sighed and gave a tiny nod.

"Me?" Michael's eyebrows drew together. "If they are questions about the search, I'm really not the best person to ask. I don't think I can help you."

"You're the only one who can help me."

"Okay," Michael said, bemused. "Let's sit down."

Chase and Wilder sat together on the couch while Michael pulled up the office chair. He crossed his arms, waiting for her to start. But *how* to start? There was so much to say, so many threads that Chase needed to weave together into a tapestry of understanding.

She decided to start with what she knew.

"I know that you found Tessa Shaw's body. And I also know that after you found it, you started sleepwalking, and you saw things in the woods. Things that upset you."

Michael's face drew in on itself until it was like a crumpled piece of paper. Chase could sense Wilder's heartbeat picking up, his breathing going shallow as they waited for Michael to answer.

Finally, Michael looked at Chase from hooded eyes. "You want me to tell you what I saw."

Chase nodded. "In the woods. And when you were sleepwalking."

He shook his head. "I'm sorry, but there's nothing to tell." He spoke in the same steady, soothing voice that he used with upset campers, but his gaze was flat and far away. He reminded Chase of Guthrie when she was trying not to be seen.

"Yes, there is." Thoughts of her sister spurred her on despite the tension in the air. Wilder shifted next to her, his fingers flexing into a fist against her leg. Chase took a deep breath. *Back off a bit*, she told herself. She couldn't force Michael to tell her about his experience any more than she could force Guthrie to talk again. If she wanted him to open up to her, she needed to do the same thing.

"Look . . ." she pleaded. "I know finding Tessa's body must have been traumatic. This isn't me trying to make you relive that just because of morbid curiosity. It's the only way I know how to save my sister. And I have to save her now, because before, I walked away from her and left her alone in the woods." Her voice shook, but she kept going, purging her guilt like it was poison. "She couldn't find her way back, and she screamed for me until she lost her voice. It's my fault that she stopped talking. It's my fault we're here at all."

There. She had said it out loud, for the first time since that night. The aftertaste of the words was oily and slick. She felt like she might throw up.

Wilder reached for her hand and she let him take it, her fingers limp. "Why didn't you tell me?" he asked.

Her breathing locked up. "I don't know. I just . . . couldn't."

Couldn't admit to him that she had left Guthrie the same way his mother had left him . . . couldn't let him know that most secret part of her, the thing she was most ashamed of, the thing that made her so undeserving of his love. She couldn't be vulnerable to that kind of rejection.

His grip tightened on her and he leaned closer. "It doesn't change how I feel about you," he said, low and soft. Just for her. "Not at all."

Their eyes met. Something inside Chase's chest loosened, and she flexed her fingers around his.

Wilder cleared his throat. "Please, Dad. Tell us what you saw."

Michael closed his eyes. His head was still wagging back and forth in slow, steady shakes. "It wasn't real. *None of it was real.*"

"It was real in every way that matters," Wilder said gently. "I've seen things, too. So has Chase."

Michael's head jerked to a stop and his eyes flashed to his son. "What have you seen?"

"A door." He said it like a confession. "The front door from our old house. Where we used to live before Mom left."

A spasm of grief flickered across Michael's face as he turned to Chase. "And you?"

"The staircase from my grandparents' house in Boone.

I saw it in the woods a few weeks ago . . . and again this morning when Guthrie disappeared. It was right outside her window, and she was going down it." Chase's heart started to pound, a ragged thump that felt more like a car accident than a heartbeat. "I tried to stop her, but I couldn't. When she got to the bottom, she—" Her throat worked as she forced the words out. "She was just *gone*. And I need you to tell me where she went, because I think it's the same place you went when you were sleepwalking."

It's like he went somewhere else.

Michael was quiet for a long moment before he answered her. "I don't know what was real, and what the woods took out of my head. And I don't know if where I went really existed, or was nothing more than the place between waking and sleeping, life and death. The moment in time that separates heartbeats."

His words sent chills creeping up Chase's spine. There was a poetic kind of beauty to them that she knew her father would appreciate.

"But I do know this," Michael continued. "Wherever I was—whether it was real or just a figment of my imagination—it was the same place Tessa Shaw is." Chase felt the truth of this in her bones, just as she knew that it was where Guthrie was, too.

"I thought you found Tessa Shaw's body in the tree roots," Wilder said. There was an edge of suspicion in his voice.

"I did," Michael said. "But Wilder, a body and a consciousness . . . they're two different things. A body without a consciousness is death. But a consciousness without a body lives on."

"So that's where you went?" Chase asked. "To a place created for your consciousness?"

"I don't know," Michael said, shaking his head as if to clear it. "I saw it in my dreams, and I saw it in the woods.

An elevator, the doors opening so slowly that it felt like I would never see what was inside. I hadn't gone anywhere, but everything had changed. The air was thicker. The birds were still singing, but their song made me feel . . . made me feel . . . made me feel—" He hooked his fingers into claws and dragged them down his face, leaving angry red furrows. His mouth sagged open, and a creaking sound escaped into the air like the bend of the trees in the wind.

"Dad." Wilder put his hands on his father's cheeks and leaned forward. "Are you okay? Do you want to stop?"

That horrible sound faded away as Michael fought to steady his breath. "I only lingered on the edge. It was a liminal space. A threshold. That's where I was when I was sleepwalking. I didn't go into the elevator. If I had, well . . . I don't think I would have made it back."

Out of all the questions that Chase needed to ask, there was only one that mattered. Could Guthrie come back to her? They were all quiet for a moment before Michael said what they were all thinking. "If Guthrie went down the stairs, she's already crossed that threshold. She's somewhere else now. She's in the lonely places."

Chapter Thirty-Eight

Chase brushed her teeth while Wilder grabbed fresh sheets from the closet. He was making up the bed when she came into the bedroom a few minutes later. Her entire body felt like a static shock after their conversation with Michael. She knew there was no way she would be able to fall asleep.

"I had to ask him," she said to Wilder, dropping onto the newly made bed and pulling her knees to her chest. "I'm sorry, but I had to."

"I know you did." He sat down on the edge of the mattress, his head in his hands. "I know. It's just . . ." he shuddered a little. "I hate seeing him like that. It scares me. I was so close to losing him too, Chase."

She moved closer, resting her cheek against his back and wrapping her arms around him from behind. "But you didn't. He's still here," she murmured. Wilder squeezed her hands, lifting them to his mouth to press a kiss to her palms.

They sat in silence for a moment, taking comfort in the press of their bodies and the steadiness of their breath, until Wilder sighed and straightened up, turning to look at her. "So what do you think?"

"I don't know," Chase admitted. "An elevator? I saw stairs because they represent home, and you saw a door because it represents your mom . . . so why do you think your dad saw an elevator?"

"His family got stuck in an elevator during a power

outage when he was a kid. Something went wrong with the emergency lights so they were trapped in the dark between floors for hours before being rescued. I don't think he's been in an elevator ever since."

"That's horrible." Chase shivered, imagining the air in the elevator going stale, the walls seeming to creep in as the hours passed. Her lungs tightened in response to the thought—it felt just like that night.

A line from one of the articles she had printed about Tessa Shaw swam up out of her memory, a mention that the Shaw family had come to the lookout after a car accident had killed their older daughter.

So they had been fleeing trauma, too.

Each one of them—Chase, Guthrie, Wilder, Michael, Tessa—had been affected by trauma. And while she didn't know for sure, it was easy to imagine Tessa coming across the crumpled car that her sister had died in; easy to imagine the overwhelming draw of the vortex, the hint that her sister was waiting for her. If she had crawled into that car—crossed that threshold—that would explain how she vanished from sight without leaving footprints.

But where had she gone?

"Ren said that our minds are metaphysical," Chase said. She was talking more to herself than to Wilder, but he leaned in just the same. "They create their own reality. And here in Pando, it's like the vortex has worn the fabric of reality so thin that it's possible to slip into a place created by our consciousness . . . maybe to help us deal with trauma from our past."

A liminal space, Michael had called it. And hadn't Chase felt that herself, the first time they had entered Pando? She had known, even then, that they were on the edge of something.

The stairs were the way to Guthrie—she knew it in her

bones and in her soul. Her mind and Guthrie's had created the same image, the same threshold, and that meant Chase was the one who could go after her and bring her home.

But if unresolved issues from the past were the doorways that opened into those lonely places, why had Guthrie gone down their grandparent's staircase, when Chase was the one who was desperate to go back to Boone?

Chase thought she wouldn't be able to sleep, but she fell into unconsciousness as soon as she said goodnight to Wilder. It was a heavy, dreamless sleep, but not restful. When she woke in the morning, her limbs were stiff, her head fuzzy and dull. It took her a long time to force her eyes open, in hopes that when she did, she would be back in the lookout—that she would look across the room and see Guthrie bouncing on her bed.

There was a part of her that wanted to keep them closed forever so she could hold on to that possibility.

But when she finally opened them, it was Wilder that she saw.

He was standing in the doorway, his mouth just slightly open, watching her sleep. "Chase," he whispered when he saw she was awake.

She sat up, wincing at the ache in her jaw. She must have been grinding her teeth in the night. "Did you hear anything from my parents?"

He shook his head. "No. Dad just radioed up to double check, but there's no news."

Her heart sank like a rock in the green glass lake. She flung off the blankets. "I have to go back up there." Another twinge of pain. It felt like she had a mouthful of crushed rocks.

"I'll drive you," Wilder said. "I just need—" He motioned awkwardly toward the dresser. "Can I grab some clean clothes?"

"Oh, right." Chase grabbed her backpack. "Yeah, I'll go change in the bathroom."

She closed the door behind her, then splashed water on her face and brushed her teeth, threw on the clothes she had packed and piled her hair on top of her head in a loose bun. She was ready to go before Wilder had even come out of his bedroom.

"How are you holding up?" Michael said from the desk in the office. His voice was low and gravelly from sleep.

Chase shrugged. "I just want to get back so I can help with the search."

"I understand. It's easier to have a sense of purpose . . . to feel like you're in control of something."

You've always valued being in control—

She nodded, pretending to agree, but that wasn't the only reason she wanted to join the search. If she could get into the woods, she knew she could find the way to her sister. Somewhere in the woods, her grandparents' staircase would appear like a portal into her loneliness and grief. Chase would climb them with her hand trailing on the shining wood banister, her feet leaving footprints on the carpet. And at the top, she would be in that other place that only existed in their minds.

She was tempted to crash headlong into the trees from the trail along the lake, like she had so many times before, but the sheriff had warned them of disturbing the search grids. If she left footprints or broken twigs in an area that hadn't been searched yet, it could compromise the integrity of the operation. She wouldn't risk that, so she waited impatiently for Wilder and Michael to finish getting ready.

When the three of them got back to the lookout half an

hour later, the clearing was crowded with cars and a few dozen people milling around, including Willow and Sasha.

Willow threw her arms around Chase, hot tears wetting her shoulder. "I can't believe it. We came as soon as we heard. Chase, we're so sorry."

"Thank you," she said automatically. "Did Wilder call you?"

"No, Sasha heard from Kathy Larson—you know, the librarian in Fitzgerald? She closed the branch today so she could come help out." Willow pointed to a middle-aged woman that Chase recognized from her afternoons at the library. In fact, as Chase glanced around the clearing, she recognized at least half of the volunteers waiting to sign in at the white tent as people from town and counselors from Spruces.

Mom and Dad were standing with the sheriff under the white tent, clutching Styrofoam cups of coffee. Chase had never seen them look so small before.

Mom kissed her cheek with dry lips. Her eyes were shadowed and sunken. "The search and rescue captain is just about to brief us."

The SAR team and volunteers gathered together by the mobile command unit. Chase stood with Wilder like they were at some twisted version of Morning Welcome at Spruces.

The captain went through CAL Topo with them, showing them the mapping program that the SAR team used. Each team captain logged in to the program on their satellite phones, allowing the command post to show everyone's position and track them live. The program even saved everyone's tracks, overlaying them at the end of each day so that it was obvious at a glance what areas had been covered.

The SAR captain's voice was toneless, like a sound underwater. Chase tried to listen, but she caught only phrases that seemed to drift like ashes on the air.

"... in line ... scan the ground at your ..."

The hairs on the back of her neck stood up as the familiar sense that she was being watched stole over her. She turned to look behind her. The clearing was crowded with people handing out water bottles, deputies and forest rangers bent over maps, volunteers waiting solemnly for their assignments. No one was watching her; no one was even looking at her. But as she scanned the crowd, a dull ringing filled her ears, deadening everything but the chatter of the birds overhead. Their song gradually intensified into a piercing cacophony that Chase could feel in the marrow of her bones.

Then she saw her.

She was on the other side of the clearing, standing just inside the tree line: a stick-thin figure, her hands knotted together, wide black eyes weeping blood.

The world narrowed to an indistinct blur of anonymous figures in orange vests as Chase stared at Guthrie. The birds were screaming now, wheeling in the sky like a black cloud. Dread twisted down Chase's spine as they spiraled toward the trees where Guthrie stood with twigs tangled in her hair.

Chase's legs were stiff, like Pando had reached up out of the ground and caught her in its grip, rooting her to the spot where she stood. She tried to force herself to move, to run across the clearing and snatch Guthrie out of the forest before she could disappear back into it, but it was like she was standing on the edge of a dream. The world spiraled around her, sunlight flashing off the windows of the lookout, birds flying in tightening circles overhead. Chase opened her mouth to scream to her sister, but the dull roar of the vacuum sucked away her voice, and all she could do was reach for her, fingers clawing desperately at the air.

Her ears popped as the shrill blast of a whistle burst through the soundless hum. She cried out, clapping one hand against her aching ear. No one else seemed to have noticed anything strange: not the dissonant, soundless hum, not the wild calling of the birds or their desperate murmurations. It was like Chase had gone somewhere that was halfway to a dream.

"Oops, sorry about that," the captain said roughly, letting his whistle fall out of his mouth. "Didn't mean to startle you. Just demonstrating what you should do if you see anything unusual in your search grid. Remember, three short whistles."

Chase blinked at him as everything came back into focus: the distinctive quaking of the silver-green leaves, the army of trees ranked around the clearing. The shadowy space where Guthrie had stood.

Chapter Thirty-Nine

Chase let herself be herded into place as the regiment set off, taking slow, careful steps and methodically studying the ground. Clambering through the underbrush made it hard to follow the deputy's instructions to stay in formation, and the line turned ragged as they entered the woods. Chase stumbled as her boot broke through brittle branches, her ankle turning when a hidden hole swallowed her foot. She braced herself against the paper-white trunk of a tree, grunting as she jerked free of the hole. Her laces were a snarled knot of twigs and thorns that had collected in the woods.

Her lungs worked overtime as she struggled to catch her breath. Everything ached: her neck from staring at the ground, her hip where she had knocked it against a jutting branch that she swore came out of nowhere. Her shoulders slumped from the oppressive despair that weighed them down.

She didn't see the stairs.

She didn't see anything that would lead her back to Guthrie.

"We should go back to Spruces," Wilder said, reading the exhaustion in her eyes when they came out of the woods at the end of the afternoon. "You need to rest."

"I should stay here," Chase said. "I should keep looking. I should—"

"You should take care of yourself," Wilder argued. "You're

not going to be able to help Guthrie if you push yourself too hard."

He was right. The SAR team kept pressing water and granola bars on them, and they had a policy that volunteers could only spend so many hours per day participating in the search. Chase understood this—it didn't make sense to have to pause one rescue operation to help someone who had overdone it—but it still made her feel helpless and selfish to take a break while her sister was still out there.

"Let me just go grab some more stuff and say goodnight to my parents," she told him.

She was halfway up the stairs to the lookout when she noticed the familiar arch of a skoolie's roof tucked against the trees in the clearing below. She froze, her nails digging into the soft wood of the railing. It was a faded blue, not the pale pink that she had helped Wilder paint Georgia Pie. It looked just like the one she had lived in for so many years. Her heart felt like it was plummeting over the railing to the hard dirt below. What was the skoolie doing here? Had Dad sent for it from the storage facility in Nevada?

Chase didn't even feel the slivers of wood that had worked their way under her nails as she tore up the rest of the stairs. She wouldn't leave. It made her sick to even consider it, to think of leaving this place while Guthrie was still out there in the woods, alone and silent. Her stomach cramped with anger at her parents.

The door to the lookout stood open, and voices drifted out like smoke on the summer air: Mom's, Dad's, and two others that Chase didn't recognize. She hesitated in the doorway, her forehead pinched. Besides the sheriff and deputies yesterday, no one had been up to the lookout besides Chase and her parents. Even the SAR volunteers had stayed down in the clearing.

"Mom?" Chase said.

Mom hurried across the room to tug her inside. She brushed tears from her cheek with one hand, but she was smiling. "Chase! Look who came. It's Natalie and Joe."

A woman with close-cropped black hair and light brown skin came hurrying across the room. She wrapped her arms around Chase, kissing her on the cheek and rocking back and forth slightly. "Oh, Chase. It's so good to see you."

"You're here?" Chase said dumbly. They hadn't seen Natalie and her husband in at least a year.

"We're here," Natalie confirmed. "We drove all night after your mom texted from the police station to let us know what happened."

A wave of dizzy relief swept over her. "So that's *your* skoolie down in the clearing."

"Yep," Joe said. "Luckily, we weren't too far—just Montana. And I'm sure we won't be the only ones from our old skoolie meetup group who come. Your mom's post about Guthrie already has thousands of likes."

A flicker of guilt flashed across Mom's face. Chase still remembered the accounts that Mom had set up to chronicle their skoolie build and travels. The following she gained had paid the bills when Dad was between projects, but he didn't like it. It was an invasion of Chase and Guthrie's privacy, he had argued, but he had a distaste for social media in general. He didn't even have a website for his art.

There was a *thud* as Dad set a cup down on the counter hard enough for water to slosh over the top. His jaw was clenched, the lines on his face like brushstrokes.

"You posted about this online?" he said in a tight voice. "I don't want people following this like it's some scripted reality show for their entertainment."

"I had to," Mom said. "You heard the deputy yesterday. He

said to get the word out any way we could. The more people looking for her, the more likely we are to—"

"You used your old account? Her hashtag?" Dad interrupted.

#heyheyguthrie. Mom had used it to tag any post about Gus. Chase's had been #chasingthegoodlife. That was one of the issues Dad had with social media. He said using hashtags to categorize their children was reducing them to products, something to be sold, and the accounts packaged them all for the consumer-driven society he was trying to escape.

"It's not a bad idea, Tom," Joe cut in. "With a few tweaks, I can get #findguthrie trending. It's just a simple matter of using the algorithm to our advantage."

"No offense, Joe, but I don't give a fuck about the algorithm. My children's well-being is more important than your follower count."

Mom looked like Dad had slapped her. "How could you say that?" she said. "We're doing this all for Guthrie, not to win some kind of popularity contest. Fuck, Tom, we're trying to find her."

Dad's eyes went flinty and cold. "You're just making this worse, inviting the whole world to come watch our own private tragedy," he said. He turned to climb back up to the cupola, muttering something about trauma porn.

The sharp crack of silence filled the room. Mom balled her hands into tight fists. "I'm sorry," she sputtered. "I don't know why he would speak to you like that, after you came all this way." She sounded like she was choking on the words.

"It's okay, Sadie," Joe said. "We know grief is ugly. Tom isn't going to drive us away."

Natalie wrapped her arms around Mom, pulling her down to the couch. "We're here until we find Guthrie, or you ask us to go. And even then, I might not listen."

Mom gave a watery laugh. "Chase, you should go back down to Spruces. Natalie will stay with me tonight."

"Are you sure?" Chase fought to loosen her muscles. Her stomach churned as she remembered Dad's accusations: *scripted reality* and *trauma porn.*

Natalie nodded. "We got this, sweetie. Go and try to get some rest."

Chase gathered up another change of clothes, thinking longingly of Wilder's bed. Her body was betraying her with exhaustion. How could she think of sleep at a time like this? How could she ache to get away from the constant chatter, the squawk of radios, the crunch of footsteps, when those might be Guthrie's salvation?

But she did, and if she dreamt of anything that night, she didn't remember.

Chapter Forty

In the morning, Chase's jaw hurt so much that she could hardly close her mouth. She dry-swallowed two ibuprofen as Wilder drove her back to the lookout.

"The first forty-eight hours have now passed," the captain said during the briefing. "At this point, we have not found any sign of Guthrie—"

No footprints. No cloth torn from Guthrie's T-shirt and caught in the grasping branches of the trees. No forgotten bones that had slipped through her fingers.

No stairs, burning out of their past.

"—but we will continue to work through each zone. This is a reminder to take care of yourselves. Stay hydrated, eat, rest. It's easy to get burned out, and we don't want to take resources away from Guthrie to rescue someone else."

They broke the volunteers into groups and sent them into the woods in shifts, covering different areas of the huge maps hanging in the mobile command unit. Chase, Wilder, Willow, and Sasha waited their turn in the white tent. Wilder piled a plate with bagels and fruit and pushed it on Chase. She picked at it, remembering what the captain had said about taking care of herself, but the food sat like rocks in her stomach.

"Is that the guy from the laundromat?" she said, noticing a man coming down the stairs from the lookout with a huge canvas bag slung over his shoulder. "What's he doing?"

"Oh—" Willow blushed. "I mentioned to my mom that you

shouldn't have to worry about laundry and cleaning and stuff like that right now. She said she'd take care of it. She must have talked to Kevin about doing your laundry. I know it's just a little thing." She shrugged. "I hope you don't mind."

"That's—" Chase's throat worked as she tried to swallow back tears. "That's so helpful. Thank you." Willow was right. It was incredibly ridiculous to think about those day-to-day things when Guthrie was gone, but knowing that someone else was thinking about it for them meant so much.

The next afternoon, another skoolie lumbered into the clearing. Chase recognized the family that tumbled out of it from the skoolie meetup group. When the SAR captain told them that they didn't need anyone else going into the woods that day, they weeded Mom's garden instead, harvesting the vegetables and setting them out in the volunteer tent so people had something fresh to eat along with the granola bars and prepackaged sandwiches.

Joe's prediction was coming true: More families from the skoolie community arrived over the next few days. Along with the SAR team and volunteers from Fitzgerald, there were now hundreds of people in the woods with Guthrie's name on their lips. When they weren't searching, they did things that Chase hadn't even thought of: coordinating rides from town, bringing in meals for the SAR team, taking loads of trash to the dump station ten miles away.

The kitchen table in the lookout was littered with pictures of Guthrie that Mom's friends had brought. Pictures they had taken at meetups in Iowa, Oregon, New Hampshire; pictures from campgrounds, RV parks, the bare dirt of dispersed campsites on Bureau of Land Management land. Guthrie was smiling with their children, sitting around a campfire, standing ankle-deep in a river wearing nothing but a diaper. Chase flipped through the photographs, marveling at how these people had captured her sister from a perspective she had never seen.

Chase had never thought of the people they'd met during their years of wandering as a kind of community—because wasn't that just another word for roots or stability? How could they be a part of a community that was always evolving and changing, moving from place to place instead of staying put?

Don't you see what you're doing? Wilder had said those words to her about that night, but now she realized that they applied just as much to her quest for belonging. She had been focused on nothing but Boone for so long—what it would be like to go back and how she would get there—that she hadn't seen the community that was right in front of her.

She had spent the past nine years telling herself the only connections that mattered were the ones that ran deep: friendships that lasted generations, people who knew her family before they knew her. But maybe Chase's family's roots were wide and shallow, a network of love and support that stretched across the country. And maybe that made their connections strong, just like the trees in Pando that were connected by the same root system and held each other up in the wind.

Maybe Boone wasn't the community she was looking for after all . . . maybe the roots she had longed for her whole life were just as intangible as whatever Dad was chasing.

Maybe her connection to Wilder was what she had really needed.

She took her time getting out of the truck when he parked outside the office at Spruces that night. He glanced back when she didn't follow him inside.

"You okay?" His voice was tight with concern.

"Yeah. I am." She stepped closer and slid her arms around

him, laying her head on his shoulder. He felt like home, and suddenly, everything she had been holding back came rushing in, filling her like a blessing, all-encompassing and raw. Wilder's was the first face she looked for in a crowd; his was the voice she listened for in her dreams.

"I love you," she said. She didn't even care if he said it back because it was the truest thing she had ever felt.

Chapter Forty-One

In the morning, Chase and Wilder drove back to the lookout alone. Even with the camp closed, Michael still had work to do. In fact, Chase thought with a pang, he should reopen. Every session that he canceled was money out of his pocket.

The narrow dirt driveway was emptier than it had been since the first day after Guthrie went missing; Michael wasn't the only volunteer who was spending less time searching in the woods. Chase knew that it was inevitable—people had jobs, families, and their own lives, and a SAR operation took a heavy toll both physically and emotionally. Soon the only ones left would be Mom's skoolie friends, and even they might leave someday. Then what?

Then it would just be the family left at the lookout; just Chase and her parents, frozen in limbo while they waited for Guthrie.

She wondered how long the Shaws had stayed at the lookout after Tessa disappeared.

"Chase." The SAR captain crossed the clearing as she and Wilder got out of the car, his face set in grim lines. "The sheriff is waiting to speak to your family. Your parents are upstairs."

She swallowed, holding her fear in tight until she was disoriented and gasping for breath. Something had changed in the night while she was lying in Wilder's arms, something serious enough to warrant a private conversation instead of the normal morning briefing.

Had they found Guthrie?

Her body?

"Do you want me to come with you?" Wilder asked. She nodded, gripping his hand, and they started up the stairs together.

Mom and Dad were sitting together on the couch with the deputy hovering by the table. Chase's stomach dropped when she saw that he was holding his hat in his hands, turning it convulsively. That was how cops in movies always informed the family of a death: holding their hats in what should be a sign of respect but was really just gut-punching foreshadowing.

Mom reached for her, but Chase shook her head, clinging to Wilder's hand. The other thing cops always did was ask everyone to sit down. As long as she stayed standing, he couldn't be here to tell them that Guthrie was gone.

But the deputy didn't wait for Chase to sit down. He cleared his throat and started to talk before she had properly braced herself. She swayed, dizzy, and Wilder put his hand in the small of her back to steady her. The captain's words swam up out of the disorientation.

"Mr. and Mrs. Woolf . . . Chase . . . it has been eight days since Guthrie went missing, and as you know, we have not had any leads in that time. Normally in a situation like this, we're able to establish a trail early on through footprints, hair, scent. That has not been the case here. Without any sign of Guthrie in the vicinity and our search grids exhausted, we are unable to proceed further as a search and rescue operation. What this means—"

"You're giving up," Chase said numbly. She didn't feel her lips move, but the voice was hers, and it was saying what she was thinking. "You're fucking giving up."

"No, Chase." The deputy held up one calloused hand. "We are pivoting from a search and rescue operation to a search and recovery operation."

The room was silent for a moment as they all took in his words. Search and recovery? What the fuck was that? How was that different from search and rescue?

Then Chase realized: You can rescue someone who is injured, someone who is suffering from exposure, starvation, and dehydration . . . but you can't rescue someone who is already dead.

You can only *recover* a corpse.

Mom started to cry at the same time Chase did. The tears burned as they rolled down her cheeks and gathered in the back of her throat. She struggled to breathe, but her lungs felt like they were held in a vise. Wilder crushed her against his chest, and she balled his shirt in her fists. Nothing made sense. So what if Guthrie had been alone, without food or water or shelter, for over a week? This was Pando, where the birds sang backward and the trees were always watching. Natural laws didn't apply here.

"But what does this *mean*?" Dad asked over and over. Chase was dimly aware of the sheriff's answers, staid in the face of their grief: They would no longer send search parties out after dark, they would take the mobile command unit back to the station, they would reduce the number of SAR team members involved in the search.

"We have to balance the safety of our team members with the operation," the sheriff explained again. "It is extremely unlikely that Guthrie is still alive at this point. We are not giving up on finding her, but taking these steps will mitigate the risk to our people."

Time seemed to be simultaneously running too fast and standing still. Chase clung to Wilder for what might have been moments but felt like a lifetime. People circled her family, making tea, offering food. Late in the afternoon, she heard the rumble of the mobile command unit pulling away.

The clearing looked strangely flattened without the oversize van and emergency vehicles, the loose flaps of the white tent flapping in the breeze. A handful of skoolies were still parked along the tree line, but as the sun sank toward the horizon, the rest of the cars started to empty out as well.

"I need to stay here tonight," Chase said to Wilder as they stood on the deck watching them go, the sky darkening overhead. "I need to be with my parents."

"They should come to Spruces, too." His brow was furrowed in concern. "I don't want the three of you here alone."

"There's no way Mom will leave," Chase said. "And we'll be fine. Natalie, Joe, and a couple of the other skoolie families are staying, so we won't be all alone."

His arms crept around her, and she felt the brush of his lips against her hair. "I'll be back at dawn," he promised. "This isn't the end. We're going to find her."

Inside, Mom was curled up on Guthrie's stripped bed, her cheeks puffy and red from crying all day. Her mouth sagged open in exhaustion, and her hair fluttered in the air blowing from the box fan next to the bed. Chase hovered over her for a moment, waiting for her to wake, but she was still.

"She fell asleep a few minutes ago," Natalie whispered from the kitchen where she was drying dishes. "I tried to get her to take an Ambien so she could sleep through the night, but she didn't want to. She was afraid she wouldn't wake up if something happens." She frowned.

"And Dad?" Chase asked.

Natalie nodded toward the cupola. "He's still up there."

Chase pressed her lips together and nodded. Of course he was. Because when things got hard, Dad disappeared into his art instead of leaning on his family.

"What do you need, sweetie?" Natalie asked. "Can I make you anything to eat? Or would you like some company?"

"No," Chase said. "I'm not hungry. And Wilder just went home." She was too weary to care if that was rude, but if she couldn't be with him, she just wanted to be alone.

Natalie set the last plate down and put her hand on Chase's shoulder. "Of course. Joe and I will be right down there if you need anything tonight. I'll come check on you in the morning."

"Thanks," Chase said, and as Natalie turned away, she added, "For everything, I mean. I don't know how we would have gotten through this week without you."

"It's been a shitty week," Natalie agreed. "And it's not over. But we'll get through it together."

Chase waited for her to leave, then turned out the lights and crawled into Guthrie's bed next to Mom. If she closed her eyes and breathed through her nose, she could still catch the faintest whiff of Guthrie, but the gust of the box fan was too much. Rolling over, she pulled at the cord, yanking it out of the wall, and buried her nose in the bare mattress.

Now it was still and silent enough in the lookout for Chase to hear the steady *thwack-thwack-thwack* of a paintbrush on canvas.

She jerked like the sound was a live wire.

Dad was painting up there? After listening to Mom's anguished cries, after letting Natalie care for his daughter like Chase was her child instead of his?

Her feet thumped to the floor as she rolled out of bed and crossed the room in two strides. The stagnant air of the cupola settled over her shoulders like a mantle when she emerged from the trapdoor. Dad was crouched in the corner, leaning over the bed, pillows shoved to the side to make room for the canvases spread across the rumpled sheets.

They came into focus as her eyes adjusted to the dim light.

There were at least a dozen, all landscapes as viewed from the lookout. These must be what he had been working on in the weeks they had been at the lookout—all the paintings that he had been so unhappy with, all the paintings he had refused to show anyone. Mossy rocks and the soft, leaf-strewn carpet of the woods; the lake, pink and blue from the light of a sunrise; the smooth granite face of a peak seen at a distance.

And her grandparents' stairs, painted in such detail that Chase could almost feel the carpet under her fingers. Among the aspen trees, on the shore of the lake, in a meadow of wildflowers . . . almost as though they belonged there, almost as though he had *seen* them there.

All the air leaked out of her lungs until they were as shriveled and empty as a potato chip bag thrown in a fire. She was helpless, her desperation for air as futile as though she was trying to breathe water.

Dad's eyes, wild and black as the paint smeared across his cheek, leaped to Chase's face. They stared at each other until a drop of paint dripped off the brush in his hand and landed on one of the canvases spread across the bed.

The drop spurred them both into movement. Dad let the brush fall to the floor in his rush to hide the paintings, but Chase scrambled across the bed to snatch the stack of canvases out of his arms. Oxygen swept into her lungs like a wave, bringing spots of darkness dancing across her eyes with its intensity. She gasped, gulping until she could almost breathe normally again, hissing out questions in a strangled voice.

"What are you doing?" she choked out. "What is this? What are you doing up here?"

Rough black brushstrokes covered the canvas that Dad had been bent over. The cup of paint fell on its side in the middle of the bed, and black paint rolled like a dark tide over the sheets, swallowing Chase up.

Chapter Forty-Two

In the darkness, she was in Boone.

Relief settled over her like the snowflakes that were drifting down from the sky. She had made it. She was home where she belonged, where she could be one part of a whole. The thought filled her chest with a kind of light buoyancy that she hadn't felt in years.

Home.

It was night—dark and bitter cold, the kind of cold that gets trapped inside your bones. Chase took a step forward, shielding her face from the wind. She didn't recognize anything, but her dream-self did, and that guided Chase down the middle of a street toward a house on the corner.

Home.

The wind whistled through a gap in her teeth, a fleshy crater in her gums that tasted like blood. Chase rooted around in her mouth with her tongue, exploring other holes and teeth that were loose in her jaw. One gave way under the probing pressure, and she spat it into her hand. It was small and flecked with blood and ash. A baby tooth. Chase stared at it, then curled her hand around it in a fist and looked at the dimpled knuckles of her hand—a child's hand. And she knew then that she hadn't made it back to Boone; she had never *left* Boone. There was a part of her that was still eight years old, a part of her that was still—

Home.

One of the snowflakes landed on the back of her chubby,

childish hand, and Chase hissed in pain at its sting. It was powder gray and red around the edges, and it wasn't a snowflake, it was a piece of flaming ash blowing in the wind, a piece of the flaming ash that Chase was shielding her face from. She dropped her hand, and then she could feel the heat of the fire and she could see the house on the corner engulfed in flames.

Guthrie, chubby-cheeked and screaming in Dad's arms next to her. The front door was still open so Chase could watch the stairs burn. The yellow and pink roses that were woven into the carpet had gone shriveled and black; the polished wood banister was dripping with golden flames. The fire swept through the door like a bride to her wedding. Her grandparents' voices rose from the top of the stairs, panicked cries that grew to shrieks as the flames reached them. Chase tried to run as the skin on her face blistered, but she was rooted in Dad's arms, and the fire consumed them like grief.

Chapter Forty-Three

The present came rushing back in. Chase's stomach turned with the memory's sensory details: the citrusy scent of polish mixed with smoke, the sting of the heat on her skin, the roar of the flames that was almost, *almost* loud enough to drown out the sound of the screams. It was a punch to the gut, sucking the air out of her lungs.

Dad stood on the other side of the bed, paint dripping to the floor. He reached for her, but she was already scrambling back down the ladder, betrayal sparking in her chest. All this time, he had known something was wrong here, but even after seeing the staircase in the woods, that manifestation of their collective trauma, he still couldn't face their past. He would rather hide it under heavy, smeared brushstrokes than admit the pain that had shaped the last nine years.

And that denial had almost been enough to close the door to Guthrie forever.

"Wait—" Dad slid down the ladder after her, landing heavily in the middle of the floor. Mom sat up, blinking at the sudden noise.

"What's happening?"

"I'm going to bring her back," Chase said roughly, yanking on a pair of shoes and grabbing the sweatshirt draped over her bed frame.

Mom cried out in shock, but Chase didn't pause to explain. She flung open the front door and disappeared into the inky black night, dimly aware of Mom and Dad clattering down the stairs after her.

She had buried the memories of what had happened in Boone so deep that they almost didn't feel real. But the trauma of that day was still there, like shrapnel embedded in her soul. And while Guthrie had been little more than a baby at the time, her entire life had been shaped by losing her grandparents. The shadow that had cast over their family had darkened with every mile they drove, every conversation Dad refused to have, every memory Chase buried. Guthrie may not be able to consciously remember what had happened, but something deep inside her did. Her soul knew the truth. She had internalized the pain of that day the same way Chase had, and the vortex had brought it out. Taken their festering wounds and projected them in the physical plane, giving them the opportunity Dad had denied them for so long: a chance to come to terms with what had happened to their family.

"Chase, stop—" Dad caught up to her in a moonlit copse of trees, grabbing her hand and yanking her back. "What do you mean, you're going to bring her back? Do you know how to get to her?"

"You do, too, Dad." Chase jutted out her chin. "You painted it, over and over. All those weeks that you refused to let us see what you were working on—all those *years* that you refused to tell me the truth about what happened in Boone." She was shaking—hot, sick anger swooping through her stomach. The woods bloomed with her pain: silver-green leaves rippling like flames under the moonlight, dark sap running from the knotholes like the smears of black paint on Dad's painting. Mom stumbled to a stop next to them, wincing as she tripped barefoot through the underbrush. Her face went sickly gray-white as Chase said to her, "Ask him what he's been painting since we got here. Ask him what he's *seen* here."

Mom looked at Dad like she was begging for something she knew he couldn't give her.

"It wasn't real. It was just in my head," he mumbled. He pressed his bandaged hand to his brow, and something else clicked into place for Chase.

"It was real enough to burn your hand," she said. "Those blisters appeared after you saw them for the first time, didn't they?"

"Saw *what*?" Mom hissed. "Tom, what is she talking about?"

"Saw the stairs from my parents' house engulfed in flames, just like they were that night!" Dad burst out. He said it the way Chase always did in her head when she thought about what had happened in South Dakota. "I saw them in the woods, and then I started painting them. I couldn't stop it. It was like I was sleepwalking. They just kept appearing under my brush."

"The stairs from your parents' house?" Mom stumbled. "But how—"

"Because our minds are metaphysical. They create their own reality. Negative vortexes can tap into that," Chase said, biting back a bitter *I told you so*. Now wasn't the time. "Pando takes things from our minds—memories, unfulfilled wishes, trauma—and projects them as physical doorways into a place created by our consciousness. That's what the stairs are. A way into the lonely places. We share the same trauma as Guthrie, which means we can go after her. We can bring her home."

"But Guthrie was just a baby—" Mom protested. "She doesn't remember the fire. *You* barely remember the fire."

Chase stiffened as another visceral wave of memory swept over her: panic and smoke choking her lungs, the sting of ash on her face.

"It doesn't matter," she insisted. "People think that trauma doesn't affect babies, but that's not true. I read in an old psychology textbook that early trauma can impact lifelong learning and mental health. It's called precognitive trauma." Her voice was rising now, shrill over the drone of the night insects. "Besides, don't you think that night influenced how you and Dad parented us, which in turn affected both me and Guthrie? You can't just ignore things and expect them to go away."

Shock. Silence. The air was a still and empty hum. At first Chase thought it was just because she had shouted, but no—the sounds all around them were fading, like a record player being turned down, leaving only her voice ringing through the trees.

"*—affected both me and Guthrie—*"

"*—ignore things and expect them to go away—*"

"*—precognitive trauma—*"

The echoes splintered apart, words overlapping and intertwining to form new phrases: *ignore me* and *lifelong trauma* and *expect* that night *to go away.*

It was everything she had been afraid to voice—afraid to even *think*—since that night. That she had irreparably damaged her sister, that her parents had already written her off. That even though Guthrie was the one who had gotten lost, Chase would never escape what had happened in the woods.

Chase's throat swelled as she fought back a pit of self-loathing that threatened to swallow her. How could she expect her parents to forgive her for that night when she couldn't forgive herself? A whiff of artificial citrus drifted on the air. Mom's head swiveled, nose wrinkling as she tried to identify the pungent scent, but Dad breathed it in like it was his mother's perfume. Moonlight rippled on the air like water and caught on a glossy curve just through the trees: the staircase with its intricately turned spindles and old-fashioned floral carpet.

The three of them turned toward it in unison. At first

Chase didn't think Mom would be able to see it—she hadn't been there at the fire, after all—but the pull of the staircase was evident in the shine of her eyes. Perhaps she had lived with the byproducts of her family's trauma long enough that it had become her own.

Mom clutched at Chase's hand, mouth sagging open and throat working in shock, but all Chase felt was relieved that the way to Guthrie was open to them. The air was as clear and still as the moment after a funeral knell, and the staircase beckoned.

She took one step forward, and then another, put out her hand, stroking the smooth wood banister, and began to climb, flanked on either side by her parents.

Memories of her life in Boone rose through the cobwebs of trauma that had hidden them for so many years. She remembered sitting on a bench in the back hall of her grandmother's house, crying as her mother tried to take her temperature with an old-fashioned thermometer, Mom and Grandma arguing over how long she had to hold it in her mouth. She remembered her father holding her on the porch swing, wrapped in a quilt while lightning forked white-hot all around them. She remembered Grandma and Grandpa waving at her from the front door as Dad unbuckled her baby sister from the car seat.

Wisps of smoke shrouded the faces in these memories, only parting enough for her to glimpse one feature at a time: her grandfather's square chin, the creases at the corners of her grandmother's eyes when she smiled. Chase moved faster, trying to piece together the picture little by little, until she was racing up the stairs, sure that if she could just make it to the top, she would find them.

But when she reached the top, the only thing there was more trees.

She and her parents stood with branches tangled together,

sentinels of the lonely places. Chase felt the difference as soon as they climbed the last step. The air was no longer an imperceptive thing, anonymous and indefinite. It crawled over her skin. She was suddenly aware of every individual molecule. There was something different about the moonlight, too. It felt . . . flat. Like someone had added all the shadows by hand.

Mom drew her back protectively, eyes fixed on the staircase descending behind them. Chase could still see it if she concentrated, but it was already fading into the strange half-light of this place, shimmering like it wasn't fully there. Though it felt like they had climbed an endless flight, they were still standing on the soft, cushiony ground of the forest. At first glance, it looked like every other anonymous aspen grove that surrounded the lookout. But when Chase put out her hand, instead of the papery bark she was used to, she felt smooth bone.

"What is this place?" Mom asked, eyes darting around the grove of bone trees. Her mouth didn't open; no sound came out. Yet the question seeped into Chase's bones, the words swirling and meeting again, an echo that would exist as long as she did:

this place,

this place,

this place,

this place . . .

"The lonely places," Chase answered. *"Created from our fears and insecurities. Our unresolved trauma."*

"This is where she is?" Dad's voice joined theirs, thin with foreboding. *"How do we find her?"*

We're *all connected*, Chase thought, but here her thoughts were words and her words were ripples. *Like the people, the trees, the birds, the bones.*

She dropped to her knees next to a slim sapling as tall as

her waist. A twisted spiral of femur with the ball-and-socket joint still visible under the silver leaves.

The bones had grown into the roots and the roots had grown into the bones . . .

And Guthrie had gathered bones from the dirt like wildflowers.

Chase clawed at the soil at the base of the tree, scraping it away in furrows until she exposed the roots. Like all the bones Guthrie had collected on her windowsill, they were warped and misshapen. Crooked fingers and knobs of spine and a single, distorted jawbone. Twined among them were the network of tree roots that joined Pando into one vast, living organism.

Guthrie had always been so connected to the forest—she had almost seemed like one of the trees herself. Here, in this place, maybe she really was a part of Pando.

Chase plunged her hands into the dirt, wrapping her fingers around the tangle of roots and bone. Her body gave a single involuntary jolt before she was carried away on a wave of consciousness.

The awareness was all-consuming, crackling across her skin like static electricity. She could feel everything that made the lonely places what they were: anguish, fear, isolation. It was like tuning in to a radio that was broadcasting on a thousand frequencies.

"Guthrie." Heart pounding, she sent the word into the confused tangle. Like before, she made no sound, but she could feel her sister's name coursing through the interconnected roots until it reached every corner of Pando. *"Where are you?"*

Clinging to the network of roots, she waited for a reply. When it came, it wasn't an answer in words, but a collection of feelings: disappointment, shame, growing panic, confusion, resentment, and deep, bone-chattering sorrow that contrasted sharply with the warm solace that Chase felt at the response. Guthrie was here, and this time Chase wouldn't go back without her.

She rose to her feet. Now that she felt Guthrie's presence, it pulsed under her skin, calling her forward and leading her through the maze of trees and bones. The whispers of the leaves grew into a gale, but the only thing she was aware of was her sister waiting for her.

The trees clutched at her as she pushed through them, bones like twigs and twigs like bones tangling in her hair. Chase ducked out of their grasp impatiently, pressing forward through the forest of empty eyes with Mom and Dad trailing behind her. Flowers bloomed on skeletal stems, clusters of skull-shaped snapdragons that chimed like bells, and daisies rising out of rings of vertebrae. The bare eye of a black-eyed Susan, petals plucked and lost to the wind, blinked up at her from the leaf-strewn ground. Chase bent to pick it up and caught sight of an uprooted mushroom just a few feet ahead. Beads of blood-like sap rolled down its cap. The clear, gelatinous fins of another fungus came next, then the crushed phalanges of a coneflower, corpse gray under the moonlight. Scattered proof that Guthrie had gone this way. Chase gathered them into a loose bouquet, and with each one, she felt her sister more fully.

When they came to Guthrie, she was sitting in the dirt, leaning against a tree with the same knothole markings as the one by the clearing where she liked to play—the one that had watched them for all those weeks. Her eyes flicked to Chase and their parents but passed over them like she didn't recognize them. She didn't respond when Chase dropped the flowers, when Dad fell to the ground, weeping, when Mom wrapped her in her arms with a cry of relief. Her eyes were wide and blank, roving through the forest like she was dreaming, the pupils dilated to dark moons that Chase could see herself in.

The four of them held each other, sharing memories in a tangled, wordless jumble that pulsed between them like a heat signature.

A flash of flame.

A figure retreating through the woods, through the smoke, through the pain.

A ribbon of leaves, a ribbon of road.

A harsh cry stopped by lungs filling with smoke.

A sunrise, a sunset, a shooting star glimpsed through the trees.

A spark, a scream, a blaze of heat.

A memory that was just a dream.

Finally, Chase spoke, forcing out the words that a part of her had always known. "*Grandma and Grandpa burned to death, didn't they?*"

She felt the truth of it rippling through the bone-like trees, the whispers in the leaves confirming it before her parents could speak.

Guthrie's eyes fluttered, darting from side to side, sending fear and anguish pulsing through their veins like adrenaline. The lingering scent of smoke grew stronger, and the constant whisper of the leaves overhead grew to a shrill shriek that set Chase's teeth on edge.

"*You told me they died in an accident,*" she said. "*Why did you lie?*"

"*It* was *an accident.*" Mom's voice was hushed inside Chase's head. Tears streamed down her cheeks. "*A horrible accident.*"

"*The fire was caused by faulty wiring.*" Dad was quiet, somber, like he was whispering. "*They had spent years restoring a historic Victorian home, and my father refused to hire anyone. He did it all himself. I was worried about the electricity in a house that old, but he swore that he would take care of it. I kept meaning to get a second opinion when he wasn't around, but I never did. And then it was too late.*"

"When we told you that Grandma and Grandpa were dead the next morning, you didn't seem to remember what had happened," Mom said. Her voice shook and she reached for Chase like she was asking forgiveness. *"We thought it was a blessing. We thought it would be easier for you if we left it vague, let you think it was a car accident. We didn't want you to remember what you had seen—"*

"Because I remember everything," Dad said, low and harsh. He sounded like he was choking on smoke. *"Everything. The screams, the—the smell."* His voice broke. *"I was going to go back for them. They were calling to me. I was going to go back as soon as I got you and Gus out. But I couldn't leave you two. I couldn't risk going back into that house."* He was pleading now, like he was trying to convince Chase of something he didn't quite believe himself. Mom gripped his hand, her eyes swimming with tears. *"The stairs were on fire. I couldn't have made it up to where they were. I had to stay alive so I could be there for you and Mom and Gus. So I carried you girls out to the street, and I stayed there and watched it burn."*

Chase's stomach clenched as the gravity of what Dad was saying struck her full force. No wonder he had always shut down any conversations about his parents or how they had died. For nearly a decade, he had been suffocated by the guilt of not saving them, no matter how impossible that might have been.

All these years, she had thought her father was chasing something unattainable—something unfathomable, something he would never find—but she suddenly realized that he had really been running from scars that went so much deeper than just the memory of the fire. *You haven't even begun to unpack your trauma.*

"We can't keep leaving things behind," Chase said. *"Not each other, and not the things we did."* She closed her eyes, allowing the memory of that night to rise up in her mind, pungent and

bitter. Every one of her molecules screamed at her to push it away, to claw her way out of the suffocating guilt, but she had done that long enough. Guilt and what she wished she'd done differently weren't enough. It was time to face what had actually happened; time to face how she had made a bad decision with consequences she had never anticipated, how leaving Guthrie in the woods had changed her in a way Chase didn't understand.

Cold tears ran down her cheeks as she relived that night in a way she had never allowed herself to. Mom brushed the tears away, melting the trails of ice they left behind, her hands warm and her emotions soft and blurred around the edges. Words were in Chase's head, words that she didn't recognize as her own. *I should have listened to you*, they said. *I'm sorry*, they said.

"I should have listened to you." Chase repeated her mother's thoughts to Guthrie. For months she had told herself she was protecting her sister, when really she had been trying to control her; trying to fix her instead of being a safe space for her. *"I'm sorry. No matter how much I try to put things back to how they were before, we'll never be the same, and it's not fair to expect us to. Instead, we have to move forward."*

Guthrie flexed her fists in response, and Chase felt a pulse of something that felt like a reprieve; this was what Guthrie needed.

This was what they both needed.

"How?" Dad's voice was small. *"How can we move forward from something like this without running?"*

Mom lay her hands on his, her eyes blazing, and this time when she spoke, her voice echoed aloud in the still air. "By moving forward together."

Chapter Forty-Four

The sun was rising as they stumbled down the stairs and out of the lonely places. Chase's ears popped painfully when she took the last step, but the staircase didn't disappear the way it had before. She still felt its inexorable pull, like spiderwebs trailing over her skin, and she lingered at the bottom, gazing up into the shifting air. She could almost see the four of them still crouched there, arms around each other and thoughts binding them together. A part of their family—a memory, a ghost—would always remain in the lonely places.

"Chase," Mom said in a hoarse voice. She and Dad were already a few feet away, Guthrie crushed against Dad's chest. Mom reached for her, her hand hanging in the still air like an offering, but Chase couldn't take it. Not yet.

The cardboard book of matches that she had taken from Guthrie the night before she disappeared was still in her sweatshirt pocket. Chase's hand went to it unconsciously, fingering the pulpy packet as her parents watched, poised on their toes as though they expected Chase to disappear back up the stairs. Leaving this manifestation of their trauma wasn't the end—they had only just begun facing their past. There were years of work and therapy ahead of her and her family, but Chase knew how she wanted to start.

A whiff of phosphorus, a sudden flare.

She dropped the match, and the staircase burst into flames.

The SAR captain had just arrived when they came out of the woods. He scrambled for his radio, for the first aid kit, for answers, but they had none to give. What had happened in the woods was unfathomable. Just for them.

The rest of that day was a blur of rushing Guthrie to the hospital in Fitzgerald, where she was admitted for forty-eight hours and given a complete physical workup that bewildered all the doctors. She wasn't suffering from dehydration or exposure. She hadn't lost any weight. She had no injuries, not even minor scrapes or bruises. It was as though she had simply vanished and reappeared nine days later.

But not all of her had made it out.

She walked when led; she ate when fed. At night, her tense fists relaxed, and her breath fluttered in sleep, but her eyes continued their blind rolling. She didn't react to their voices or any other stimuli. It was as though she was still sleepwalking.

"It's rare for children to exhibit symptoms of catatonia, but not unheard of," the doctors said when they released her. "And after two traumatic events in a relatively short period of time, Guthrie is probably experiencing severe PTSD. With time, she may recover. Right now, the best thing you can do for her—and for all of you—is settle into a routine and get into therapy."

Therapy. Chase was wrung out at the end of their first family session later that week, limp with exhaustion from the range of emotions it had brought up—and not just about that night or the fire. She hadn't expected every mention of the skoolie to fill her with simmering rage, or to cry as she told the therapist the most benign facts about her childhood, but the tears had started as soon as the session began, racking sobs that felt like they were turning her inside out.

It hurt, but there was healing in the sting, too. Like using alcohol to clean a wound, or a fire burning away the diseased part of a forest so that something fresh and living could take root.

At the end of it, she picked herself up and stitched the pieces back together, knowing she would have to do it all over again at her individual session in just a few days.

None of them had gone back to the lookout. Mom's skoolie friends had packed their belongings while Guthrie was still under observation, and Michael had offered to let them stay at his house in town for the rest of the summer. Wilder was there, waiting for her on the front steps, when they pulled into the driveway after therapy.

He stood up and shoved his hands in his pockets. Mom dropped a kiss on Chase's forehead and Dad squeezed her arm as they murmured hello to Wilder and led Guthrie inside. Chase watched them go, her chest hollowing as Guthrie's eyes drifted blankly over her, pupils blown out just as they had been since Dad had carried her out of the lonely places.

"Hi," Wilder said. His breath stuttered as she wrapped her arms around him. It reminded her of the first time they had kissed, the inevitability, the revelation of it.

This was where she belonged.

"How was it?" Wilder asked after a moment.

"Horrible," Chase said honestly. "But also good. Really, really good. We talked about things that we've never been able to say out loud before."

"I'm glad," Wilder said. He glanced toward the house. "And Guthrie?"

Chase shook her head. "She's the same. It's like she's not even here anymore." Her throat tightened and she swallowed hard, leaning into him.

"Give her time." Wilder stroked her hair.

"How did your dad . . ." She paused, thinking about how Wilder had phrased it: *I was just here, hoping he would come back to me.* "How did he make it back to you after everything that happened when he found Tessa?"

Wilder sighed. "Patience. Therapy. Family. My mom left, but he had me and my grandma. There's no easy fix here, Chase. All you can do is be there for her. Support her on *her* terms, whatever that looks like."

Her lips sagged into a frown. She had never felt so helpless. If only there was something she could do, a way she could reach into Guthrie's soul and take the pain from her.

You've always valued being in control . . .

But this was something she couldn't control, and she was finally starting to understand what that looked like.

It looked like sitting quietly with Guthrie, bathing in her silence instead of constantly feeling the need to fill it.

It looked like walking with her to the park and watching the other children play without pressuring her to join their game.

It looked like not doing things for her that she could do for herself.

It looked like talking about their future—for once something more than just the abstract lines on a map.

And slowly, little by little, Chase started to recognize Guthrie all over again.

Mom joined a community garden and was making friends who all had dirt under their nails and an overabundance of zucchini; Dad was preparing for an art show at a gallery in Salt Lake City. He was going to call it "lonely places" and planned on donating any proceeds to the search and rescue organization that had put in so many hours looking for Guthrie.

Chase was moving forward, too. She didn't need the credits to graduate, but she registered for her senior year at Fitzgerald High School anyway. Wilder and Willow promised to help her make up for all the high school experiences she had missed out on so far—Friday night football games, ditching class, studying over coffee. Prom and graduation and yearbooks in the spring.

And then there was the question of college and Boone.

What had been an all-encompassing goal for Chase for so long now seemed flat and hollow. Things were different now . . . *she* was different. For the first time since she was a little girl, she knew where she would be in six months. The future—the immediate future, at least—was laid out before her, but she had never felt so lost.

"Do you need to decide right now?" Mom asked when she brought up her concerns. "You've been through a lot of change recently, so your plans for the future might change, too. Honor your emotions, even the messy ones."

As the summer ended and Chase started her first and last year of high school, she tried to follow that advice, dissecting her complicated feelings about Guthrie with her therapist and untangling how she really felt about Boone. She saw now that going back wouldn't be the clear-cut answer that she had always imagined, because home was so much more than a place. Maybe she would go to Appalachian State University right after graduation like she had always planned; maybe she would take a year to figure things out. Maybe she would choose a completely different school, somewhere closer to Fitzgerald and her parents and Guthrie and Wilder. She wasn't sure what she wanted anymore, but she would figure it out.

One night in October, Chase and Wilder were lying on the trampoline in the backyard of the rental house where Chase's family had moved at the end of the summer. The mountain air was crisp and cool, perfect for cuddling under a blanket and watching the Orionid meteor shower. Chase wriggled closer, laying her head against Wilder's shoulder so that she could feel the steady rise and fall of his chest. Everything was still and quiet, the sky filled with lights falling, some trailing bright tails, others so small and fast that they were nothing more than a blink above them.

Home, Chase thought, as she always did when she was lying in Wilder's arms.

Something moved behind them. Chase recognized the brush of bare feet over grass, the slight shift of molecules rearranging themselves. She felt the stutter of her heart as it synced to another.

She rolled onto her elbows, already reaching for her sister.

Guthrie stood outlined in the light from the back door, her hair a wild halo around her face. Her eyes were clear and deep as the lake, and Chase let herself fall into them.

"Chase," Guthrie said in a sweet, clear voice.

It was like birds singing.

Author's Note

Many of the places mentioned in this book are real, though I took liberties with location to allow Chase and her friends to experience them more easily.

While I created the town of Fitzgerald and the fire lookout where Chase and her family live, Pando is a real place along the shores of Fish Lake in central Utah, as is Mystic Hot Springs in nearby Monroe, Utah. Mystic Hot Springs is the Grateful Dead–themed campground of your dreams, including a custom double-decker bus called the Ben Bus that proprietor Mystic Mike drove when he followed the Grateful Dead on tour.

Found in northwestern Utah near the Nevada border, the salt flats are forty square miles of blinding white salt, not far from Sun Tunnels, a mind-blowing land art installation by Nancy Holt. Originally placed in the mid '70s, these four massive concrete tubes still draw visitors all throughout the year, but especially on the solstices when the sun is centered through the tunnels. Like Chase, I had a special experience camping at Sun Tunnels, coming together with a group of strangers to witness "the sun rising and setting, keeping the time of the earth" (Nancy Holt, from "Sun Tunnels," originally published in *ArtForum* Vol. 15 No. 8 April 1977).

Other Utah favorites that didn't make it into this book include the bright pink water of the northern half of the Great Salt Lake; Moab, with its red rocks and arches; and the mountain lakes and wildflowers in Logan Canyon.

One last thing about Utah: Don't knock fry sauce until you try it.

Acknowledgments

Eight years ago, *Lonely Places* was the first story I ever finished. It was not very good. But like many new writers, I was convinced it was ready to send out to agents immediately, and I threw myself into the query trenches with a whole lot of blind optimism. Three days in, I received a full request from a well-respected agent. Wow! I was so talented that I was going to sign my very first book with no revisions and no rejections!

That did not happen.

The agent passed on it, as they absolutely should have. That version of *Lonely Places* was a meandering mess with no plot structure. I was prone to head hopping and switching tenses. But most of all, the story was flawed in a way I just didn't know how to fix.

Over the next five years, I kept writing and learning. I attended conferences. I found critique partners. I was selected for WriteMentor. I queried other projects. Dozens of people read my work, encouraged me, brainstormed with me. They each deserve my deepest gratitude because I would not be a writer without them.

Thank you to early readers of that original version of this story—Amanda, Madison, Ali, Kiera, and Sarah. And thank you to that first agent who expressed interest, because the thrill of that full request kept me from giving up as rejections poured in.

My biggest thanks to my sister Kelsey, who was the first person who told me I should finish my story and has been my biggest supporter and critique partner ever since. I'm so grateful for your enthusiasm and love. Also, when do I get to read more of your family horror WIP so I can figure out which character is based on me?

I'm grateful for the other critique partners and publishing

friends I've found in the last few years: Shannon, Crystal, AJ, Katie, and Renae. I'm honored to be able to collaborate with such talented people! Thank you to my writing group (the Typewriters) and my book club (Overbooked) for all the support, friendship, and love. I love nerding out about books with you!

Thank you to Sergeant Doug Howell, who answered my questions about search and rescue operations clearly and in such thoughtful detail. I appreciate the time you took to help me understand the process and the work you do to keep us all safe!

Thank you to my agent, Sharon Belcastro, for her guidance and support in this journey. Thank you to my editor, Ashtyn Stann, and the team at Flux for making publishing such a joy—Meg Gaertner, Taylor Kohn, Heather McDonough, and Sam Temple. And the design team, Kate Liestman and Andrew Selbitschka. Thank you to illustrator Kelsey Oseid, who brought my vision of Pando and the fire lookout to life for the cover.

I have to thank my favorite place in the world to write—Split Leaf Coffee in Bountiful, Utah. Thank you for creating an amazing community space. I never write better than when I'm sipping on a peach horchata chai latte!

And of course, so much love and gratitude to my family. Thank you to my parents, the most selfless, giving people I know. Thank you to my in-laws for loving me like your own. Thank you to all of my siblings, both those by blood and those by marriage. You're the best!

And finally: To Jason, thank you for always believing in me and supporting me in whatever scheme I'm currently pursuing. Thank you for taking me to the mountains when I feel like my soul is withering away. And to Tempe, Helena, Juno, and Pearl, thank you for being the best kids on the planet. I love you so much!!

About the Author

Originally an East Coast girl, Kate Anderson now lives in Utah with her husband, four children, and a much-loved cat. When she's not reading or writing, she loves exploring the mountains and desert, and planning road trips to places off the beaten path—like Pando or Sun Tunnels. *Lonely Places* is her second book. Find Kate on Instagram @kateanderwrites.

Kate Anderson

Here Lies Olive

A 2023 Foreword INDIES Book of the Year Awards Finalist

"Anderson presents a fresh, multilayered exploration of grief and trauma set against an engaging supernatural mystery that evokes urban legends and ghost stories in this atmospheric debut." —*Publishers Weekly*, starred review

Growing up in the dark tourism capital of the United States, sixteen-year-old Olive should be comfortable with death. But ever since an allergic reaction almost sent her to the wrong side of the grass, she's been terrified that there is no afterlife. And after the death of her surrogate grandmother, Olive has kept everyone at arm's length because if there's Nothing after we die, relationships and love can only end in sorrow.

When she summons a spirit to answer her questions about death, Olive meets Jay, a hitchhiking ghost trapped in the woods behind the poorhouse where he died. Olive agrees to help Jay find his unmarked grave in exchange for answers about the other side and what comes next.

Meanwhile, someone—or something—is targeting Olive's classmates, and the longer Jay lingers, the more serious the attacks become. Blaming herself for having brought Jay back, Olive teams up with maybe-nemesis, maybe-crush Maren, ex-best friend Davis, and new girl Vanessa to free Jay's spirit before he's trapped as a malevolent shade and the attacks turn deadly. But in doing so, Olive must face her fear of death and risk losing another person she loves to the Nothing.